By Eliana West

THE
WAY
Beyond

MOCKINGBIRD BRIDGE
BOOK THREE

ELIANA WEST

Published by
SECOND PRESS
info@secondpress.com

The Way Beyond
© 2024 Eliana West

Second Edition
First Published by Tule Publishing, September 2021

Cover Art
© 2024 Elizabeth Mackey
Cover content is for illustrative purposes only and any person depicted on the cover is a model.

Trade Paperback ISBN: 9781963011074
Digital ISBN: 9781963011067
Digital eBook published July 2024
v. 2.0

For Grandpa, who always believed that West, Mississippi,
could thrive and grow.

ACKNOWLEDGMENTS

ONCE AGAIN I have to give a shout-out to my sisters in words. Anne Turner, Aliyah Burke, and Carmen Cook, thank you for standing by me through all the laughter and tears bringing this story to life.

Neva West, for always being an inspiration.

To my husband, David, thank you for always believing in my dreams and understanding when I talk about my characters as if they are actual people. I am so grateful to have you by my side on this journey. Jackie and Satchel, your words of encouragement and support mean the world to me and it is such a joy to be your mom. Thank you.

CHAPTER ONE

THE LATE spring air was filled with the scent of honeysuckle, jasmine, and lavender. Mae Colton stood under the gazebo in Colton Park, watching her friends exchange their vows. There were so many flowers under the canopy, there was barely any room for the bride and groom. The rest of the wedding guests sat in white folding chairs that ringed the gazebo. Almost all of the small town of Colton had turned out to wish the bride and groom well.

Mae glanced over at the groom's side, where Jacob Winters stood in his gray suit with a sage-green gingham tie that matched the sash on the strapless bridesmaid's dress she wore. Her breath caught when their eyes locked for just a fraction of a second, and the heat that flared in his let her know that she'd be gazing into them longer at the end of the night.

She turned her attention back to the bride and groom, who were following local tradition and getting married under the gazebo in the town square surrounded by their friends and family. Mae was happy to see the bride wanted to follow local custom. Mae never thought much of the legend that Colton brides who married under the gazebo would have a long and happy marriage. But standing in this special place, watching another friend say her vows, she wondered if maybe there wasn't just a little bit of magic at work. She eyed her best friend and cousin, who'd become a Colton bride just a year before. She was looking at her husband standing across the aisle, her face practically glowing with love, and he was looking at her with the same intensity.

Country star Lucas Monroe, a friend of the groom, walked down the aisle strumming the first chords of Stevie Wonder's "As" on his guitar. Tillie, the owner of the Catfish Café, came next, with her head held high, wearing a sage-green silk suit that had a matching gingham camisole under the jacket. Her freshly dyed bright red hair was styled into an elegant updo, and she was beaming from ear to ear. She'd been crowing about being the maid of honor for weeks now. Jo came up the stairs, and Mae swallowed the lump in her throat, seeing her on her father's arm. She wore an ivory lace fitted blouse with a high-necked lace collar. The blouse was tucked into a full silk skirt with a train. Her hair had been swept up with yellow roses and white camellias clustered on one side. The dress and hairstyle matched the picture of her ancestor that was found during the restoration of the plantation house Halcyon.

Mae observed the groom wiping his eyes as his bride approached. As Jo walked up to him, the scent of eucalyptus overpowered all the other flowers that surrounded them. Watching them, Mae felt a slight twinge of jealousy at how open and honest they were with their love.

Judge Beaumont cleared his throat and began the ceremony. There was a lovely reading of the Paul Lawrence Dunbar poem "Invitation to Love" before the judge asked them to repeat the traditional vows. Mae had been busy sneaking glances at Jacob and almost missed the moment when the groom's brother handed him a simple platinum band that he slid on the bride's finger, next to her beautiful diamond engagement ring. Mae blinked back her tears as they were pronounced man and wife.

A broom was placed in front of them, decorated with flowers and gingham ribbon. Taylor Colton took his bride's hand, and they both jumped to cheers and applause, and the DJ started playing PJ Morton's "Only One." Each groomsman escorted a bridesmaid, dancing down the aisle. When it was her turn, Jacob held out his hand for Mae with a smile. For a large man, he could move surprisingly well. He swiveled his hips and spun her around, making her breathless before they descended the gazebo steps.

Tilly insisted on hosting the reception, so the street in front of the park was closed off, lights had been strung in a zigzag down one half of the block in front of the café, and a large tent was set up at the other end. Mae watched with amusement while the café owner directed the students from the culinary program at the trade school in Greenwood as if she were the conductor of an orchestra. She waved her arms around while the students scurried about, bringing out platters of food. The culinary students presented the three-tiered cake covered in confectionary flowers in yellow and white as their wedding present to the newly married couple.

There were the traditional toasts and speeches, and then it was Mae's turn to come to the microphone. She'd been working with the governor's office for months to arrange this moment, and she'd managed to keep it a secret, wanting to surprise her friends.

She stepped up to the microphone and cleared her throat. "Ladies and gentlemen, I'm happy to be here with you all tonight. Although my role on this occasion is a bridesmaid, I hope y'all will indulge me for just a minute while I put my mayor hat on."

She reached down and pulled out the plaque she had hidden earlier by the podium. "Will the new Mr. and Mrs. Colton please come up here with me?" They came forward, looking at her with curiosity. "Taylor and Jo, it is my great honor as the interim mayor of Colton to announce that the governor of Mississippi has signed an executive order renaming Colonel Absolem Madden Colton Park, the Ada Mae Riley Park." There were gasps and murmurs of approval as she held up the plaque so everyone could see.

Jo pulled her into a hug. "I don't know what to say. Thank you. This is an incredible gift."

Taylor was next to wrap her in his arms. "Thank you, Mae. Just when I thought this day couldn't get any better."

The three of them stood with their arms wrapped around each other, posing with the plaque for the photographer. The bride and groom took the plaque over to show their parents while Mae made her way back to her table.

Her mom and dad came over when she was finished. "Oh honey, I'm so proud."

"Thanks, Mom."

"That's a pretty big secret," her dad said. "How in the world did you pull it off?"

Mae gave her dad a wry smile. "I didn't let any email or phone calls go through the office, so my office manager didn't know."

Joseph let out a hearty laugh. The same woman had been running the office at Town Hall since the days when they were called secretaries. The woman was a notorious gossip, and in a small town where secrets didn't stay secrets for long, she transmitted information faster than the new high-speed internet they'd just brought to town.

"Well, good job, baby girl."

"Excuse me." Jacob came over. "I thought the mayor might like a glass of champagne to celebrate both the wedding and her hard work."

His hand briefly touched hers as he handed her a glass, sending a shiver of desire through her. As much fun as the evening was, she couldn't wait for it to be just the two of them.

Her parents drifted away to visit with Jo's parents. Jacob drained the rest of his glass and set it down on the table. "May I have this dance?"

Mae set her glass down and slipped her hand into his. He pulled her onto the dance floor just as the tempo changed. He drew her closer and clasped her hand to his chest, while her other hand rested on his shoulder.

"You smell like summer," he whispered in her ear.

"People are staring."

"No, they aren't, they're watching the bride and groom."

"Behave yourself, Mr. Winters. It was your idea to keep our relationship on the down-low."

"It was both our idea."

Mae pulled back and scowled. He was right, but he didn't have to remind her about a decision she was beginning to wonder if she regretted. Looking around at the other couples dancing and occasionally kissing, she wondered why she thought she couldn't have what they had.

"Is there a problem, Pixie?"

"Children, don't fight," Dax admonished as he danced past them with Callie.

Jacob looked down at her, his lips curling into that smile that always made her stomach dip. He leaned forward and whispered one word in her ear that set her entire body on fire.

"Foreplay."

"We can't leave yet. It would be too obvious."

Jacob nodded, the song ended, and the tempo changed again. Mae watched Jacob break out some serious dance moves that she honestly didn't think a White man could be capable of before she met him. She already knew the man had mastered the electric slide from his performance at Callie and Dax's wedding. Jacob was full of surprises. Mae cherished the brief glimpses of carefree moments when he let his guard down.

Her dad came over when the next slow song started. "Do you mind if I have a dance with my little girl?"

Jacob nodded. "Of course."

Joseph Colton clapped his hand on Jacob's shoulder. "You'll understand one day when you have a little girl of your own."

Mae looked down just in case there was a hole nearby she could jump into. She watched helplessly as Jacob walked away while her dad twirled her around the dance floor.

"You shouldn't have said that, Dad. What if Jacob doesn't want to have children?"

"He'll settle down one day, just like you will once you've established yourself in DC."

"Can we take a break from talking about my future and just enjoy the party?"

"All right, all right, I'll stop." He chuckled. A minute later, he looked toward the gazebo. "Just promise me when it's your turn, you'll come home from Washington and get married under the gazebo."

"Of course, Dad."

Mae added her dad's request to the impossibly long list of her sister's failings she'd have to make up for.

The song ended, and he let her go. She stood on tiptoe and gave him a kiss on the cheek. He could be annoying sometimes, but he was her dad, her hero. He was the first man she'd ever danced with, standing on his shoes in the living room, giggling while he waltzed her around. No matter how hard it was to carry the weight of her parents' expectations sometimes, she loved them.

Suddenly, it felt like there were too many people around her, and the air was too hot, too sweet from all the flowers and the spring air. She backed away from the dance floor and headed into the park and the gazebo.

She stepped under the canopy adorned with flowers, reaching up to caress one of the cherry blossom branches that had been artfully arranged to become part of the ceiling. When it was her turn, she didn't want so many flowers or people; just her with the man she wanted to wake up to every morning and create a lifetime of memories with. The truth was, Mae never thought she'd be a Colton bride; she'd always pictured herself single, living in the big city. But just over a year ago, a giant of a man who reminded her of an angry lumberjack the first time she saw him walked into her life. Now, she had a job she loved and a relationship that held promise. Her life had changed, and now she wondered if her hopes and dreams were really hers or what other people expected her to do.

"Hey, Pixie, what are you doing out here?"

The nickname Jacob gave her on the first day they met wasn't as annoying as it used to be. She'd grown to like it as much as she liked the man who made it sound so sexy when it came from his lips.

She turned around, and Jacob was leaning against one pillar of the gazebo with his arms folded in front of him. How long had he been there watching her?

"I just needed a break from all the people."

He poked his thumb in his chest. "I'm the one who's antisocial. You love this stuff."

"You're not antisocial, you're just... grumpy."

"You didn't think I was grumpy the other night," he said with a cocky grin.

Mae glanced around to make sure they were alone before she stepped toward him and kissed him, nipping at his bottom lip before she moved away.

"I happen to like grumpy."

He reached out, linking her pinkie with his. "I don't understand why."

His gaze was filled with sadness and something that she could only think of as longing.

"Because you may have fooled some folks around here, but I know your secret." Jacob's eyes widened just a fraction. "Grumpy is just an act. The real Jacob Winters is a thoughtful man, who can be a romantic when he wants to be."

"Mae, I—"

Whatever he was about to say was interrupted by a *pop* and then a burst of color overhead.

"Come on, let's go watch the show," Jacob said, letting go of her hand and shoving his into his pockets.

Mae walked alongside him, wondering how they had made their relationship so complicated when it was supposed to be so simple. *A summer fling*, that's what she told herself when Jacob roared into town on his motorcycle. From the very beginning, he'd told her he didn't know if he'd be staying, and he wasn't a commitment kind of guy. That was fine with her; she wasn't looking for two-point-five kids and a white picket fence. But now here they were, a year later, and Jacob had bought the hardware store and put down roots.

She glanced at his profile, lit up with a rainbow from the glittering lights in the sky. His jaw was set, and his eyes were locked straight ahead. Jacob always had a way of moving like he was headed toward a target. Most of that came from his years in the military, but some of it was just a part of who he was. Just one more part she'd given her heart to.

Thoughtful and *romantic* weren't the words she'd use to describe him; she wanted to say *loving*, but she couldn't bring herself to. That was a bridge they'd agreed not to cross. Summer flings didn't end with her under the gazebo in a white dress, but summer flings weren't supposed to last once the leaves turned from green to gold and back to bright again, either.

JACOB BURROWED deeper under the covers, wrapping his arms around the warm body pressed against him. Mae turned with a soft sigh, reaching up to cup his cheek.

"I'm sorry," she said, brushing her thumb over his lips.

No other woman could bring him to his knees with a simple touch the way she could. He grasped her hand and pressed a kiss to her fingertips.

"I'm sorry too."

It was a silly argument over whether they had left the wedding party too early or not. They both liked to push each other's buttons. He did it just because he liked to see the fire in her eyes. Deep-brown eyes that were filled with so much life. Humor, passion, pain, everything Mae experienced was reflected in her eyes. He'd become addicted to looking into them, as he had everything else about her.

"We have to stop," she said, pulling her hand out of his. She sat up and started looking around the room for her clothes.

Jacob ran his hand through his hair and sat up, leaning against the headboard. "I'm not being rude. I'm being honest."

Mae scooted back until she mirrored his position. "We can't keep sleeping together when we both know nothing is going to come out of it."

He hated the way she spoke with a tinge of sadness. He didn't want to hurt her, but he'd made it clear from the first night their fighting escalated into something more that he wasn't interested in a relationship. He didn't want to make memories he'd never be able to forget.

Mae jumped out of bed and began gathering her clothes that were strewn around the room. She glowed in the morning light. Shorter than average, when he first met her he thought she was all sharp angles. Over time, that opinion had changed. He relished how soft and warm she felt in his arms every time they were together. His fingers itched to reach out for her and pull her back into bed so he could run his hands over every inch of her dark brown skin. He couldn't keep her, but he didn't want to let her go. These were the only moments he regretted taking the assignment that brought him to Colton.

CHAPTER TWO

"MORNING, MAYOR," Ben, the oldest of the three Anderson brothers who owned Mockingbird Orchard, called out while he lifted a crate of apples out of his truck. "Looks like we're gonna have another busy weekend."

Mae smiled and waved. The Colton Farmers Market had only been going for a couple of months, but it was already a success. Every Saturday, the newly renamed park buzzed with activity as local residents came out to sell their wares.

She skirted away from where June Palmer was setting up her table filled with jars of honey and homemade granola. Ms. June had been given many labels over the years—town kook, radical hippie, and do-gooder among just a few. Yes, she might be a bit quirky, but the woman had a heart of gold. Her long silver-gray hair was in its usual fishtail braid, and she was wearing her trademark outfit of a denim shirt with a long, flowing batik skirt and Birkenstocks. It was a sure sign that winter was over when Ms. June stopped wearing her sandals without socks. When Mae became mayor, she came out of the self-imposed isolation she'd been in since her husband died a few years ago, with many helpful suggestions for town improvements. It didn't matter if Mae avoided her today; Ms. June would be in her office first thing Tuesday morning with a list of ideas, as she had done since Mae's first week on the job. It wasn't so bad really, and it was important to her to be accessible to the people she served, especially after the chaos the old town council left behind. They ran the town as more of a dictatorship than a democracy, and ethics weren't high on their list of priorities.

It had been almost a month since the night of Taylor's and Jo's wedding. They'd returned from their honeymoon, and the sounds of saws and hammers echoed from just a few blocks away, where Taylor Colton was filming another episode of his home improvement show. Bringing his show *History Reborn* to Colton had been a big boon and bolstered efforts to rejuvenate the town. They'd even started having a few fans of the show coming to visit.

Slowly but surely, Colton was transforming from a brief stop on a long railway line into a destination. A place where people would want to stop and stay a while. Morning dew clung to Mae's sneakers as she made her way across the park toward her best friend Callie's storefront. The Spring Street Bookstore and Coffee Shop was one of the first new businesses Colton had seen in decades. But if Mae had anything to say about it, there would be more to come. The jangle of the bell above the door brought a smile to her lips, and the smell of fresh baked goods made her stomach rumble.

"Morning." The barista gave her a smile from behind the espresso machine.

"Morning, how are you doing today?"

"Just fine, ma'am, thank you."

"Oh, please"—Mae waved her hand at the young woman—"I am not ready for ma'am-hood yet."

Steam rose from the milk the barista was heating, and she carefully poured it into the cup, creating a pretty leaf design before handing it to Mae.

"I figured you'd want your usual, a latte, right?" She chewed on her lip. "I shouldn't have assumed." She tried to take the cup back.

"Nope"—Mae took the cup from her—"this is perfect."

The young woman hesitated for a second. "I just wanted to say thank you for all you're doing to make things right here in Colton. There's a group of us at the trade school who are looking for a place we can rent. We all want to do our part to help the town grow."

Mae's heart filled until she thought it would burst with pride. "Thank you for saying that. I really appreciate it."

She took her coffee and said goodbye while thinking about what the barista had said as she wandered through the bookstore toward the library. There were other buildings in Colton that had empty second stories. Maybe she could talk to Dax about investing in remodeling some of those spaces into apartments the way he did with the Barton Building. Mae gave herself a mental shake. She was doing it again. Dreaming and scheming when she wasn't sure if she would be around to see her dreams realized.

Mae paused at the magazine rack to glance at the latest issue of her favorite knitting magazine before she headed through the doorway that connected the bookstore to the town library. She left the magazine on the rack, not wanting to tempt herself with a new project until she was finished with the sweater she was making for Jacob. It was a well-known rule among knitters that you should never knit a sweater for someone you were dating. The superstition was that you would break up with the person you were seeing before you finished the project. But since Jacob and Mae weren't "official" and she was almost finished, she didn't feel like she was tempting fate.

Her best friend Calle was perched on the edge of her desk, making out with her husband when Mae walked through the doorway. She observed them for a moment with a pang of envy. Mae was tired of sneaking around with Jacob. It was fun when they started, but now she felt a little embarrassed. She was a grown woman and deserved better than a fling. She'd never thought of herself as the kind of person who made ultimatums, but it was time to talk to Jacob.

Mae cleared her throat to announce her presence. "Sorry to interrupt, y'all, but do you think you can keep your hands off each other for five minutes?"

Callie's husband Dax chuckled and gave his wife a kiss on her forehead before heading toward the door.

"Have a good day, ladies." He saluted before heading out.

"Honestly, you two are worse than the high school kids necking in the park after dark."

Callie blushed. "Sorry, I guess we're still in the honeymoon phase."

Mae's heart softened. She was happy for her best friend. Callie and Dax didn't have the smoothest road to romance. As happy as she was for her friend, she couldn't help the tinge of sadness she felt. While Callie gained a loving husband and partner, Mae had lost her wingman. Of course, they would always be best friends, but Callie spent most of her time with Dax now. And that was the way it should be. It's what she would do if she found a partner to spend the rest of her life with.

"Hopefully, that phase lasts for as long as you're married."

Her friend looked at her thoughtfully. "I'm not sure it's supposed to. I think there'll be ebb and flow, good days and bad days. It's knowing that even when you're going through a rough patch, the person you're with is who you want to have by your side. Even when Dax and I disagree, he's still the person I want to wake up to every morning."

Mae thought about waking up in Jacob's bed that morning. It was time to admit to herself she wanted what Callie and Dax had. She was ready to share her life, the good and the bad, with someone. And that someone was Jacob. It wasn't supposed to be him. He wasn't her type. She'd always dated polished, put-together professional men. Usually people who hung out in the same political circles she did when she worked for Senator Weems in Jackson. But none of those men with their sharp suits and perfect haircuts made her heart beat faster the way a certain grumpy, bearded man who looked like a lumberjack with his flannel shirts stretched across his broad shoulders did.

Callie waved her hand in front of her face. "Mae... earth to Mae."

"What? Oh, sorry."

"You were awfully distracted just now. Anything you want to share?"

Mae shook her head. "Just distracted with work."

"How's life in Town Hall?"

"Not too bad, actually. There's a lot of infrastructure work that needs to happen."

"Do you need another donation from the Colton Foundation?"

Mae shook her head. "I appreciate the offer, but the entire town needs to be involved. This has to be a community effort to succeed. I sent out a questionnaire to everyone asking what they would like to see prioritized, and there are a lot of state and federal grant programs we can take advantage of. It's just a lot of paperwork and phone calls."

The library door opened and a group of children came in with their parents, full of energy and filling the quiet room with their excited chatter.

"I'll let you get to work." Mae waved to Callie and headed back out to the town square. She quickened her step, wanting to sneak in one more kiss from Jacob before the day swept them away.

Friends and neighbors called out greetings as she made her way down the block. Sometimes it could be a nuisance, but Mae loved living in a community where everyone knew each other. It was that love of community that motivated her to accept the governor's request.

Just over eight months ago, the state senator she'd been working for called her into his office and made a bombshell announcement.

A year ago, Colton was rocked by the biggest scandal the state had seen in many years. Two members of the town council, one of them being the sheriff, were in jail, and the third was facing corruption charges. The state had pressed racketeering charges against all three. The day Mae was summoned into Senator Weems's office, she found the senator and the governor of Mississippi himself waiting for her. The Colton town council had been dissolved, and the senator had put her name forward to serve as interim mayor of her hometown. Her degrees in business management and political science, combined with the fact she was a Colton, made her a perfect fit. It didn't hurt that the governor liked the optics of promoting a young Black woman for his own political career.

You could have knocked her over with a feather, but once she got over the initial surprise, she jumped at the challenge. She'd spent years watching her hometown mismanaged. The corruption was even worse than she'd realized. Her first few weeks in office had been consumed with wading through old, outdated contracts and finding out what happened to all the missing town funds. Eight months later, she could see the results of all her hard work. They'd recovered some of the town funds, and the Colton Foundation had provided additional money to support revitalization efforts. The one-man fire department was now a two-man fire department, and the town had a new sheriff who had integrity and honored the office he held. They also had a new doctor, and the clinic had reopened.

She stared at the hardware store at the end of the block for a minute. Jacob would probably be busy and annoyed that she was interrupting, but she didn't care; it made little sense, but spending time with the surly lumberjack made her day a little brighter. She snorted a laugh. Of course, he wasn't a real lumberjack, but that's what he reminded her of the first time they met. Tall, with dark hair that wasn't long, but long enough that she could run her fingers through it. He had a thick beard and mustache; she'd always liked clean-cut guys before, but there was something about those full lips surrounded by those whiskers. Her stomach did a little dance thinking about how those lips felt when they'd kissed the inside of her thigh that morning.

She walked into Winters's Hardware and glanced around to see if there were any customers. Confirming that they were alone, she slipped behind the counter and stood up on her tiptoes to give her big burly lumberjack a quick kiss on the lips.

"What was that for?"

Mae shrugged. "Just because."

"You're getting awfully bold, Ms. Colton," he said with a teasing smile.

"Maybe it's time to be bold and stop sneaking around."

Jacob's expression grew serious, and Mae's heart constricted.

"Mae, I—"

The door opened and the Jewels walked in, interrupting whatever it was he was about to say. That was just fine with Mae. She had a feeling she wasn't going to like what Jacob was going to say.

She stepped back and poked her finger at Jacob's chest. "I expect to see you at the next business association meeting, Mr. Winters. No excuses this time," she said in a stern, no-nonsense voice.

She gave him a quick wink before spinning around to face the three sisters known as the Jewels.

"Morning," said Opal, the oldest.

"We just need to pick up some oilcloth," Pearl, the middle sister, said, pointing to the barrel of checkered oilcloth rolls in the corner.

"We thought it would look nice on our table," Ruby, the youngest, added.

"What are you ladies offering at the market today?" Jacob asked.

"We've got a fresh batch of strawberry jam and some raspberry cordial today."

"Tell you what, I'll trade you some cordial for as much of that oilcloth as you want. That batch of blackberry you made last summer was some good stuff."

The Jewels beamed with pride and bustled off to the display and started arguing over colors.

Jacob leaned across the counter. "I'll see you later tonight?"

Mae nodded and headed out of the store. She squinted against the bright blue sky before slipping on her sunglasses. She wandered back into the park, meandering through the vendors at the farmers' market. Buying a few things here and there was another way she could support her community.

She wanted to stroll through the park hand in hand with Jacob instead of by herself. *No more sneaking around*, she decided. It was time to take their relationship public.

CHAPTER THREE

THE NEXT morning, Jacob sat on the rooftop deck he'd built when he helped his friend Dax rehab the old three-story cotton trading building into apartments, with an office on the ground floor Dax could use for his business. He loved this view, looking out over the treetops of Colton's town square. Sipping at his coffee, he watched the sky brighten from lavender gray to a bright blue. He shook his head with a slight smile. There were days when he still couldn't believe he would find a place that gave him a sense of peace the way Colton did. He'd gone from being a loner to being surrounded by friends and people he thought of as family. And then there was Mae. She was in a category all her own. The only problem was, he wasn't sure what that was. She wasn't his girlfriend, or at least he wasn't willing to give her that title. Doing that would go against one of the rules he made for himself. No girlfriends, no serious relationships.

The two of them were like a string of firecrackers, igniting sparks every time they were together. She pushed all of his buttons, and he kept coming back for more. Mae brought him back to life again. The years he'd spent trying to stay aloof and alone, all the walls he'd built around his heart, were all ruined the minute he met her. And to be honest, it pissed him off. Even though he should, he couldn't stay away from her. His Pixie, he chuckled, thinking about her reaction the first time he'd used the nickname for her. Those dark brown eyes ringed with thick black eyelashes flashed with protectiveness and care for her friend. Her pink lips formed a perfect *O*, her oval face transformed with emotion. He recalled every detail of that moment because his photographic memory allowed him to.

A slight breeze ruffled through the treetops. There were days like today when he still felt guilty. There would always be that part of him that didn't feel like he deserved this life after what happened to his parents.

As if on cue, the access door to the roof opened, and Dax stepped through. He nodded and said thanks when Jacob held out the thermos he'd brought up with a spare cup. Dax reached into his jacket pocket and pulled out a flask. This had been their ritual since the first time they'd shared this day together.

The first time they'd spent this day together, Dax found him on a different rooftop on the other side of the world, watching the sunrise the same way he was now. Dax didn't ask questions that first morning he found him; he just sat down next to Jacob, watching the sky. It was the first time he'd shared with anyone the significance of the day. Now, more than a decade later, Dax was still at his side, supporting him while he mourned.

Dax opened the flask and poured a shot into each of their cups. Lifting his, he said, "For Naomi Sarah Winters, may her memory be a blessing."

It was an odd way to observe his mother's Yahrzeit, the anniversary of her death. But they had never been a traditional kind of family. He wasn't religious, but he kept this tradition out of respect for his mom.

His mom came from a religious family, and when his Italian father, a rookie in the fire department, had a call in her building, it was love at first sight. When his mother's family discovered she had been sneaking out to meet a boy, they made an ultimatum—stop seeing him or she would be shunned. She chose love, and it cost her. Her parents sat Shiva for her, mourning her loss as if she were dead, and she never saw them again. Even when his dad died, they didn't send their condolences. When the cancer finished its terrible war against her body, they didn't come to her funeral. But the members of the women's league at the reform synagogue where she had found a new religious home had. Every member of the synagogue was there, and all of his classmates from Hebrew school, his teammates from the football team, along with Coach Murphy and his wife, who took him in after his mom died.

They finished the rest of their coffee in silence. When Jacob set his empty cup down, Dax followed suit and asked, "Are you ready?"

He nodded, and they stood up in unison and turned to face the East.

"*Yitgadal v'yitkadash sh'mei raba b'alma di v'ra...*"

Dax's voice joined his in the mourners' Kaddish, the traditional blessing for someone who had died. Jacob exhaled on the word *Amen* and looked at his friend.

"Thank you."

Dax put his hand on his shoulder. "You never have to thank me, you know that."

Most of the time, Jacob kept his grief to himself, but twice a year, he shared it with Dax. No matter where they were in the world, on 9/11—the day of his father's death—and the anniversary of his mother's passing, Dax was with him. It was the only time he allowed himself to feel the pain, and it was just as fresh today as it was all those years ago.

He'd thought about inviting Mae to the rooftop with him this morning and quickly rejected the idea. He'd already broken his rule when it came to Mae. Don't let people get too close, so that way it won't hurt so much if you lose them.

"You don't have to keep doing this, you know."

"Yeah, I do," Dax said quietly.

A look of silent understanding passed between them.

"I wish I could stay, but I've got to get back—"

"Don't," Jacob interrupted. "You don't owe me any explanations. Besides, I've got some new inventory I need to take care of before I open."

Dax smiled and shook his head. "I never imagined you'd turn into a respectable business owner when I talked you into coming down here. I didn't think you were ready to give up being a Ranger and going out into the field." Dax huffed a laugh. "You were always happier sleeping in a cave somewhere than in a bed."

Jacob forced himself to smile even though Dax's words felt like a knife in his heart. His best friend didn't know the truth, that he hadn't given up covert operations but had just changed the agency he was working for.

"Sometimes, when an opportunity presents itself, you have to take advantage of it."

"I'm glad you did. I'm thrilled you've made Colton your home."

What should have been a compliment sat like lead in Jacob's stomach. Would Dax feel that way if he knew Jacob had been lying to him the entire time?

He ran into Mae when he came downstairs with Dax. He eyed the black knit dress that did a crossover thing over her breasts, creating a deep vee that tied on one side. It didn't show much skin, but it was enough for him to start thinking about undoing the tie and peeling the dress off to reveal all of her, because that one small glimpse wasn't enough. It was never enough. His gaze roved down from the tempting patch of skin at her throat to the patch of skin between the hem of her dress and the top of her boots.

"I don't know why you insist on being so… fancy all the time," he grumbled.

Mae frowned and looked down at her outfit and back at Jacob. "This isn't fancy. It's professional. Maybe you should think about wearing something other than an outfit that makes you look like a lumberjack." She eyed him up and down. "There's going to be a shortage of flannel if you keep this up."

"There's more than enough left to keep sheets on your bed."

He watched the flush of pink spread over her cheeks. Mae might have a tough exterior, but he'd seen the real woman who was all softness and floral flannel sheets.

His eyes flickered to Dax, who watched them with amusement. He was playing with fire, and it was going to bite him in the ass if he wasn't careful.

"I don't have time for this," he ground out. Turning on his heel, he marched out and headed toward his store. Good Lord, he couldn't manage to be in a room for one second with that woman without wanting her.

Guilt made his footsteps heavy as he made long strides across the park toward his store. He wasn't proud of lying to Mae, Dax, and everyone else in Colton; it was one of the worst parts of his job. But seeing the bright blue letters outlined in orange that proclaimed Winters's Hardware every morning always gave him a sense of satisfaction. He blinked at the glint of sunlight on the letters. His father would have been proud. He didn't regret the impulse buy, even though he shouldn't have made the commitment when he didn't know if he would stay, or if he could stay, when the real reason he came to Colton was revealed.

He opened the door to the hardware store and flipped on the lights. Every time he completed that simple action, he felt a small swell of pride. The chaos the previous owner left behind had been transformed. The walls were painted white, and new lighting meant customers could actually see what they wanted to buy. He'd added a small selection of housewares, fishing, and gardening supplies, something that had made him a favorite among the members of the Colton gardening club and Mae's mother. And yes, maybe it was important to him to make a good impression on Mae's mom.

He replayed the memory of waking up in bed with Mae that morning while he went through his opening routine. He didn't like the mornings he woke up without her by his side. Mae brought warmth and joy to his bed and his life. For anyone else, that might seem like a good thing, but it didn't suit the life he'd chosen for himself.

He'd just flipped the Closed sign to Open when Isiah came in.

"Mornin'," Isiah said, touching the tip of his hat with his fingers.

"You sure have gone all-in on the small-town sheriff thing."

Isiah chuckled. "It's crazy, I know. It couldn't be more different from working as a fire marshal in Chicago, but I like it."

"Colton's lucky to have you after that asshole Crosby."

"Well, he's making a lot of new friends down at the prison," Isiah said.

"The list of corruption charges ensures he won't be a free man for a very long time," Jacob said with a smirk.

"Let's hope so."

"What brings you in this morning?" Jacob asked.

Isiah's expression grew serious. "I wanted to make sure you haven't had any trouble."

"What kind of trouble?"

"A few of the businesses and a couple of churches in the area have been hit with racist graffiti. One church in Wynona was set on fire. Thankfully, someone was in the building, and they caught it before it could do any real damage. There's been some rumors around that there's a white supremacist group in the area that's flexing their muscles."

Jacob's gut clenched. "No, I haven't had any trouble."

"Good, I'm letting all the businesses and houses of worship in town know. Thankfully, with Dax setting up business here, we have security cameras in the town square."

Jacob nodded. "Helps to have a friend who specializes in electronic surveillance and cybersecurity."

"Having the cameras is a good thing, but the entire community is going to have to be vigilant."

"I'll keep my eyes open."

"Thanks man, I—"

Isiah's words trailed off as a streak of bright yellow sped down the street, catching his attention.

"Goddammit," Isiah muttered, heading for the door. "I'll catch up with you at the Buckthorn," he called out over his shoulder.

Jacob shook his head with a wry smile. Isiah had been chasing Presley Beaumont and her yellow convertible and handing out speeding tickets since the day he started the job. It was a game of cat and mouse that, at the moment, the mouse was winning.

With a sigh, he pulled out his phone and dialed a number. A man on the other end answered on the first ring.

"Any updates?"

Jacob frowned when the voice on the other end said no. He hung up and stood at the store window, watching the comings and goings. His gaze traveled over to the town hall, and he wondered what Mae was doing. More importantly, he wondered if Isiah had shared the same news with her. He turned away. This was why he needed to end his relationship with her—she was a distraction he didn't need right now.

So why was he hesitating? He'd never had a problem keeping his romantic entanglements brief. It was careless to let himself take his relationship with Mae this far. Looking around the store, he sighed. He wasn't planning on putting down roots in Colton either, but somehow he'd found himself a home here, something he'd sworn he would never do.

The store was one thing, but the situation with Mae was different. He had to end it with Mae. It wasn't fair to her, and it was too hard on him.

CHAPTER FOUR

THE BUCKTHORN buzzed energy; it seemed like most of the town had kicked off their weekend at the juke joint that Friday night. Jacob nodded to Mr. Wallace as he served up whiskey and beers from behind the bar with Reid Ellis. An old Muddy Waters song played in the background, mingling with the conversations from customers.

Dax waved at Jacob from the table toward the back where he sat with his wife, Callie. Peanut shells crunched under his feet as he wove his way through the picnic tables toward his friends. He'd just sat down when Mae's laughter drifted toward him as she walked in with Isiah. Jacob clenched his hands into fists under the table, fighting the wave of jealousy that took him by surprise. Her eyes lit up when Isiah leaned over to whisper something in her ear, making her laugh again. He had no reason to be jealous; he knew that, but it didn't stop him from wanting to drag Mae away from Isiah and stake his claim. Ignoring the curious look from Callie, he pulled some peanuts away from the larger pile in the center of the table and focused on removing the nut from its papery shell while Isiah and Mae took their seats.

Reid joined them, handing Jacob a beer.

"Good to see you," Jacob said as Reid took a seat next to him. "I haven't seen you much since you made your move. How are you settling in?"

"I've been spending most of my time here. Primus and I are working on a few new ideas. I sold my condo furnished back in Chicago, so it was a pretty simple move."

"Is this going to be something full-time for you?" Jacob asked, waving his hand toward the bar.

Reid frowned down at the glass of whiskey in his hand. "I'm not sure. I transferred my law license just in case something came up that I'm interested in." He glanced back toward the bar. "I'm happy being an apprentice and learning everything I can about making whiskey from Primus. That man is an encyclopedia of knowledge. I already have one journal filled with notes, and I'm starting another one. I'm taking my time before I decide what my next steps are going to be."

Jacob nodded. "Colton's a good place to figure things out. You've got family and good friends here."

"Thanks, I appreciate that."

"Oh, I'm so glad you're here!" Presley exclaimed, bouncing up to their table with her brother Ashton.

Jacob watched Colton's resident beauty queen and all-around troublemaker smile at Reid, completely unaware of the looks of disdain from the rest of the table.

She plopped down next to Reid. "I need a new dress for the Moonlight and Magnolia dance at the country club, and I thought we could go shopping together."

Mae barked out a laugh.

"Please tell me you're not asking Reid to be your gay best friend," Callie said.

"I hate to break it to you, Presley, but not all gay men like to shop," her brother Ashton said with a wry smile.

"Well, you do," Presley shot back, "but you won't help me."

All eyes at the table turned to Ashton as his face became flushed. "I can't believe you just did that," he choked out.

"What?" Presley blinked at him, completely unaware that she'd just outed her brother.

"Ms. Beaumont, I'd like to have a word with you." Isiah stood up and walked over to Presley, grasping her by the elbow and pulling her out to the patio.

Jacob watched along with his friends as Isiah pointed at Presley while she stared up at him open-mouthed.

"I'd pay money to hear that conversation." Mae chuckled.

Ashton sat with his head bowed, picking at the label of his beer. "I wasn't hiding it, I just—"

"Ash, I think I can speak for everyone here.... We respect your privacy, and your love life is none of our business," Dax said.

Ashton nodded but didn't say anything.

"So are we still friends?" Dax broke the awkward silence.

Ashton looked at everyone at the table. "Thanks, y'all," he said in a quiet voice.

The patio door opened, and Presley came back in with Isiah behind her. She approached their table, twisting her hands with a nervous glance at Isiah standing behind her with his arms folded.

"Ash, I would like to apologize. I was selfish and—"

"Inconsiderate," Isiah prompted.

"Inconsiderate," Presley parroted.

Ashton looked from his sister to Isiah and back again.

Presley's chin trembled. "If y'all will excuse me…." Whatever else she said was lost as she turned and fled from the bar.

Isiah sat down with a sigh while Ashton stared at his retreating sister with his mouth open.

"Should we call you Professor Higgins?" Mae quipped.

Jacob shot her a look.

What? she mouthed back at him.

He shifted in his seat, his body already anticipating the argument they would have later that would lead to Mae ending up in his bed again. He'd given up trying to make sense of their relationship. They were fire and ice, and Mae usually won whatever argument they were having, melting his heart in the process.

Ashton looked at Isiah. "You're a goddamn miracle worker. I've never been able to get my sister to apologize for anything."

Isiah shrugged and downed the contents of his glass. His eyes grew wide, and he put his hand to his chest, sputtering and coughing. "Damn, what in the world are you putting in that stuff?"

Reid grinned. "That, my friend, is one of the best-kept secrets in Mississippi."

Jacob smirked. *If only they knew.*

Conversation around the table resumed, and Jacob was happy to sit back and let the chatter flow around him while he observed the people coming and going from the bar. There were always a few familiar faces around. A couple of older guys were sitting at a corner table with a couple of other men telling tall tales from their latest fishing trip, while another table full of students he recognized from the local trade school burst into raucous laughter. One of the first things he did when he took over the hardware store was to offer a discount to the students who went to the trade school; it was an easy thing he could do to support them.

The door opened, and all conversation stopped. Jacob leaned forward in his seat, watching the group of young men file in. Tension filled the room, and every customer watched the group approach the bar. There were a few hushed whispers, wondering what this particular group was doing in the Buckthorn.

"I can't believe they have the nerve to come in here," Mae said, glaring at the group.

"Who?" Reid asked.

"I don't know the others, but that one is Rhett Colton," Dax said, pointing to one with dark blond shaggy hair.

Reid shook his head. "I don't remember him."

"He's a distant cousin, very distant." Dax frowned. "His family has a farm between here and Greenwood, but last I heard, they'd all shunned Rhett."

Callie's eyes grew wide, and she gasped when Mr. Wallace turned off the music and pulled out a bat. Setting it on the bar, he glared at the group with a thunderous expression.

Isiah jumped up and put his hand out when Reid followed. "I've got this," he said.

Even out of his uniform, there was no mistaking that he was giving a command. Reid sank back down into his seat with his fists clenched. Jacob's body tensed, instantly reverting to his military training. He kept his eyes trained on Isiah, watching him go behind the bar to stand with Mr. Wallace. One man, clearly the ringleader, took a step forward, and the skin over Mr. Wallace's knuckles stretched taut as he gripped the bat tighter.

"I don't serve racist trash in my bar," Mr. Wallace said between clenched teeth.

"You don't get to tell us what we can do, old man," the ringleader sneered.

Isiah pulled out his badge and slammed it on the bar. The man frowned and stepped back.

They stared each other down for a minute until the leader jerked his head, and the group followed him out the door. Mr. Wallace turned toward Isiah and shook his hand; then he reached under the counter and pulled out a bottle of whiskey, pressing it into the sheriff's hands.

The music started up again, and Jacob cracked his neck, trying to release some of the tension. There were murmurs of "Good job, Sheriff" and other words of appreciation as Isiah made his way back toward them. He sat down and set the bottle in the center of the table.

"You okay?" Jacob asked.

Isiah gave him a wry smile. "Part of the job."

"I haven't seen those guys in here before," Reid said.

"That's the problem," Dax said between clenched teeth. "That was a sampling of our local white supremacist group. Klan, Proud Boys, or whatever they're calling themselves these days."

"I'm so damn disappointed in Rhett," Mae said.

Reid stood up from the table. "If you'll excuse me, I'm gonna go back and help at the bar."

"Damn," Ashton muttered. "I really hate those guys. I agree with you, Mae, I can't believe Rhett would fall in with them. But I have to admit, I've had moments when I've been worried about Presley."

Isiah's forehead wrinkled, and he sighed. Jacob groaned inwardly. He knew that look. His friend was a fixer, and for whatever crazy reason, he'd decided he could fix Presley. God help him.

"Isiah, do you think we're going to have any problems?" Mae asked.

Jacob's stomach clenched. Mae had just voiced his constant worry.

"I'm keeping an eye on it," Isiah said.

"We all will," Dax added.

The intrusion took the fun out of the evening, and they all headed home after another round of drinks.

Isiah and Mae pulled up to the Barton Building the same time as Jacob, their three car doors slamming in unison. Jacob pulled out his key and opened the door, and Isiah headed over to the keypad and entered the security code.

Isiah and Mae chatted about the new deputy candidate they would interview the next day as they made their way upstairs. The sound of music from the fourth apartment, where Taylor Colton's assistant Chloe lived, drifted down the hallway. They each went to their apartments.

"Good night," Isiah said, nodding.

Jacob gave a brief wave and glanced over at Mae.

"Good night," Mae called out. She opened her door and looked at Jacob over her shoulder with a wink before she closed the door.

MAE SHIMMIED out of her clothes, anticipation thrumming through her body. Sometimes she wondered if Jacob felt the same need. She hoped he did; she wanted him to.

Seeing Callie and Dax at the library the other day made her realize she might miss out by not being in a committed relationship. From the first night they'd spent together, she and Jacob agreed they were just having a fling. It was supposed to be nothing serious, and they could stop anytime. Only they didn't stop, and after sleeping together for a year, she realized she might just want to keep this fling going for the rest of her life. At the time, it seemed like a good idea to keep their relationship a secret. The idea was they wouldn't have to answer questions when it was over, and they wouldn't have to explain themselves to anyone.

She slipped into a pair of black leggings, threw on a T-shirt, and slowly opened the door, peering down the hallway to make sure the coast was clear. The second the door closed behind her with a soft click, Jacob's door jerked open. His eyes roved over her in a way that made her breath catch. It took just a couple of steps, and she was pulled into his arms. He wore only a pair of plaid pajama bottoms that sat low on his hips. Even in the dim light, she could make out every plane and muscle on his bare chest.

"What took you so long?" he asked in a low, husky voice that took away any concern that he desired her as much as she wanted him.

He nipped at the space behind her ear, the spot that always made her weak at the knees. Jacob made her feel feminine and soft in a way that no other man had ever done.

"Jacob." She gasped his name when he picked her up and walked backward to his bed, falling so that she stayed on top of him. She sat up, her thighs pressing against his hips, reveling in the feel of his hardness against her core. She pressed her palms against his chest, losing herself in his dark blue eyes and feeling his heartbeat under her fingertips.

The urge to say "I love you" sat on the tip of her tongue, but she couldn't bring herself to take that step across the precipice into uncharted territory.

"Come here," he murmured.

He pulled her down, his lips capturing hers. All these months later, her body still burst into flames with his kisses.

He slipped the strap of her camisole off one shoulder and then the other, and reaching up, he tugged it down into a puddle around her waist and palmed her breasts. Mae threw her head back, reveling in his touch.

With an impatient grunt, Jacob rolled them over, trying to pull at her leggings at the same time he shoved at his own pajama bottoms. They became a tangle of arms and legs, trying to get out of their clothes. He leaned over her, kissing the space between her breasts, and then making a trail of kisses down her belly.

"Jacob," she gasped, wriggling under him. "I need you now."

She cooed and arched her back when his fingers stroked over her most sensitive parts and then slid into her.

"You're always ready for me." He groaned.

"That's because I always want you."

His fingers left her. He looked up at her, his eyes glittering with lust, and his beard tickling the inside of her thighs when his mouth replaced his fingers. The warmth disappeared.

She heard the condom packet being opened, and her body pulsed with anticipation.

"Open your eyes," Jacob said in that deep commanding voice that she secretly loved. "I always want to see your eyes when this happens."

He slid into her softness, filling her, making her complete. No other man made her feel this way, soft and taken and yet so powerful.

She tried to hold back the tide that threatened to sweep over her as Jacob thrust into her. She grasped his shoulders, but it wasn't enough. She wrapped her legs around his, feeling the tension coursing through his body. Jacob kissed her, and she could only cling to him. It was always like this. She wanted the feeling to last forever, but she always lost herself in him, this pleasure, this want, this need.

"Mae, sweet Mae, hold on, baby."

And she did, digging her fingers into his back. Jacob pulled out, hovering over her for just a second, and then pushed into her with one hard stroke. "Now," he ground out between clenched teeth.

And the wave crashed over them, pulling her under and taking her breath away with color and light. When she could breathe again, she reached up and stroked his beard. He nuzzled her nose and pulled himself away from her. With a groan, he got up and disposed of the condom before returning to the bed and pulling her to his side. That was how it was. The first time was always fast and frantic; the second time they would take their time, touching, exploring, and just feeling.

Jacob kissed the top of her head, and she snuggled into the warmth of his chest, her hand splayed over the coarse hair on his chest.

"How was your day today?"

Mae's lips curved into a smile. This was just one more thing that endeared Jacob to her. He always asked how she was doing, and when she told him, he listened. And not like listening and then telling her what he thought she should do. He listened and asked thoughtful questions and always made her feel... supported.

"Was that a sigh of contentment I just heard?" He chuckled.

"Don't get cocky."

Jacob rolled them over so that they faced each other lying side by side. "I'm not being cocky. If I make you happy, then I'm happy."

This time she did sigh. Reaching out, she traced the lines across his forehead. "I'm happy."

"Are you sure?" He arched an eyebrow.

Her lips twitched. "Well... I could be happier."

He made a low, sexy sound that reverberated through his chest. "Let me show you just how happy I can make you, Mae Colton."

"I think we should stop sneaking around."

Chapter Five

"WHAT?" JACOB sat up like he'd just heard the starter pistol at a race.

Mae scooted up so she was sitting against the headboard. "I think we should stop sneaking around."

"So, you want us to stop"—Jacob waved his hand between the two of them—"doing this?"

She felt the heat rise in her cheeks. "No, I don't want to stop sleeping with you. I just want to do it as a couple. A real couple. I want to hold your hand or give you a kiss whenever I want."

Jacob frowned and shook his head. "I don't think that's a good idea."

The blood pounded in her ears, and her face grew hot. "Why not?" She was thankful they were both sitting facing forward. She couldn't bring herself to look at him.

"We... I... we talked about this, Mae. This thing between us was never going to be long-term. If we went public, it would be awkward with our friends when it's over."

"What if I changed my mind? What if I don't want this to end?" she asked quietly.

Jacob's head whipped toward her. "I—"

She sat up on her knees facing him, grabbing a pillow to cover herself. She couldn't say what she wanted to say naked; she didn't want to be that exposed.

"I know this was supposed to be just a fling, but—" She blew out a shaky breath. "—I know we don't make sense; you're not even my type. But I like us together, I think we could be a good couple, and I can see myself in a relationship with you... long-term. I love you."

There, she said it. Maybe it wasn't the most eloquent or romantic. She wasn't going to come out and say she was head over heels in love with him, for God's sake, not yet anyway.

Jacob ran his hand down his face. "Mae, I'm just not a relationship kind of guy. I can't do the whole wife and kids, white picket fence thing."

"I'm not asking you for that. I'm not a white picket fence kind of girl, you know that. Actually, I was thinking we could see if Reid would consider trading with one of us, and we could live on the top floor together." Her voice faded as she watched Jacob get out of bed and start to pull on his pajama bottoms.

"I think it's best if we end this now so we can still be friends."

Her eyes darted around the room, trying to locate her clothes, but her body was too numb to move. She took a few deep breaths and got up. Her hands shook as she pulled on her underwear and leggings. She didn't bother to put on her bra. Tugging her T-shirt over her head, she headed toward the door.

Jacob reached for her arm. "Mae, wait, let's talk about this."

"No," she said, wrenching her arm out of his grasp. "You made your point. This is over."

"Don't go. I want to make sure we're okay. Please, Mae, can we still be friends?"

She stiffened. "You'll be lucky if I consider you an acquaintance."

Mae wrenched the door open and hurled herself across the hall. It took her an extra minute fumbling with her keys through the sheen of tears she refused to let fall. She finally got the key shoved into the lock and pushed the door so hard it banged against the doorstop and bounced back toward her. Mae rushed inside, closing it behind her. The click of the deadbolt unlocked her last bit of composure. She let out an anguished groan and sank to the floor.

How could she have been so dumb?

There was a soft knock on the door.

"Mae, are you okay?" Jacob asked.

"Go away."

When she didn't hear his retreating footsteps or his door shut, she yelled, "I mean it, Jacob, go away." She said it with such force she felt her vocal cords pop.

There was a heavy sigh, and then she heard him walk away. Pulling herself off the floor, she stumbled into the bathroom, ripping her clothes off along the way. By the time the water ran cold, she still hadn't washed away all of her tears. Eventually, she found her way into her bed and pulled the covers over her head. She sniffed and then let out a frustrated moan. Forcing her weary body to move, she started stripping the bed. She'd be damned if she was going to sleep on sheets that smelled like him. She dug out fresh sheets, tripping over the ones she'd just discarded, and threw them on the bed staring at them, waiting for the bed to make itself. Heaving a sigh, she went over to the couch and grabbed the afghan her gran knitted for her when she was in college. Wrapping herself in its softness always brought her comfort when her heart was hurting. She closed her eyes, exhaling once, twice, and the tears began again.

This wasn't the first time she'd been dumped, but this was different. She didn't really care about the other guys that she'd broken up with. But the big surly lumberjack across the hall was different. He pushed her buttons. He was stubborn and refused to let anyone help him. It made her so angry she could spit. But then he could be so tender and push a different set of buttons in the most delicious and sexy ways. She knew in her heart he cared about her, or at least she thought he did. So why wouldn't he want to date her openly?

Mae grabbed her phone, thinking she would talk it out with Callie; after all, that's what she always did. Her finger hovered over Callie's number. She chewed on her lip and, with a sigh, put the phone back down. She blinked back another round of tears. Telling Callie was out of the question. She'd have to explain that she'd been sneaking around with Jacob before she could tell her they broke up. It was all just too… humiliating.

Mae cracked one eye open. She didn't remember falling asleep, but at some point, she had no more tears left to shed, and exhaustion took over. She sat up, rubbing her eyes that felt like sandpaper. For one second, she hoped she remembered the events from the night before differently, but she knew it was true. She'd offered Jacob her heart, and he'd rejected her… them.

Mae took a deep breath and forced herself to get up. She stumbled into the shower and let the hot water soothe her bruised heart. She got ready for work on autopilot, going through the motions while she thought about how she was going to move forward. How was she going to act like everything was fine in front of her friends when her heart had been smashed to bits?

Dressing for her mood, Mae pulled on her favorite pair of black boots, black leggings, and a black short-sleeve cashmere sweater. Despite her best efforts, the mirror didn't lie. No amount of concealer was going to hide the dark circles under her eyes. With a sigh, she grabbed her bag and headed out the door.

Of course, Jacob's door opened at the exact same time, and they both froze, staring at each other.

"Mae—"

Hearing her name on his lips broke the spell, and she rushed past him, down the stairs.

"Mae, is everything okay?" Dax looked up from his desk with concern as she rushed past.

"It's fine," she said between gritted teeth.

She burst through the doors and onto the sidewalk. The sun was shining, and the birds were singing, which only made her even more miserable. She made a beeline for her office, ignoring her administrative assistant's disapproving look over the rims of her bright red reading glasses at her outfit, and headed into her office, slamming the door behind her. Today was not the day for Grace to give her one of her lectures on how a lady should dress properly. Mae slumped into her desk chair and dropped her head in her hands. She needed to get her shit together. This wasn't the end of the world. She would get over that big dumb lumberjack. She'd become caught up in a fantasy as she watched her friends pair off. What was good for them wasn't necessarily good for her, she reminded herself.

After that little pep talk, she got down to work. She'd made a lot of progress getting the town accounts back in order and connecting with state resources that would benefit Colton. But there was still so much more that needed to be done to fix the years of neglect, and she couldn't do it all in just a few months. Mae reviewed the new state policies on land management and did some research on the city infrastructure, prioritizing what needed to be fixed now and what projects could wait. Sadly, there had been so much mismanagement, it felt like nothing could wait. The town needed a new sewage system and electrical and cable upgrades. She worked until her stomach reminded her that she hadn't eaten since the night before. Unable to bring herself to face anyone, she grabbed her phone and called the Catfish Café across the street.

"Catfish," the owner Tillie Reynolds answered.

"Hi Tillie, it's Mae. Can I get a turkey sandwich with an extra pickle?"

She needed comfort food.

"Sure thing, honey. Y'all want some pie to go with that?"

"Do you have any chocolate cream?"

"I sure do."

"Can I have two slices?"

She might not be able to tell anyone what happened, but that didn't mean it did not entitle her to some breakup food.

"I'll have it ready for you in ten minutes."

"Thank you, Tillie."

Mae gathered her things and left her office.

"Grace, I'm heading out for lunch."

The older woman looked at her over the top of her glasses with a frown. "Please try to be back on time."

Mae sucked in her breath. The administrative assistant she inherited when she took on the job was the poster child for White Southern women of a certain age.

She looked around the office. "I'm sorry, I didn't see a time clock. Should I be punching in somewhere?"

"I'm just trying to make sure you manage your time well. Some of you people—"

Mae counted to ten before she interrupted. If she could, she would have fired the woman when she became mayor, but Grace also served as Judge Beaumont's administrative assistant, and it wouldn't be fair to the judge to make that decision without consulting him.

"This conversation is over. You know what, I haven't taken a day off since I started this job. I'm not going to lunch, I'm leaving for the rest of the day."

She left the office before Grace could put her foot any further into her mouth. It was quiet at the Catfish, so she could grab her order without being stopped too many times. Everyone always wanted just a quick word that usually ended up taking at least ten minutes. But in less than half an hour, she was zipping across Mockingbird Bridge with Lucas Monroe blasting on the radio. Mae pulled down the narrow dirt road that most folks forgot was there, and a few minutes later the trees thinned, revealing a glimpse of Turtle Pond. She parked and climbed out of her Jeep and grabbed her lunch and a blanket she always kept in the back of her car. She made her way along the narrow pathway through the brush until a small clearing appeared to reveal a large black granite rock. The minute she walked out onto the flat smooth surface, some of the tension left her body. She sighed—this was her special place. She'd been coming here since junior high whenever she needed a place to be alone.

Mae spread out the blanket and sat down. She opened up her lunch and nibbled on her sandwich. True to its name, there was a row of turtles lined up on a log at Turtle Pond, sunning themselves in the afternoon heat.

Mae set down her sandwich and leaned back on her elbows, mimicking the way they stretched their necks toward the sun. She took a deep breath and fought back a fresh wave of tears. She'd never cried over a breakup before, but she'd never really fallen for someone the way she had with Jacob.

"Stupid lumberjack," she muttered.

But that was a lie; Jacob was smart and observant. He didn't use a bunch of fancy words and try to impress her with grand ideas, the way some of the other men she'd dated had. There was no expensive cologne or silk ties where Jacob was concerned. She may have given him a hard time, but she liked his flannel shirts and the way he smelled like cedar and sandalwood. But as her dad taught her, clothes don't make the man. Underneath all that flannel was a thoughtful man, and underneath that gruff exterior was kindness and passion that took her breath away. She groaned and sat up, wrapping her arms around her legs and resting her cheek on her knees. There would be no more of those breathtaking orgasms. Maybe she could learn to live with that, but she didn't know how she would learn to live without those quiet moments when she got to see the real Jacob Winters and the little pieces of his heart that made him whole.

One turtle turned its long neck, blinking at her with its glittering black eyes.

"What happens now?" she asked.

Her terrapin friend just blinked at her before pulling its head back into its shell.

"You've got the right idea."

Mae packed up her things and drove home, where she climbed into bed, curled herself into a ball, and pulled the covers up over her head.

Chapter Six

THERE WAS miserable, and then there was Jacob Winters after breaking up with someone he wasn't willing to admit he'd been in a serious relationship with in the first place. He'd worked late in his shop every night in the week since he'd turned Mae away, taking out his anger carving pieces of southern pine and mahogany. Even though he knew breaking up with Mae was the right thing to do, he couldn't stop wanting to go back and tell her he was wrong, beg for forgiveness, and hold her in his arms again. He hovered in front of her door every night, his hands fisted so tight they were numb to keep himself from knocking. It was best for both of them if he didn't.

By the end of the week, he was worn down and distracted, wondering how Mae was doing. The smooth, soft leather of the pair of work gloves he was restocking reminded him of Mae's skin when felt under his fingertips.

He didn't know how long he'd been standing there missing her when a voice asked, "You okay, Jacob?"

He jerked his head up to see the town's fireman, Nate Colton, looking at him with concern.

"Sorry, I was just thinking about…." He rubbed the back of his neck. "I was… I don't know what I was doing just now."

"We all get a little distracted sometimes."

Jacob grimaced. "Thanks."

"I was just asking if you got that order of lineman's pliers in yet?"

Jacob made a few keystrokes on the computer. "They're due in day after tomorrow."

"Great, I'll stop back by."

Nate waved and walked out. Jacob turned back to his computer and added a reminder to call Nate when the order came in. He could remember minor details, but sometimes things got lost in the bigger picture.

There was a steady flow of customers for the rest of the morning and into the afternoon, not enough to keep Jacob's thoughts from Mae, but enough to keep him busy.

The few customers in Winters's Hardware paused when three men entered. They strolled in looking like a group of college students—to anyone who wasn't paying close attention. Despite their khaki pants and polo shirts, they had a slightly grungy appearance. One had hair that was just a bit too shaggy and long, another had a tattoo peeking out from the bottom of his shirt sleeve that revealed the bottom half of a swastika, and the third one glanced toward Jacob and flashed the upside-down okay symbol. All of them were part of the group that had come into the Buckthorn.

Jacob came out from behind the counter and stood with his arms crossed, watching. All three jerked their heads toward the door when Isiah came in. His eyes narrowed while watching the group cluster around a display of new chainsaws. He moved next to Jacob and mirrored his stance.

"Any trouble?" Isiah asked, keeping his eyes trained on the young men.

"No, and there won't be."

He winced, watching one of his customers shy away when one man walked past her. It was rare to see them in town. Whatever was going on, it must be important for them to come in.

One of the men broke away from the group—Rhett Colton. Jacob kept his eyes locked on him as he headed toward the counter, moved behind it, and braced his hands on the worn wood countertop while Isiah stepped to the side. Rhett's gaze flicked toward the sheriff before he slammed a box of nails on the counter with a scowl and slid a twenty-dollar bill toward Jacob. His light hazel eyes locked on Jacob's for just a minute before taking his change.

Jacob watched the three men file out of the store and climb into a beat-up Jeep parked outside. Isiah followed them out, standing on the sidewalk with his holster unsnapped while they started the engine and drove away. He turned and tipped his hat with a grim expression.

Jacob finished up with the rest of his customers, and once he was alone in the store, he opened the register and pulled out the twenty the young man had handed him. Turning it over, he carefully peeled away the false back and read the note.

"Shit," he muttered under his breath.

THE MEETING point was an hour outside of Colton, and they'd only used it once before until tonight. That was the first time he'd met Rhett Colton, the man Jacob had been assigned to as his handler.

Jacob shut off his headlights and turned off the main road, heading toward a grove of trees in the middle of nowhere. There was no sign of Rhett when he pulled up, but the minute Jacob shut the engine off, he emerged from behind a kudzu-covered tree.

"You look like hell," Jacob greeted him.

"I'm fine, and you don't look much better," Rhett replied, his voice low and threaded with tension.

Jacob observed the haunted look in Rhett's hazel eyes and the lines bracketing his mouth. They needed to get the evidence to end this operation for both their sakes.

He'd been leery that the FBI was asking too much from Rhett from the beginning. Jacob's job as his handler was easy compared to what Rhett had sacrificed to embed himself into the group of White supremacists.

"I don't have much time." Rhett reached into his jacket and pulled out a flash drive. "They're getting bolder, and they're planning something big, but I don't know what it is yet."

"Anything else?"

Rhett hesitated for just a second. "Yeah, and you're not going to like it."

"What's going on?"

"There's been some talk about Mae and the sheriff."

Jacob's heart sped up. "What kind of talk?"

"Some folks aren't happy having a Black woman making changes. Renaming the park got them pretty riled up."

"How bad is it?"

"Bad enough that I passed you that note. There's a few others saying that a Black man isn't the law where they're concerned."

He had to stay calm. This was the job. He knew that going into it, and it was another reason why he didn't do relationships. He couldn't get close to anyone. But it was too late. Mae Colton had wormed her way into his heart. More like shoved and kicked her way in, but that's what he liked about her. She had spirit. Unfortunately, that was going to make his task that much harder.

"Anything else specific you can tell me?"

"Nothing yet. You know if I hear any definitive threat, I'll get word to you."

Jacob nodded. "You need anything from me?"

"Just pass that on and be careful," Rhett said, pointing to the flash drive in Jacob's hand. "We're getting close. What's on that drive should be enough, but"—he glanced over his shoulder, affirming they were alone—"I'm staying in as long as I need to. Until these guys are arrested, and now with the threat against Mae, I want to do everything I can to make sure these guys don't follow through on their threats."

"That's not your call to make," Jacob reminded him. He reached out and put his hand on Rhett's shoulder. "Listen, if you need extraction at any point, you make the call."

"Got it."

Rhett backed off and turned, walking away into the kudzu forest.

Jacob pocketed the flash drive and got back into his truck. He drove out the way he drove in, with his headlights off until he hit the main road.

Worry knotted in his stomach on the drive back to Colton. He bypassed town; it was late but, as if he knew Jacob was coming, Uncle Robert was sitting on the porch when he pulled up to his house.

Robert Ellis, known as Uncle Robert to everyone in Colton, was the one person who knew his secret.

He got out of his truck and walked up to the porch, dropping into a rocking chair next to the man who'd become a mentor and the only person he'd allowed to take the role of father figure in a very long time.

In his usual style, Uncle Robert didn't say a word. He just rocked and waited.

Jacob exhaled. "Got an issue."

Uncle Robert nodded and waited for him to continue.

"There's talk about Mae and Isiah."

Uncle Robert stopped rocking and leaned forward. "How bad?"

"Bad enough that Rhett asked to meet with me. I'm as worried about him as I am about Mae and Isiah."

"He knew what he was signing up for."

"That doesn't mean it's taking any less of a toll."

"Fair point."

Uncle Robert got up and went inside, returning a minute later with a bottle of whiskey and two glasses. He poured out two fingers in each glass and handed him one.

Jacob downed the contents, adding to the fire already burning in his belly. "She's not going to do anything to make keeping her safe easy."

"Nope."

"Damn it." Jacob pinched the bridge of his nose.

"When it all comes out, and it will, they'll understand."

"They'll understand that I've been keeping it a secret that I've been working with the FBI this whole time?"

"I ain't gonna lie, they'll be bitterer than greens for a while, but they love you. You're family."

Jacob tried to swallow past the lump in his throat. As hard as he'd tried to avoid it, he'd found a community and people he cared about... loved. That's what made this assignment his hardest one yet. And why he knew it would be his last one.

"I'm surprised Dax and Isiah haven't figured it out yet." He glanced at the older man next to him. "I wasn't here more than a couple of weeks before you called me out."

Uncle Robert leaned back in his rocking chair and took another sip from his glass. "I got thirty years of service on you boys."

Even with his security clearance, Jacob didn't know exactly what Uncle Robert's position in the intelligence community was. FBI, CIA, or some other agency, Uncle Robert's record of service to his country was a closely guarded secret. Most folks around Colton heard the rumors that he'd worked for the government at some point in his life. But the majority just thought of him as a local farmer and occasional curmudgeon.

Jacob was furious when Uncle Robert let on that he knew Jacob didn't move to Colton just because Dax had suggested it. Jacob had been in town less than two weeks before Robert sought him out and told him he knew Jacob was working with the FBI tracking the White supremacists in the area. Robert had also been observing what was happening in his community and alerted the Bureau office in Jackson about several people he thought might be connected with the Klan or some other organization.

Dax asking Jacob to move to Colton was an added bonus that helped solidify his cover story. He was a fraud. Jacob came to Colton on an assignment. He'd fallen in love with the place, and that was his first mistake. Then he started putting down roots, something he swore he'd never do.

"I'm scared," he admitted.

"It's when you stop being scared that you know it's time to get out," Uncle Robert said quietly.

"I thought taking one last assignment as a handler would be a good way to ease out."

"You're the right man for the job. I'm glad you're lookin' over Rhett."

"I just hope he doesn't crack. He didn't look good tonight."

"I've taken on some ugly assignments in my day, but I have the utmost respect for the guys who are willing to go undercover with scum like the KKK."

"He's sacrificed a lot."

Uncle Robert nodded. "The men and women doing this work, all of you are helping keep this country and our town safe."

"We don't always succeed."

"The weight shouldn't all be on your shoulders. It's up to all of us to help. Folks here in Colton are going to have to fight to make sure this is a town that welcomes everybody."

The little town of Colton had made a lot of progress in a short amount of time. Getting rid of a corrupt town council had a lot to do with that. Recently Taylor Colton, star of the home improvement show *History Reborn*, moved his production office into town after restoring the old plantation house Halcyon and turning it into a trade school with his fiancée, Jo Martin. Taylor's brother also moved to Colton to reopen the medical clinic. Every day, there were small signs of progress. And a lot of the credit went to Mae. She was a force to be reckoned with.

The rocking chair creaked in protest as Jacob leaned back and scrubbed his face with his hands. "How am I going to keep Mae safe without her knowing what's going on?"

"I've got to be honest with you, I'm not sure you can. That's one savvy woman you're dealing with."

One savvy woman who currently refused to acknowledge his existence, let alone heed any warnings he might give. He needed to talk to his superiors. It was time to bring Isiah into the loop. He pulled out his phone. It was late, too late to call, but he was eager to pass the information he had up the chain of command.

"Nothing you can do tonight, son. I'll cover for you at the hardware store in the morning so you can head to Jackson."

"I'd like to bring Isiah in the loop, but so far I can't get approval."

Uncle Robert nodded. "I expect they will. You know how things can go at the Bureau. Let me know if there's a problem and you need me to pull any strings for you."

"Thanks." His years in the service had tempered his independent streak, but it was still hard for him to accept help.

"You wanna bunk here tonight?"

"If you don't mind."

"You should know better by now."

Jacob took Uncle Robert's admonishment for the compliment it was.

"I just wanted to make sure I wasn't interrupting anything," he said with a sly smile.

Uncle Robert stroked his beard and looked at him thoughtfully. "I made a lot of sacrifices for my country, and I don't regret any of them except one. I shouldn't have sacrificed the woman I loved. I wish I'd known then that love means sharing burdens, not keeping them all to yourself."

"Did you ask for a second chance?"

"It's been over thirty years, and I still haven't worked up the nerve yet."

Jacob saw the flash of pain and regret in the older man's eyes.

There was a slight tremor in Robert's voice. "Don't make the same mistake I made, son."

CHAPTER SEVEN

"GRACE, WHAT is this doing on my desk?" Mae fought to keep her voice calm as she held up the wig catalog.

Her office manager lowered her reading glasses to the tip of her nose.

"I thought it would be a good idea for you to consider a more professional hairstyle that would be more suitable for your position."

Mae sucked in her breath and counted to ten. It didn't work.

She straightened her shoulders and started to address her office manager as calmly as possible. "Ms. McConnell, I am assuming you are not aware of the Crown Act—"

Before she could continue, Judge Beaumont cleared his throat, announcing his presence. He moved to place himself between her and her assistant. He gave Mae a brief nod before he turned to face Grace.

"Ms. McConnell, I'd like to see you in my chambers."

It was clear from his tone that it was a command, not an invitation.

"If you'll excuse us, Mayor Colton, I'll be with you in just a moment," the judge said, pushing Grace toward the door.

As soon as the judge ushered her office manager out of the room, Mae sighed with relief. She'd inherited Grace McConnell when she took on the job, and the older woman had given her grief since day one. She was just one of many who didn't think Mae was a suitable candidate to be the mayor of a small town in the Mississippi Delta. Those were the people who thought she was too young, had no experience, and the one unspoken mark against her for many people, too Black.

Mae shoved the wig catalog off her desk and sank down into her chair, dropping her head in her hands. Grace was just as bad as some men she'd dated. She'd gotten used to the remarks over the years. "You could be so much prettier if you let your hair grow," she'd heard more than once.

She ran her hand over her close-cropped curls. She liked her curls just the way they were. For years, she watched her sister waste hours every morning trying to get every strand perfectly placed. Mae didn't have the patience for that; she liked the freedom that came with her short hair.

"You were born wantin' to get somewhere quick," Mae's grandmother told her. It was true. Patience wasn't her strong suit. Once she figured out where she wanted to go, she wanted to get there as quickly as possible. Keeping her hair cut short saved her time, not just getting ready in the morning, but also having to drive over an hour to get to a salon. That was life in a small town with limited resources. Colton hadn't had a salon for women in years, and as much as she loved Hank, she didn't want to get her hair cut at the barbershop her dad went to. Sometimes, a girl needed a little bit of pampering.

Her lips curled into a smile. Jacob always told her how much he liked her short hair. She closed her eyes, remembering one night in bed when Jacob whispered in her ear how her short hair made her eyes look big and how he could see everything in them.

Someone cleared their throat, and she opened her eyes to see Judge Beaumont standing in the doorway.

"May I come in?"

"Of course you can. You never have to ask."

He took the chair across from her with a sigh. "I have an unpleasant habit of turning a blind eye to things that are... inconvenient. You never should have been saddled with Grace in the first place. It just seemed like the most convenient thing to do to keep her on and have her work for both of us."

"Judge—"

"Please, how many times do I have to ask you to call me Harrison?"

Mae smiled. "Harrison, having Grace work for both of us made sense, especially while we're trying to get the budget back on track. You have nothing to apologize for. But Grace is just not working out."

"You're absolutely right. I've had a talk with her, and Grace agrees that it's time for her to retire. We need to find you someone who is going to support your work, not hinder it. Colton is lucky to have you here, and I want to do everything I can to support you."

Mae's chin trembled. Judge Beaumont had been her cheerleader from the start. It turned out along with Senator Weems's recommendation, he'd also written a glowing letter to the governor recommending her for the position.

Blinking back tears, she said, "Thank you, Harrison. I feel bad. You've been working with Grace for years now."

"Honestly, I like to do things for myself most of the time." He gave her a wry smile. "I'm an old curmudgeon set in my ways."

"I still want to make sure you have help when you need it."

"I know you will. Now, it's a beautiful day. I've got a fish with my name on it. Not to be presumptuous, but I figure you could use a break. How about we take the rest of the day off, I can wrestle with that slippery devil, and you can take some time for yourself. Unless you want to go fishing with me," he added with a conspiratorial wink.

Mae couldn't help but smile. She'd come to care about the judge in her time working with him in Town Hall. He was a fair man who cared about the community just as much as she did.

She looked around her office and sighed. "I don't think an afternoon off would hurt anybody, but if you don't mind, I think I'd rather spend some time reading a good book than baiting hooks."

The judge got up from his chair, and Mae grabbed her bag and followed him out of the office, locking the door behind her.

"I'll put a note on the door for you before I leave."

"Thank you, Jud—" He cut her off, putting his finger up and waggling it. "Thank you, Harrison," she corrected herself. "I appreciate everything you've done for me."

Harrison gave her a fatherly pat on the shoulder. "You go have yourself a relaxing afternoon, and we'll start again tomorrow."

Stepping out of Town Hall and into the bright sunlight, Mae took a deep breath and looked around the square. She glanced toward the library. She could go see what Callie was up to, but she didn't want to have to explain why she was taking the afternoon off. Not that it would matter. The news about Grace would be all over town by the time she sat down to dinner.

She refused to look toward the hardware store to see what Jacob was doing. It didn't matter anymore. Fighting back the urge to cry again, she headed toward the Barton Building. Thankfully Dax's office on the main floor was empty as she made her way upstairs.

She changed into a pair of shorts and a T-shirt and her favorite pair of beat-up purple Converse. Food wasn't that appealing, but she made herself a sandwich and grabbed a pop on her way out. Five minutes later, she was headed toward her favorite spot at Turtle Pond.

When she rounded the corner to her thinking rock, she stopped short. Her place was already inhabited. Presley Beaumont sat with her legs crossed, hunched over a book, her forehead wrinkled and her narrowed eyes darting back and forth across the page. Whatever she was reading, she was clearly struggling to understand it. Mae's groan of frustration must have been louder than she intended, because Presley's head jerked up just as she was about to turn away.

Presley jumped up. "I'll go," she said, gathering the blanket and book at her feet.

"No, it's fine. I'll go."

Presley stopped and chewed on her lip. "I don't mind sharin' if you don't mind."

Mae did mind a lot. This was her rock; it had always been her favorite place to come and think. She eyed Presley, who was watching her with a hopeful expression that made her stop and not reject the offer outright.

It was probably a bad idea, but she didn't want to head back into town. With a shrug, Mae headed toward Presley, stopping a couple feet away to spread out her own blanket.

Presley's eyes grew wide for a second before she broke into a smile, rearranged her blanket, and sat back down.

"Can we just... I just need a little peace and quiet. It's already been a day," Mae said.

Presley nodded. "Okay."

Presley was the town beauty queen and all-around nuisance. Over the years, she'd managed to offend or piss off just about everyone who had an ounce of common sense in town. That left her with a group of friends who were just as addlebrained and willfully ignorant as she was. Which is why Mae couldn't help wondering what Presley was reading that required so much of her concentration.

Mae watched her for twenty minutes before her curiosity finally got the better of her.

She propped herself up on her elbows. "Whatcha reading?"

Presley looked up at her and then back down at the book in her lap with a frown. "It's just a book."

"I can see that. What's it about?"

"Well, it's, um, about racial stuff."

Mae crinkled her nose. "Racial stuff?"

Presley held up the book so Mae could see the title—*I've Got the Light of Freedom: The Organizing Tradition and the Mississippi Freedom Struggle.*

Mae sat up. "What in the world are you reading that for?"

"Someone told me I shouldn't be so ignorant. I saw this in a bookstore window in Greenwood, and I thought... I'm tired of people thinkin' I'm just some dumb blond beauty queen. But"—she looked down at the book with a frown—"I'm not sure I understand all of it. I mean, I've never heard about a lot of this stuff. Why didn't we learn about this in school?"

Mae rolled her eyes. "Schools around here like the sanitized version of history, and most folks don't ask. They'd rather remain ignorant about parts of history that make them uncomfortable."

"Oh."

"I can't believe I'm having this conversation with you, of all people," she muttered.

Tears hovered at the corners of Presley's eyes. "How am I supposed to change if no one will talk to me? I want to be more than a Southern belle. Ever since Ms. Ellis got sent to jail, no one will talk to me, and I never say anything right. I want to be better, but I don't know how.... This is hard."

She had a point. Mae hated to admit it, but Presley was right. Most of Colton had been wishing she'd act like she got some sense, and here she was finally trying.

"Okay." She sighed.

Presley scrunched up her nose. "Okay what?"

"You're right, you can't change if no one will give you a chance, so I'm willing. But"—Mae waggled her finger at her—"I expect you to watch your tongue and think before you speak."

She bobbed her head. "I can do that."

Mae gave her a skeptical look.

"I mean I'll try," Presley corrected herself.

"Realistic expectations are a good place to start."

Mae drew her knees up to her chest and wrapped her arms around her legs. This was her favorite view of the pond. She missed the days of hunting for turtles with Callie and Sunday afternoons fishing with her grandpa.

"It's peaceful here, isn't it?" Presley said.

"Maybe that's why I've always thought of this as my thinking rock."

Presley frowned and got up. "I didn't mean to take your place—"

Mae waved her hand. "Sit down, it's fine. I mean, I didn't expect to see you here, and it's… well, you gotta admit this is pretty awkward, but it's not the worst thing I've had to deal with today."

Presley plopped back down with a smile.

"I said you could stay. I didn't say you could be happy about it," she said with a slight smile.

Good Lord, what have I gotten myself into, Mae thought, while Presley fussed and fidgeted until she had herself situated just right. Presley had been putting on airs since they were in kindergarten. Mae didn't cross paths with her often, and when they did, Colton's resident beauty queen usually said or did something that put Mae's teeth on edge. But today, there was something about the way Presley seemed so happy to hang out with her that made her curious. Besides, Mae was too wrung out to be upset with anything foolish that might come out of Presley Beaumont's mouth.

Presley returned her attention to her book, her face a mask of concentration.

They sat quietly, long enough for some of the tension to ease out of Mae. She resumed her position, stretching her legs as she leaned back on her elbows and lifted her face to the sun.

She was able to enjoy just a few moments of blissful silence before Presley cleared her throat.

"Yes," Mae said, keeping her eyes closed.

"Well, I was just wonderin'… Why do y'all lay out in the sun?"

Mae opened one eye. Presley was looking at her with a picture of confusion and curiosity.

She sighed and shut her eye again. "Black people can get suntan and sunburns just like White folks, Presley."

There was a beat of silence before she said, "Oh." There was another moment of stillness, and then she said quietly, "Thank you for not yelling at me for asking."

"You're welcome."

She laid back down, opening her eyes to gaze at the white cotton candy clouds in the sky, smiling at the memory of how she and Callie would look for animals in the shapes when they were little. After a while, her muscles began to unbind in the warm sun, and her eyes drifted closed.

"Mae... Mae." Someone jiggled her shoulder.

She popped her eyes open and sat up, looking around.

"You fell asleep, and I didn't want to leave y'all alone."

Mae rubbed her eyes. "Thanks, I would have been okay though."

"Well, I didn't want to be impolite."

She nodded to the book in Presley's hand. "How was the rest of your book?"

"I'm learning some things." Presley bit her lip. "I was wonderin' if... I wanted to ask if y'all would be willin' to talk to me again sometime."

Presley was looking at her with so much hope in her eyes, Mae couldn't help but feel a little sympathetic.

"I'll probably regret this, but sure. You can buy me lunch sometime, and we can talk."

Presley's eyes lit up. "Okay, I could bring you lunch at your office. I know you're busy."

"That is very considerate." Mae bit back a smile.

Mae watched Presley bounce off, the rhinestones on her T-shirt sparkling in the sunlight. Shaking her head, she laid back down on the blanket. This day could not have been any crazier. She watched the clouds floating by, wondering if Presley could change. Was there any hope Jacob might change too? Did she still want him to? Maybe she should let go of that small piece of hope she'd been holding in her heart and move on. A flash of brown crossed her path, and a mockingbird swooped down and perched on the rock next to her and started squawking.

"Yeah, yeah, I know, I need to move on and forget that ornery lumberjack."

The black-and-brown speckled bird cocked its head, hopping along the granite surface. He let out one more long series of squawks before taking off to yell at someone else.

CHAPTER EIGHT

IT HAD been a hell of a day. The store was busy, which was a good thing, but the constant flow of customers didn't keep Jacob's mind off Mae. He'd only caught brief glimpses of her since he rejected her offer of making their relationship more permanent. He couldn't stop seeing the look of hurt on her face as he replayed the moment over and over in his head. The one he put there. Damn it, Mae was stubborn, reckless, insufferable, kindhearted, and smart. He blew out a sigh and ran his hands over his face. Every time he tried to list all of Mae's faults to convince himself that he did the right thing, all the things he liked… no, loved about her managed to slip into the list.

The bell over the door jangled, announcing another customer.

"Hey, Jacob, I just wanted to stop by and say thanks for the display of fire extinguishers," Nate said, gesturing to the items Jacob had put in the window for Fourth of July.

"I figured it would be a good idea after all the calls you got last year."

"Whew-wee, you'd think folks would act like they have some sense."

"People don't think one little sparkler is going to do any harm."

Nate shook his head. "I still can't get over how Floyd thought it was a good idea to put a ring of rockets around his flagpole and light his own damn flag on fire."

"Not exactly patriotic." Jacob chuckled.

"That's the other reason I stopped by. I was hoping you wouldn't mind helping keep an extra eye out on the Fourth. I'll manage the fireworks show for the town from the station, and I'd like to have a few extra hands on deck if Floyd or anyone else decides to make a fool of themselves."

"Sure thing, happy to help."

"I've been meaning to ask if you'd volunteered before. I've never had a civilian who knows their way around a fire truck the way you do."

"My dad was a firefighter."

Nate's face lit up. "He was? Where was his station?"

"FDNY, Ladder Company 3," he said quietly.

Nate's face fell. "Oh hell, son." He reached out and put his hand on Jacob's shoulder. "You know, in Judaism they say, 'may his memory be a blessing.'"

Jacob smiled. "Yes, we do, thank you."

Nate's eyes grew widened for just a fraction of a second before he smiled back and gave Jacob's shoulder a squeeze. "You let me know if it's ever too much for you."

"I enjoy it. Like I said, I'm happy to help."

And he truly was. He liked helping Nate out as a volunteer firefighter. It made him feel close to his dad. He waved goodbye to Nate, remembering the exact same way his father would walk with his hands in the pockets of his station-wear pants the way Nate did. He remembered the way his father would polish his belt buckle and shoes the night before his shift. Those were the wonderful memories, the ones he didn't mind not being able to forget.

He caught sight of Mae coming down from the courthouse steps. Today, she was wearing a pair of black jeans and blazer over a Democracy Now T-shirt, paired with leopard-print heels. She glanced in his direction with a frown before lifting her chin and heading toward the library. All confidence and swagger. It was that poise and determination that he found so compelling. He closed his eyes and let the memory of the first day they met wash over him. He'd met her on the day he arrived. Mae stood at her best friend Callie's side against the head of the corrupt town council, who also happened to be his friend Dax's mother. He'd never encountered a woman quite like Mae. Those large dark brown eyes took in everything around her. And she loved her friends and family with a fierceness that scared him as much as it endeared her to him. His mom loved like that. He'd served with hardened soldiers who still took the time to think twice before heading into battle. But not his Mae. He sighed, running his hand through his hair. She wasn't his. The door opened, and another customer came in. He pasted on a smile and turned to face whatever the rest of the day would bring.

By the time he flipped the Open sign to Closed, he'd had enough of people and sought solitude in his workshop. He eyed his woodworking tools and a particularly beautiful piece of walnut, and then his gaze swiveled to the new inventory that had come in that morning. The step stool Mae's father ordered for his wife would have to wait. He needed to get the shelves restocked before he opened in the morning.

Jacob walked into what he thought of as the heart of Winters's Hardware. The long space ran the length of the building. He'd painted the walls a creamy white and updated the lighting with large industrial glass fixtures with modern LED elements, taking the dark, dingy space into a light, bright workspace. It had taken weeks to sort through the jumble of tools that the previous owner left behind. Now he had everything neatly put away and organized on the two large pegboard panels he'd attached to one wall. At the end of the room, he'd built large brackets that held his supply of wood, some old and some reclaimed. There was a metal garage door on the opposite end that was used for deliveries and made it easy to load and unload his finished projects.

Grabbing his pocketknife, he went over to the pallet of boxes sitting by the garage door and sliced open the first box from that morning's delivery. He unpacked the gardening gloves and seed packets and was just about to open the next box when he heard rustling and a squeak. With a frown, he looked around. He'd be damned if he was going to allow mice back in. They had infested the place when he'd first taken over. He was just about to head for the shelf where he kept the mousetraps when he saw a minuscule triangle of fur/ A second triangle joined the first one and the next thing he knew, two green eyes popped over the lid of one of the boxes in the pile. He blinked at the furry creature for a minute and then jumped when it let out a brief howl and ran toward him.

Tiny daggers pierced his skin as it began to climb his leg. He watched with a mixture of shock and horror as it came closer until it reached his shoulder. A loud purr filled his ear as it curled up into a ball and nestled itself in the crook of his neck.

Jacob stood motionless, Black spots began to dance in front of his eyes. He didn't realize he'd been holding his breath until the room started to tilt. It came out in a whoosh, and his shoulders sagged. He straightened back up immediately, straining his neck and looking out of the corner of his eye to see if the intruder was still there. In a slow shuffle, he made his way across the workshop until he reached his workbench and leaned against it. As gently as he could, he reached up and pried the creature from his shoulder and held it in his palm. The small body, with brown-and-gray striped fur dotted with white patches, let out an indignant cry and rearranged itself, curled in his hand, and restarted its miniature motor.

"Where in the hell did you come from?"

He walked around the workshop, holding his hands cupped in front of him with the little fur ball curled up inside, looking for any sign of a mother or its siblings. Circling the room twice, he saw no sign of any other little creatures. He ended up back where he started, looking down at the sleeping kitten.

"What am I supposed to do with you?"

Carefully transferring it to his other hand, he reached for a sweatshirt lying close by and wrangled it into a little nest before gently depositing the kitten onto the soft fleece. It lifted its small head, blinking at him for a minute before closing its eyes and tucking its tail over its nose.

Jacob rested his hands on his hips, looking from the little cat to the pile of inventory he had to take care of and back again. With a long exhale, he went back to the stack of boxes and finished unpacking the new stock, sneaking peeks at his intruder every few seconds to make sure it was still where he left it. He managed to get everything unpacked, but he stopped there, not wanting to leave the room to put the stock out on the shelves in the other room. He spied his heavy-duty waxed canvas work apron on the hook by the door. Eyeing the pockets, he pulled it on and picked up the little piece of fluff, depositing it in one. There was a little mew of protest before he felt a vibration against his thigh. With the target secure, he went to work getting the shelves restocked.

When he finished, he peeked into the pocket where the kitten was still sleeping. He made a slow circle in the store. "What do I do with you now?"

He pulled the little fur ball out of his apron pocket and pulled the apron off with one hand. With a grunt of exasperation, he turned off the lights and carried the kitten home. He hesitated when he reached the top of the stairs and thought about knocking on Mae's door. Maybe he could persuade her to take it for the night, and then he'd have an excuse to talk to her. No, she was so mad he doubted even a kitten would work. He turned to his own door and went inside. He set the bundle of fur down. It wobbled for a minute before it plopped down on its butt.

Jacob carefully stepped over it and headed for the kitchen, realizing he hadn't eaten all day. He found some leftover fried chicken in the refrigerator and pulled out a beer.

"Ouch!" He looked down, and the little monster was climbing up his leg again. It squealed a mewl of protest when he plucked it off his leg and set it on the floor. Then it let out the closest thing to a roar its tiny body was capable of.

"I guess you're hungry too, huh?"

He searched through the cupboards and found a can of tuna. "This will probably work for now."

The meows grew louder as soon as he got the can open, and it circled his legs as he scooped a little out onto a plate and set it on the floor. As soon as it was within reach, it attacked it, making little growling noises while it ate.

Jacob leaned against the counter, picking at some chicken while the kitten ate. He'd given up eating at the kitchen table. Without Mae sitting across from him, there didn't seem to be much point.

He glanced down at his intruder.

"Aw, hell."

The little monster was licking itself next to a puddle on the floor.

After he cleaned up the mess, Jacob found an empty box and ripped up some paper. He set the kitten inside and ordered, "Next time, use this."

It blinked up at him and then climbed out of the box and headed toward his leg again. He picked it up before its tiny little daggers could dig into him and carried it around while he got ready for bed. When he finally climbed under the covers, it settled in the crook of his neck again, its motor vibrating.

"One night, buddy, that's all you get. I don't do long-term relationships."

He gritted his teeth as the kitten stretched and then began to knead at his neck.

CHAPTER NINE

"WHAT CAN I get for the mayor and the rest of you lovely ladies for lunch today?"

Tilly stood at the table with her coffeepot in hand. Today, her checkered shirt was a shade of orange that matched the brightness of her freshly dyed red hair.

"You can just call me Mae, Ms. Reynolds."

Tillie set the coffeepot down with a thump and rested her hands on her hips. "This town hasn't had a proper mayor in years, and I'm damn proud to have one of my girls sittin' in that office." She jerked her head toward the courthouse. "I'm gonna call you the mayor out of respect." She picked her coffeepot back up. "I expect y'all want sweet tea. I'll start with that," she announced, walking back to the kitchen.

Emma Walker smiled and nodded her head while Callie beamed at her with pride in her eyes. Heat bloomed over her cheeks, and Mae picked up her menu as if she didn't have the contents memorized since she was ten years old just to have something to hide behind.

Tillie returned with their drinks, and they had just finished placing their orders when Jo Martin came in and slid into the booth next to Emma.

Tillie patted Jo on the shoulder. "What can I get you, honey?"

"Ham and cheese sandwich with a side of potato salad to go. Thank you, Tillie."

Tillie headed off with their order, and Mae turned to Jo. "How are things going at Halcyon?"

"Great. We're expecting our first group from the trade school next week. We only have room for six students right now, but as soon as we get the rest of the second floor restored, we'll be able to have as many as twelve students when we put bunk beds in some of the larger rooms."

Emma shook her head. "I never imagined the old plantation house being used as a trade school. It's a wonderful idea. I... I thought that if you ever wanted to have a class on the history of the plants and herbs that would have been grown and used on the plantation, I... I could do that...." Her voice faded away as she finished speaking.

It would be good for Emma to help at Halcyon. She barely had any life outside of working for her father and stepmother at their drugstore as a pharmacist. Mae would love to see her push back against her dad's domination and get out more.

"I think that's a wonderful idea, Emma. Why don't you come by the house one evening, and we can have a glass of wine on the veranda and work something out," Jo said.

Emma nodded. "I'll try to get away."

Mae exchanged worried glances with Callie and Jo. They were all concerned about Emma living under her father's tyrannical thumb.

Jo got up from the table when Tillie dropped off her order. "I'll see you later. And Emma, you're welcome at Halcyon anytime."

"Thank you," Emma said quietly.

Mae had just taken a bite of her sandwich when Jacob walked in with Isiah. She forced herself to keep chewing and swallow.

She didn't want to face him, couldn't face him yet, or maybe ever.

Pulling out her phone, she pretended to see a message that didn't exist. "Oh, I forgot I've got a meeting." Mae reached into her handbag and grabbed a few bills, throwing them on the table before she rushed past the two men, out of the restaurant, and made her way quickly back to Town Hall.

She breathed a sigh of relief when she reached her office. Now that Grace was gone, she didn't have to explain her premature return from lunch. Mae dropped into the chair behind her desk and let out a frustrated groan. At some point, she was going to have to be in the same room with Jacob. Colton was just too small to hide.

There was a soft knock on her door. Mae jerked her head up and eyed Callie and Emma standing in the doorway.

"Tillie packed up our food so we can have an office picnic," Callie said, holding up a large brown paper bag.

"Come on in," Mae said before sighing and pushing away the papers on her desk.

"You just sit while Emma and I unpack the food." Callie pulled containers from the bag.

Mae nodded, biting her lip. "Jacob and I... I ended it," she blurted out.

Callie froze, a sandwich dangling from her hand, staring at Mae wide-eyed.

Emma began to sputter and cough, trying to choke down the sip of tea she'd just taken.

"What in the…. Lord have mercy," Callie said, dropping into a chair. She set her sandwich down and wiped the mustard off her hands with a frown. When she looked back up at Mae, there was a note of sadness in her eyes. "You're my best friend, and I didn't know."

Mae sighed. "I didn't mean to hurt your feelings. It was supposed to be a summer fling, and then it got… complicated."

"When did it begin?" Emma asked.

"Pretty much the day he rolled into town. We agreed it was just going to be for fun. I figured we'd get it out of our system and then move on, but it didn't." She looked at Callie. "I see how happy you and Dax are, and Jo with Taylor. I decided I'm ready for what you have, and I thought I wanted it with Jacob, but he…."

She dropped her chin and blinked back her tears.

"Oh, honey." Callie jumped up and came over to kneel by her side. She pulled Mae into an embrace and despite Mae's best efforts, a few tears escaped.

"When did it happen?" Callie asked.

Mae sniffed and pulled out of Callie's embrace. "A couple of weeks ago."

"You've been keeping this to yourself this whole time? First, you had a secret relationship, and now, you had a secret breakup," Emma said.

"You could have talked to us," Callie admonished.

Mae shrugged. "I didn't want to burden you—"

"Don't you dare. You're my best friend. You are never a burden to me."

"Me neither, Mae," Emma said. "I'm always here for you no matter what."

"I appreciate you, both of you. I guess I was also a little embarrassed."

Callie wrinkled her forehead. "What in the world for?"

"I poured my heart out to that stupid lumberjack, and he turned me down. I'm so sick and tired of never being enough where men are concerned. I'm too smart, too educated, or too opinionated. I'm too Black or not Black enough. I just can't win." She threw her hands up in frustration.

"I don't think Jacob thinks any of those things about you."

"Then what is it?" Mae asked Callie.

"He's scared," Emma said quietly.

Mae and Callie both stared at her.

"I can see it in his eyes," she continued. "I... I can't explain it, but it's more than just being in a relationship. There's something else there."

Mae wrinkled her forehead. Emma was right. She'd been so caught up in what she wanted, she didn't think about what Jacob's concerns were.

She sat, balled her napkin, and threw it down on her plate. "I'm an idiot. I've been so caught up in my wallowing I didn't think about that." She exhaled. "It doesn't matter. If he's scared or whatever the reason is, I'm not going to wait around for him to figure it out." She forced a smile. "Besides, I've got my hands full here. I don't have time for a relationship."

Callie gave her a pat on the shoulder and returned to her seat.

Emma cleared her throat. "Since you mentioned it, you were asked to serve as mayor until the next election. What are you going to do in November?"

"Well, I've been thinking about that. I think I want to run for re-election."

Emma blanched.

"Em, what's wrong?" Mae asked.

"I... my dad has been talking about running. He, he said if he ran, no one would dare run against him, and he had friends who would make sure of that." Emma's eyes grew bright, and a tear formed on the edge of one of her pale lashes. "Oh, Mae, I'm so sorry—"

Mae got up and sat on the arm of Emma's chair and put her arm around her. "You have nothing to be sorry about."

"Emma, you never have to worry," Callie added. "No one around here holds you responsible for the way your dad behaves."

Mae wanted to help, but she and Callie didn't want to do anything that might make it worse for their friend. She chose her words carefully, not wanting to offend Emma. "I have to say I'm surprised to hear that he wants to run for mayor. I thought he'd be preoccupied with all of the legal problems he has."

"Dad says he has friends who can fix that," Emma said.

Mae exchanged a worried look with Callie. "Promise you'll come to either one of us if you're in trouble." Mae gave Emma a stern look. "Promise me, Em."

"Yeah, okay, I will." Emma smiled and took Mae's hand in hers. "This isn't about me. This is supposed to be about you. Let's be honest, we all know my dad isn't a good man, but I don't think he'll really run for mayor. He likes to brag, but deep down, I think he knows he's in trouble. Now, what can we do to help you with Jacob?"

"There's nothing to do. The only thing I'm asking is if y'all can act normal when we hang out," Mae said.

Callie frowned. "It's going to be hard to pretend I'm not mad at him."

"I'm the one that gets to be mad, and to be honest, I'm not even mad anymore, just… sad." Mae sighed.

Callie and Emma gave Mae a sympathetic look.

There was a knock on her office door, and Ms. June stuck her head in. Little bells at the bottom of her flowing skirt in shades of red and purple tinkled as she swept into the room.

"Oh, hello, girls. Mae, I wanted to stop by and talk to you about the Fourth of July celebrations. I was thinking we could set up a station in the park where children could make art projects about tolerance. And then I was thinking, wouldn't it be a good idea if someone did a reading about the brotherhood of man, or"—she clapped her hands, her eyes sparkling with excitement—"a Maya Angelou poem. Oh, and I thought we could have some Black Lives Matter T-shirts made to pass out. I just think it's so important for everyone to understand that liberty is for everyone, don't you think?"

Mae plastered on the patient smile she had mastered since Ms. June started her weekly visits. Ms. June had a new list of ideas for her every week, and while she appreciated her enthusiasm, there was no way she could incorporate every idea she had into the Fourth of July celebrations.

"Those are all interesting ideas. It's so fortunate that Mrs. Ellis is here, since she's on the planning committee for the celebrations."

"Oh, wonderful, dear." Ms. June linked arms with Callie. "You know, I just finished reading an article about children of mixed-race couples, and I have so many questions."

"Why don't you and Callie head over to the library to talk?" Mae asked. "As much as I'd like to chat, I'm afraid I have work to do."

As Callie was being led away by Ms. June, she paused in the doorway. "Don't forget about dinner. You promised to come, and Dax has invited Jacob."

Once Ms. June had Callie out the door, Emma laughed. "I love you guys. You're so brave."

Her heart went out to her friend. "Oh, Em, so are you."

Emma ducked her head. "I'm trying."

Mae walked Emma out and watched her head back toward Walkers's from the top of the town hall steps. If she were still with Jacob, she'd have asked him for help keeping an eye on her, but that wasn't an option. She paused before heading back inside, taking in the surrounding activity. Now that all the ridiculous rules the town council had put into place were gone, there were people enjoying the park again. Children were playing around the gazebo. She smiled when she saw a couple sitting on a blanket sharing a picnic lunch. She was happy with everything she'd accomplished, but there was something missing, and as much as she didn't want to admit it, that something was a big surly lumberjack.

Speak of the devil. She glanced toward the hardware store and saw Jacob leaning against the doorjamb with his arm crossed, watching her. Mae lifted her chin and marched back into her office. Jacob Winters had no right to care about her anymore.

Now, all she had to do was stop wanting him to.

CHAPTER TEN

"YOU MIGHT want to rethink the name," the vet said with a chuckle.

"What's wrong with Busta?"

"There's nothing wrong with Busta. I mean, who doesn't like Leaders of the New School? I love old-school '90s rap. It's just that Busta here is a girl."

Jacob frowned down at the little kitten who was chasing the vet's laser pointer across the exam table. He'd brought the kitten to the animal shelter with every intention of surrendering it, but the minute he saw the other animals watching him with sad eyes, he tightened his hold on the kitten in his arms until he... *she* let out a little howl of protest.

One vet at the shelter offered to give her an exam and her first round of shots. "You've got yourself a good dad, take care of him," the vet said, chucking her under the chin.

Jacob tried to rub away the tightness he suddenly felt in his chest. The right thing to do would be to leave the little ball of fluff here. He didn't do commitment, it wasn't his thing. Commitments made memories. He'd remember every moment he had with Mae. So far he'd been lucky and those memories were all good, filled with light and joy. But what if he couldn't prevent something bad from happening? It was better to avoid starting a relationship so he wouldn't have to live with the memories when it was over.

As if she knew he was wrestling with his decision, the kitten abandoned the vet and walked over to Jacob, butting his hand with her head. He scooped her up and she stood on her hind legs, placing her paws on his chest and nuzzling his chin.

"Come on—" He sighed. "—let's get you home."

Jacob paid the bill and stopped at the pet store the vet recommended. He left with his pocketbook considerably lighter.

On his way home, he looked up at one of the large hanging baskets with colorful flowers tumbling over the edges that hung from the lampposts lining the street.

"Petunias are my favorite because they're fragile but hearty at the same time," Jacob remembered his mother saying while she reached out to gently cup a paper-thin bloom in her hand. He recalled the memory of his mother holding his hand as they walked through the park on their way to the playground.

There was a little *meow* from the new carrier he'd just purchased. He got in the truck and set the carrier on the seat next to him and opened it. The little cat leaped out and into his lap, blinking at him with her green eyes. "I guess you're not Busta anymore. Why do you think of Petunia?"

He took the *meow* as a yes.

A couple of hours later, Jacob looked at the pile of cat toys with dismay while Petunia was happily playing in the bag all the toys came in instead.

Jacob huffed, shook his head, and continued pacing in front of his apartment window. He was restless and worried. It had been a week since he'd crossed paths with Mae. She was avoiding him, and doing a damn good job of it. Eyeing his motorcycle parked out front, he decided he was long overdue for a ride. Some time on the open road was just what he needed to clear his head.

THE AIR was sweet and warm as he lost himself on the back roads around Colton. It had been too long since he'd been on the back of his bike. After an hour on the road, he felt more relaxed and started to head toward home.

The minute his headlight bounced off the small figure fighting with a tire iron, all the good vibes he'd been feeling disappeared, and Jacob's blood began to boil. Pulling over, he cut the engine and swung his leg over his bike. The force of seeing Mae hit him like a punch in the gut. He'd missed her, missed having her burst into the store to share some new idea or piece of news. Most of all, he missed having her in his bed. Not even for the sex, which was off the charts. No, he missed the little noises she made when she slept and the way she laid her head on his shoulder with her hand on his chest. Which was why his heart stuttered to a stop seeing her on the dark road, vulnerable and alone.

Cursing at her recklessness under his breath, he stalked toward her.

"What the hell do you think you're doing?" he growled as he pulled off his helmet.

"What does it look like I'm doing?" Mae grunted, continuing her battle with a stubborn lug nut.

"Here." Jacob took the tire iron out of her hand and started to remove the tire.

The shove was just enough to put him off-balance and make him land on his ass in the dirt. Mae grabbed the tire iron out of his hands, holding it to her chest as if it were a shield.

"Oh no, you don't. You don't get to rescue me."

Jacob climbed to his feet. "Damn it, Mae, I'm just trying to help."

"Nope"—Mae shook her head—"no way, you don't let me help you, so why should I let you help me?"

"You're being unreasonable."

Oops, that was a mistake.

Mae's eyes grew wide. She let the tool fall to her side and put her hand on her hip. "What. Did. You. Just. Say. To. Me?"

Oh crap, this wasn't going well at all.

He ran his hand through his hair. "I shouldn't have said that."

"Go away, Jacob."

"Listen, I wanted to help because it's dark, and these roads can be dangerous. Someone might drive by and not see you. I don't want you to get hurt."

A set of headlights illuminated where they were standing, and a black pickup rolled past, slowing down just long enough for the two men inside to glare at them as they went by. Jacob shuddered. Would they have stopped if he hadn't been there? He clenched his hands into fists at his side until they began to ache. The pain grounded him and helped him push his fear down into that deep place that made him so effective at his missions, but it was almost impossible because this wasn't another mission—this was Mae.

Another pair of headlights came toward them, and Jacob's protective instincts kicked in. He moved so that Mae was behind him. This time, he exhaled when he saw Isiah pull up in his sheriff's car.

Isiah rolled down his window. "Evening. You need a hand?"

Mae stepped out from behind Jacob. "Yes, that'd be much appreciated."

Isiah nodded and pulled over.

Mae turned to Jacob, her hands on her hips in what he always thought of as her superhero stance.

"You can go now."

He ran his hand through his hair again and clamped his mouth shut. He'd already gotten himself in enough trouble tonight. With a curt nod, he grabbed his helmet and climbed back on his bike.

As soon as he got back to his apartment, he put his memory to work and emailed the Jackson office with the license plate, make, and model of the truck, and a detailed description of the occupants just for good measure. Then he paced until he heard Mae's footsteps in the hall. His breath hitched when he heard her pause in front of his door. He wanted her to knock, needed that reassurance only she could give him. A second later, the soft click of her door closing squashed that kernel of hope.

A series of small tugs on his pant leg took his attention away from Mae. He looked down at the enormous green-gray eyes on a tiny head surrounded by a fluff of fur moving slowly up his leg. He sighed and picked up the little fur ball.

"You know, most cats just meow," he said with a sigh as the kitten immediately squirmed out of his grasp to settle into the crook of his neck.

He received a loud purr in response.

Jacob carefully made his way to the overstuffed chair in the corner and lowered himself as gently as possible so he didn't disturb his little friend. He reached up and scratched the soft fur between her ears and was rewarded with tiny daggers digging into his neck as it began to knead.

"I fucked up," he said with a sigh.

The little cat nuzzled his neck in agreement. Jacob pulled out his phone and started scrolling through his music app to find the right song to suit his mood. He often used music to psych himself up for a mission and to calm himself down afterward. Most people assumed he listened to hard rock or country based on his looks, but he was a city kid from the '90s. His parents' love of music from the '80s wore off on him, and if he wasn't listening to that, it was all hip-hop, funk, and rap.

Jacob chuckled. "Here, you'll like these guys." A second later, a song from Curiosity Killed the Cat filled the room. He set the player to shuffle, and the eclectic mix of songs suited his chaotic mix of emotions. Closing his eyes, he leaned back in his chair and let the images each song evoked wash over him.

When he first met Dax, he'd asked Jacob what it was like to have a unique memory like his. He described it like having one of those old-fashioned library card catalogs in his head. He could open any drawer and pull out any card and relive that memory. Most of the time, he kept those drawers firmly shut, but tonight he allowed himself to open them. Memories flitted through his mind—his dad teaching him how to drive, coming home after school with the football team to a kitchen full of snacks and fresh-baked cookies his mother always had ready for them. He filed that card away and pulled up the memory of the night he sat on his front stoop, wondering where he was going to go, when Coach pulled up and told him in his gruff voice to go pack his things. Jacob lived with him for the rest of his senior year. Thank God he'd just turned eighteen when his mother succumbed to the cancer that ravaged her body. And he would always be thankful to Coach Murphy for giving him a home until the Army did.

Busta Rhymes came on, and he broke into a smile. Coach Murphy and his wife Carol had an open door for any of the guys on the team who needed a place to call home. His teammate Marcus was another stray Coach Murphy and his wife took in. How many nights had he and Marcus stayed up late listening to Busta and talking about their plans for the future? Marcus dreamed of a career in the NFL, and Jacob wanted to join the Army to serve his country in his father's memory. Besides Coach and his wife, Marcus was the only other person he'd stayed in touch with from childhood. He pulled up his contacts and checked the time before he hit the Call icon.

"Hey, man, how you doing?" Marcus answered on the first ring.

"Got a cat. I was gonna name it Busta."

The cat made a little mewl of protest at his friend's howl of laughter.

"Oh, man, I gotta see this. Send me a pic."

Jacob held up the phone and sent the image of half his face and a tiny kitten curled up next to his neck.

"Aww, that's the cutest dang thing I've ever seen. Hey, Stacey, come look at this."

Marcus and his wife cooed over the picture until Jacob finally barked, "You done?"

There was some muffled whispering before Stacey yelled out in a singsong voice, "Bye, Jacob."

Marcus came back on the phone, his voice dropping to a more serious tone. "You remembering tonight?"

"A little bit."

"Want to talk about it?"

Jacob thought about it for a moment. "Not really."

It was comforting to know Marcus wouldn't push. He always understood when Jacob was having a night where his memories plagued him.

True to form, Marcus said, "Let me know when you're ready. How's small-town life? You let me know if you need a celebrity endorsement for the hardware store."

Jacob chuckled. "If you know of any celebrities, let me know."

"That's just cold, man."

It was impossible to talk to Marcus and not laugh. While Jacob never really had any plans to leverage his high school football career into anything else, Marcus had bigger dreams. He might give him a hard time, but he was proud of his friend, who'd become an all-star running back for Seattle.

"Just trying to keep you humble," he teased.

"Seriously, Jake, are you okay?"

He ran his hand over his face. "I let myself get settled."

"That's not a bad thing."

"I hate that I can remember everything about my parents, everything I've ever done in battle, everyone I've cared about and lost. I don't want to make memories that will hurt, and I can't forget them," Jacob confessed.

"But what if you make so many good memories you have a hard time finding the bad ones?"

"You know it doesn't work that way," Jacob interrupted.

Marcus sighed. "Yeah, I know, but let me finish. I haven't gotten to my point yet. Everyone has good and bad memories. Hell, you know I have my fair share of bad ones. I look at my kids and think about how my father beat me and—" He sucked in a breath. "—the thing is, marrying Stacey and having our kids, those good memories make the bad ones just... it's not so bad."

Jacob swallowed past the lump that had formed in his throat. "I hear you."

"How 'bout I keep saying it until you believe me?"

"Yeah... okay."

"Now, about this cat, you said you were gonna name it Busta. What happened?"

"It's a girl."

This time, he couldn't help joining in his friend's laughter.

CHAPTER ELEVEN

"MORNING, MAYOR Colton." The new member of the Colton Fire Department waved as Mae walked past.

"Morning." She smiled and waved back.

The one-man fire department becoming a two-man department was another sign of progress and a reminder of how much the work she was doing further cemented her desire to stay in office. There was so much more that she could do to help her community.

The office was eerily quiet without Grace at her post, and Mae welcomed the solitude. She worked at the reception desk rather than in her office so that she'd be aware of anyone coming in. It was amazing how much she could get done when she wasn't having to battle her truculent former office manager.

Mae was knee-deep in reading through old emails she'd found on Grace's computer, that the woman had arbitrarily decided weren't important enough to pass on to her, when a movement at the doorway caught her eye. Her eyes widened in surprise at the visitor.

"I, um, thought that if I brought y'all lunch, maybe we could talk some more," Presley Beaumont said, holding up a takeout box.

Mae's stomach grumbled, and when she looked at her watch, she realized the morning had slipped away and it was indeed time for lunch.

"Well, that depends. What did you bring?"

Presley moved closer to the desk, and Mae grew hopeful that what she thought she was smelling wasn't a figment of her imagination.

"I brought you tamales from Tony's."

"You may remain," Mae said, gesturing to the chair across from her.

Presley grinned and plopped down, pulling out plates and cutlery along with a couple of sodas from her sparkled tote bag.

They couldn't be more opposite; Presley was all ruffles and feathers while Mae preferred clean lines and solid colors. She wouldn't be caught dead walking down the street with a bag covered in sequins, but she had to give Presley credit for being fearless in her fashion choices.

Mae cleared a space on the desk and a few minutes later took a bite of the spicy cornmeal confection.

"Delta tamales are proof there is a God," she said around another mouthful.

"Can I tell y'all something?" Presley asked.

Mae nodded.

"I'd never had one until just a few months ago. I… I always thought they were, I don't know, kind of ghetto food."

Mae's eyebrows rose. "I see, and what made you change your mind?"

"I found this cookbook about Southern cooking. I'm not really that much of a cook, but I thought maybe I should try to learn because Is—I mean, because maybe if I met someone… well, I just thought it might help make a good impression."

Mae fought back a smile as Presley rambled. Who knew it would take just a couple of stern talking-tos from the right man to turn Presley Beaumont around?

"Anyway, then I found this show called *Somewhere South,* and it's about Southern food, but it's got more than that. She talks about history and how food brings people together, different kinds of people. Did you know that almost all cultures have dumplings?" She sat back, shaking her head. "Lord a'mighty, I had no idea."

Lord a'mighty is right, Mae thought.

Before Presley left, she offered to bring her lunch in exchange for Mae talking to her more. It seemed like a fair deal, as long as she wasn't actually doing any cooking yet. Just a few minutes after Presley walked out, her brother Ashton walked in.

"Do I want to know what my sister was doing in here?" he asked with a wince.

"She brought me lunch."

Ashton's eyes widened. "You're joking, right? She's my sister, I know, and I do love her, I guess, but most of the time the porch light is on but no one's home with her, but lately…." He rubbed the back of his neck and shook his head. "You should see all the books she's been bringing home. And she keeps apologizing to me for that night in the Buckthorn. She even offered to take me to the Pride parade in Atlanta this year. Honestly, this whole do-gooder kick she's on is driving me crazy. I almost miss the old Presley."

Mae laughed. "Maybe you should just appreciate that your sister is motivated."

"But why now?"

"I think she's finally found someone she wants to impress."

"Any guesses on who it is?"

Mae shook her head. "Oh no, you won't catch me spreadin' twallop. Now, what can I do you for?"

Ashton grinned and pulled an envelope out of his jacket pocket. "I'm happy to inform you that the Colton Foundation is presenting you with a two-thousand-dollar donation to help bring back the Fourth of July celebrations."

Mae got up and took the envelope from him. "Thank you, Ashton. I really appreciate this."

"Bringing back the fireworks in the park is long overdue. Lots of folks in town are excited about it, and we want to do everything we can to help." The smile fell from Ashton's face, replaced with concern and hesitancy. "Can I ask you a question?"

Mae nodded. "Sure."

"Have you made any plans for security?"

Mae frowned. "Isiah will be there. I didn't think we needed more than that."

Ashton gave Mae a skeptical look. "A teller at the bank asked me if I thought it would be safe. She heard a rumor that some folks might want to start trouble, especially after you renamed the park." Ashton held his hands up. "Don't get me wrong, I totally support what you did, but it did piss some people off."

Mae folded her arms. "Yeah, okay, I get it. I'll look at the budget and ask Isiah if there are any additional resources we can bring in."

"We thought some of this money might help with that."

"Thank you, Ashton, it's been really encouraging to see the town come together like this."

"You're doing an outstanding job, Mae. Look, I know most folks are rootin' for you to go to Washington and become a big-time politician, but I guess I'm selfish. I'd love it if you'd stick around here. Small towns need good leadership too."

Mae gave Ashton a hug. "Thank you. You don't know how much it means to me that you said that."

"Hey, if you decide you need a campaign manager, I'd like to offer my services."

Mae pulled away, wiping her eyes. "I haven't made a decision yet, but if I decide to run, you're hired."

"WHAT IS that?"

Jacob opened his door at the same time as Mae came out of her apartment the next morning. He was cradling something in his arms, and she thought she heard a little *meow*.

"It's a kitten."

"I know that. What are you doing with it?"

"I, uh, kind of adopted it."

Mae stared at him for a minute, trying to process what she was hearing. "Wait a minute, so you can't commit to a relationship, but you can commit to a cat?" she blurted out.

He looked down at the kitten in his arms. "I... it's different."

"Did you name it?"

Jacob paused, looking down at the kitten before looking back to her with unmistakable guilt in his eyes.

She shook her head and turned away.

"Mae, wait." He followed her down the stairs.

Dax and Jo were huddled together in front of a group of computer screens when they reached the main floor. They both looked up in surprise as Jacob continued to call out to her.

She barged out of the building and marched toward Town Hall, ignoring the curious stares as Jacob, holding a tiny kitten, chased after her.

When he followed her up the stairs, she whirled around. "No pets allowed."

He looked down at the kitten tucked close to his chest. "Can we just talk about this, Mae? I didn't mean to hurt your feelings, but—"

"No buts, I get it. You made it really clear that you don't do long-term relationships." She pointed to the kitten. "What are you going to do with that when you've decided the relationship has gone on too long?"

Mae knew she was being mean, but the little kitten seemed helpless in Jacob's arms, and it made her angry to think he would walk away from it the way he walked away from her. Before he had a chance to answer, she turned and ran up the stairs and into her office, slamming the door shut behind her and burying her face in her hands.

Chapter Twelve

"MOM?" MAE called out, walking through her parents' house. She made her way through the kitchen and out the back door. Sure enough, her mom was in the garden, babying her peonies.

"Oh, sweetheart, I didn't hear you come in," Ella Colton said, getting up and brushing the dirt from her knees.

"Hey, baby girl." Her dad came out of the garage, enveloping her in a warm hug.

"Hi, Dad."

"We missed you at Sunday dinner, a. Are you feeling better?" her mom said, pressing the back of her hand to Mae's forehead.

Sunday dinners at her parents' table was a promise Mae made when she moved out. It wasn't all out of a sense of obligation; she also did it because even though she craved her independence, she loved her parents and didn't want to lose touch with them the way her sister had. Until now, she hadn't missed more than a handful of dinners. She'd made up excuses to miss the last two Sunday dinners, the last one being she had a cold when the truth was her eyes were too puffy and swollen from crying after seeing Jacob with the kitten. Mae knew she was out of excuses, so she put on her favorite T-shirt that read *Good Trouble Better South* and her most comfortable pair of jeans and headed home for dinner.

"I'm fine, Mom."

"I'm just worried about you. You're working yourself too hard."

Her dad put his arm around her shoulder and gave it a squeeze. "We just don't want you to burn out too quickly. You have bigger and better things ahead of you than being mayor of Colton."

What if I don't want bigger and better things?

Instead, she lied. "I know Dad, and I promise I won't."

"I heard Congressman Green might be looking for a new chief of staff. Maybe by the time your term is finished in the fall, you'll be able to make a move to Washington," her dad said with a huge grin.

Her parents had been encouraging and planning for Mae to make a move to Washington since she first expressed an interest in politics.

They'd even taken a vacation there during spring break when she was in high school. She soaked up every moment of visiting her state representative's office and the tour of the White House her parents had arranged with him.

When her sister decided her career was going to be an NFL wife, her parents put even more of their focus on Mae's hopes and dreams. Somewhere along the line, their goals for her became bigger than her own. She didn't have the heart to tell them that, not when her sister continued to disappoint them.

"Beth called." Her mom sighed. "It looks like she won't be able to make it for the Fourth of July celebrations after all."

Mae resisted the urge to roll her eyes. Her big sister always had an excuse for not coming home, and her parents always pretended like it was okay.

"Oh, that's too bad," Mae said.

"Maybe they'll come home for Thanksgiving," her dad tried to console her mom.

"Not if the team makes the playoffs," Mae said, wincing when she saw her mom's crestfallen expression. She shouldn't have said that. She forced a bright smile. "But you never know. And you guys could always go to Atlanta and spend the holidays with her up there."

Her mom's face brightened. "Maybe. I'll ask what she thinks next time I talk to her."

Mae silently begged for her sister to say yes, even though she knew the odds weren't good. Her older sister didn't like to have reminders of her small-town life around her, and that often included her parents.

"Can you stay for dinner?" her dad asked.

"That's why I came over. I was craving a home-cooked meal, maybe some of your biscuits and gravy," she said hopefully.

Her mom gave her an affectionate smile. "I think I can come up with something."

"Want to keep me company in the garage while your mother makes dinner?"

Mae gave her dad a grateful look. Despite her mom's best efforts, she would never be a master chef in the kitchen. She was okay at the basics, but anything more than an omelet was beyond her skill set. Spending time with her mom in the kitchen was never going to be her idea of fun. Beth was the one who'd loved creating elaborate meals with their mom.

She followed her dad into the garage and took up her spot on the worn stool in the corner. Some of her favorite childhood memories were from sitting in that exact spot, watching her dad work on his prized 1964 Mustang convertible. Sometimes she would lend a hand, but it was his baby, and most of the time it was more fun to keep him company while he worked.

It was on this stool that she learned about the history of her family and Colton. Even the car represented her family history. Her dad was the first person in his family to buy a brand-new car off the lot. That was a big reason he'd babied it over the years and only let it out of the garage when the conditions were absolutely perfect.

"I heard you lost another flag the other day," he said over the clatter of his tools.

Mae sighed. "Yeah, I'm going to have to order replacements in bulk."

After over a hundred years of Mississippi being the only state with a Confederate flag as part of their state flag, the state finally had a new flag. It featured the state flower, a magnolia blossom, on a dark blue background ringed with stars representing Mississippi being the twentieth state, and one gold star honoring the indigenous peoples who first inhabited the land. It was a flag Mae was proud of. Unfortunately, not everyone felt that way, and someone had been stealing the flags at Town Hall and at people's homes in town.

Joseph grunted from under the hood of his car. "I just hope it doesn't escalate into anything worse. I heard there were some storefronts vandalized with racist graffiti in Wynona last week."

"I hadn't heard about that."

"I got a couple of calls for insurance claims."

Mae frowned. She'd make sure to talk to Isiah in the morning to see if there was anything they needed to do to protect the businesses in town.

Her dad popped his head out from under the hood and walked over to his workbench. "I'm just thankful this won't be your problem for too much longer. Before you know it, you'll be looking at places to live in DC." He snapped his fingers. "Oh, I forgot to tell you. One of my clients mentioned he has a nephew who works as a lawyer in Virginia. I thought maybe when you move, I could set up an introduction. He sounds like a fine young man, with a law degree from Georgetown. Just the kind of person you should be dating."

"I think you're jumping the gun a little, Dad. I don't know for sure if I'll be moving to DC after the election for a new mayor is over."

"What do you mean you won't be going to DC? What else would you do?"

Run for mayor, stay here in Colton.

"I don't know." She shrugged. She couldn't bring herself to tell her dad what she really wanted to do.

Her dad studied her for a minute. "What's going on, sweetheart?"

Before Mae could answer, her mom called them in to dinner. The biscuits and gravy she'd been craving sat like lead in her stomach, making her feel queasy instead of full. She wanted to tell her parents about Jacob and her ideas for her future, instead of listening to their plans for what she was supposed to do with her life.

She went home after making up an excuse that she had a grant proposal she needed to finish. Her apartment used to be her sanctuary; she loved the exposed brick walls and the enormous arched windows overlooking the park. It was the first place she'd ever had that was just hers. She shared a dorm room and then an apartment with Callie in college, and before that a room with her sister. Mae had thoughtfully picked out each piece of furniture and decor that reflected her personality, clean and modern mixed with bold florals and rich jewel tones. Now, she looked around the space, and it felt... empty.

"Stupid lumberjack," she muttered.

In a fit of *Bridget Jones*-inspired life reboot, she grabbed her laptop, settled onto her sofa, and pulled up a dating app that she had long abandoned but never deleted. Too tall, too short, too muscular, not muscular enough. At one point, she even changed the filters and started looking at profiles of bearded White guys, but none of them had the piercing dark blue eyes and slightly shaggy dark hair that she loved to run her hands through. With a groan of frustration, she tossed her laptop to the side and grabbed a pillow, burying her face in it to let out a frustrated scream.

MORNING CAME too soon after a fitful night of sleep where she dreamed about being Bridget Jones, only instead of begging Colin Firth not to leave, she was pleading with a surly lumberjack.

She showered and changed, deciding it was a red-heel day. A woman could face anything if she was wearing a really impressive pair of red pumps. With Grace no longer around to make snide remarks about looking professional, Mae wore her favorite pair of dark slim-fit jeans paired with a T-shirt with the saying *All Y'all* printed in white on the black background. She grabbed a black blazer and her messenger bag and headed out, ready to take on a new day and determined not to think about Jacob Winters.

It was a busy day, and Mae was grateful to see Presley on her office doorstep with lunch again. They were just finishing up eating when they were interrupted.

"Mae, I was wondering if you have any thoughts on hiring a replacement for—" Judge Beaumont rounded the corner and stopped in his tracks, looking from Mae to his daughter and back again. "Presley, what are you doing here?" He sighed and pushed his glasses back on his nose. "What have you done now?"

Mae's heart went out to her when Presley's shoulders hunched.

"Presley has expressed an interest in learning more about civil rights history, so she offered to buy me lunch and ask me a few questions."

Judge Beaumont raised an eyebrow. "I see."

"I have a lot to learn," Presley added quietly.

Mae watched the father-and-daughter exchange and realized their relationship was a complicated dynamic, just one more thing she never thought she'd have in common with Presley.

The judge cleared his throat and continued, "Well, I was just wondering if you had any thoughts on a replacement for Grace. I don't want you to get buried under paperwork, Mae. You have enough on your hands as it is."

"I haven't thought about it."

"I can help," Presley said.

Mae and the judge both looked at her in surprise.

"I took a business course at the college last year, remember, Daddy?" Her eyes darted between the two of them. "It doesn't have to be permanent. I could just help until you find someone better... more qualified. You wouldn't even have to pay me. I'd just like to help."

Mae looked at the judge with a raised eyebrow. He shrugged and held his hands up.

"I'll give you a one-day trial. You can come in tomorrow. I expect you to be here at eight a.m. sharp." Mae waggled her finger. "No excuses."

Presley beamed, nodding her head. "Yes, ma'am."

Judge Beaumont cleared his throat. "Well, I guess that's settled, then."

MAE WASN'T sure what to expect the next morning. It certainly wasn't to see Presley waiting for her outside the office when she arrived. She had her hair pulled back into a low ponytail and was wearing considerably less eyeshadow than she usually did. There wasn't a rhinestone or ruffle in sight; instead, she was wearing a pair of gray slacks with a pink cashmere sweater.

By noon, Presley had proven to be much easier to work with than Grace. She wasn't perfect, and they started the morning with a lesson on phone etiquette. But she worked diligently through the morning, and other than a penchant for wanting to organize everything in rainbow colors because it looked "prettier," she was managing the front desk pretty well.

"Presley, what are you doing behind that desk?"

Mae grinned at the shock in Isiah's voice.

"Sheriff Colton." Presley's voice had a slight tremor to it. "I'm helpin' Mayor Colton out for a while."

There was just a touch of pride in Presley's voice that made Mae feel good about her decision to give her a chance.

A second later, Isiah popped his head in her door. "Got a minute?"

"Of course, come on in."

Isiah dropped into the chair across from her. "We've got a problem."

"What's going on?"

"I got a call out at the Walkers' last night. Emma had a black eye and some bruises on her arms. The abuse seems to be escalating."

Mae's breath caught. She'd been friends with Emma since childhood. She'd always been worried about her friend's home life. Sadly, she wasn't surprised Emma's father was taking out his frustrations on his daughter.

"Did you arrest him?"

Isiah frowned and shook his head. "Emma wouldn't press charges."

"Damn it."

"I'm going to monitor the situation, but I thought you should know."

Mae resisted the impulse to go over to the Walkers' and drag her friend away from her abusive father.

"Thanks, I appreciate it. I'll let Callie know, and we'll try to keep an eye on her."

"I can let Pastor Warren know if y'all think that it might help," Presley said from the doorway. "I wasn't eavesdropping, I swear. I couldn't help but overhear."

Isiah looked at Presley with a raised eyebrow.

"Thank you," Mae said. "Anything we can do to support Emma would be helpful. I really wish they'd get her dad's trial going. The sooner that bastard is in jail, the better."

Isiah nodded in agreement as he got up to leave. He paused on his way past Presley. "Thank you for your assistance, Ms. Beaumont."

Mae watched Presley flush bright pink. As soon as Isiah walked out, she asked, "Anything you want to share?"

"No, ma'am," she said, scurrying back to her desk.

After work, Mae headed to Callie and Dax's house. A groan escaped when she pulled up and saw Dax and Jacob sitting on the porch. She'd avoided Jacob since she saw him with the kitten, but it was only a matter of time before she would run into him again, and it looked like time had just run out. She forced a bright smile on her face, jumped out of her Jeep, and headed up the walkway.

"Good evening. Is your lovely bride at home?" she asked Dax, ignoring Jacob.

"You're just in time," Dax replied. "There's a 7Up cake coming out of the oven any minute now."

Mae nodded and went inside where a wave of sugary lemon scent washed over her. She wandered into the kitchen where Callie was pouring the glaze on her cake.

"Hey there, this is a pleasant surprise," Callie said, giving Mae a hug. "It's been too long since we've had a chance to catch up."

"We've both been busy."

"That's no excuse."

Mae followed Callie as she carried the cake out to the table.

"Can you stay for dinner?"

The idea of having to sit through a dinner with Jacob made her stomach churn. "No, sorry, I have some work I need to get back to. I just came to talk to you about Emma."

"What's going on with Emma?" Dax asked, walking in with Jacob.

"We can talk about it later," she said, giving Jacob the side-eye.

Dax looked over his shoulder where Jacob was standing with his arms folded over his chest, staring at her. "Knock it off." He shoved Jacob with his elbow.

"I've got to go. I'll call you later," Mae said to Callie.

"Wait, I'll walk you out." Callie rushed to her side.

As soon as they were out of earshot of the men, Callie wrapped her arm around Mae's shoulder. "What's going on?"

"Emma's—"

"Hold on, tell me what's going on with you and Jacob first."

"Nothing, there's nothing going on. I just don't need that big dumb lumberjack glowering at me like some kind of misogynist caveman."

Callie's eyebrows rose. "Misogynist caveman, really?"

Mae waved her hand. "You know what I mean. Anyway, I don't care about Jacob, but I care about Emma. Her dad gave her a black eye last night."

Callie put a trembling hand to her mouth. "No."

"Are you really surprised? We've seen bruises on her arms before. The closer his trial gets, the more he's going to escalate, you know that. She wouldn't press charges against that bastard."

Callie sighed. "You're right."

Mae sighed, too. "I didn't mean to be so harsh just now. I'm angry and frustrated."

"I understand. What can we do?"

"Isiah's going to do some extra patrols by her house. I'm going to drive by on my way home tonight."

Callie shook her head. "Mae, you can't—"

Mae held her hand up. "I'm not going to do anything crazy. I just need to check. I'll be up worrying if I don't."

"I know how you feel. I'll do what I can to keep an eye on her as well, but we can't force her to do anything she doesn't want or isn't ready to do."

"You're right. I hate that you're right," Mae admitted. "She's our friend, and I can't stand seeing her hurt. Please let me know if you see anything, okay?"

Callie gave her a half-hearted wave with a worried look on her face as Mae pulled out of the driveway.

She circled the block around Emma's house on her way home, feeling helpless. The lights were on in the ramshackle Craftsman that had been neglected since Emma's mother passed away fifteen years ago. The dove-gray paint was peeling or worn away in patches, and what used to be a bright yellow door had faded away just like the sunshine had faded from Emma's life when her mom died.

Rolling down her window, Mae listened for any signs of distress, but she heard nothing, so she headed home. Jacob was waiting on the sidewalk when she pulled up in front of the Barton Building with a thunderous expression.

"You drove by Emma's house on your way home, didn't you?" he growled when she got out of her car.

"So what if I did?"

"What were you thinking you were going to do?"

"I don't know. I just want to make sure she's okay."

"It's too dangerous. What were you going to do if you saw something? Were you going to march up to the front door and confront him? You're so damn impulsive, you don't think about the danger you put yourself in."

Mae glared at him. "What I do is none of your damn business."

She pushed past him and unlocked the door, ignoring Jacob as he locked the door behind them and followed her up the stairs. He didn't stop at his door, following her to her door instead.

"Mae, let's talk. You can't ignore me forever."

She slipped the key into her lock and let her forehead fall to the door. "Go away, Jacob. I don't want to talk to you." She blew out a shaky breath. "Maybe someday, but not today, I'm still mad at you."

His hands wrapped over her shoulders, and she couldn't resist leaning back into the warmth of his body.

"I wish we could go back to the way things were." He sighed.

Pulling away, Mae opened her door and turned to face him. "But we can't. I don't want what we had before, a relationship that we didn't admit was a relationship. I want what we could have been, a couple who loved and supported each other and did it without sneaking around. Good night, Jacob."

She closed the door and squeezed her eyes shut. *No more tears*, she told herself. Jacob didn't want her, but somewhere out there was someone who did.

The sweater she had been knitting as a surprise for Jacob taunted her from her knitting basket in the corner. She should have believed the knitting superstition. The rule was if you started knitting a sweater for your boyfriend, you'd be broken up before you finished it.

She eyed it for a few more minutes before getting up and pulling the half-finished project out with a heavy sigh. She sat down on the couch, running her hands over the deep-blue yarn she'd crafted into intricate cables for a minute before sliding the needles out of the stitches. An hour later, she had five skeins of yard sitting on her coffee table waiting to become something new. That's what she loved about knitting—taking one thing, a piece of yarn, and turning it into something else. Was that what she'd been doing with Jacob, trying to turn him into something else? He'd told her he wasn't into commitment. She should have believed him instead of thinking she could go along with it for a while and try to change later, and she should have listened to her friends. Don't knit a sweater for your boyfriend.

CHAPTER THIRTEEN

IT WAS darker than usual in the ring of trees that night, the clouds obscuring the faint light from the stars and the moon.

Rhett Colton walked into the clearing from the opposite side at the same time as Jacob. The two men exchanged their greetings with curt nods.

"Lot of guns and ammo coming in. They've got people ready to help them when the time comes. Names are here." He handed Jacob another flash drive.

"Are you ready to exit?"

"Not yet." He shook his head with an angry scowl. "I still don't know exactly what they're planning to do. Whatever they got planned, my being there might make the difference if they succeed or not."

A shiver of fear ran through Jacob. He'd faced fear before and embraced it. It was a part of the job, but this time was different. This was the fear he'd spent most of his adult life trying to avoid.

"Thank you."

The haunted look in Rhett's eyes told the story of just how much of a sacrifice he was making each day he continued to engage with the scum who considered themselves patriots. Jacob wanted Rhett to get out as soon as possible, but the work he was doing was important.

"I'll keep you briefed as much as I can," Rhett said.

"Got it."

Jacob watched Rhett disappear into the trees and tried to exhale, but the wired-up feeling flowing through his body wasn't going to go away. Until they broke up this group and Jacob knew Mae would be safe, there was no way he would be able to breathe easily.

Petunia was waiting for him when he returned to the apartment. She perched on his shoulder, watching while he connected the flash drive and downloaded the information. This time, instead of sending it directly, he read the report.

Dread knotted in his stomach while he read the list of names and their connections to local government. He sent the report and deleted everything off the flash drive—too bad he couldn't delete it from his memory.

Petunia butted her little head against his cheek. He chose to believe she was trying to comfort him. As much as he appreciated her efforts, it wasn't the same as having Mae in his arms.

He got up and paced the apartment. He needed to talk to someone, and he couldn't talk to Dax or Isiah. And he didn't know if either of them would speak to him again once they learned the new role he'd taken on after leaving the Army. He plucked Petunia off his shoulder and grabbed his car keys.

"I'll be back," he said, giving her a scratch between the ears.

Fifteen minutes later, he was sitting on Uncle Robert's porch with a glass of whiskey in his hand.

"Act like you've got some sense, boy. Did you honestly think pushing Mae away was going to keep you from remembering?"

Jacob shrugged. "Kind of."

Uncle Robert slapped his knee. "Good Lord, first Dax and then Taylor, I swear the good Lord brought me back here just to knock some sense into you boys. Mae Colton is the best damn thing that could ever happen to a man. You don't throw those memories away, you cherish them, the good and the bad."

"I can't," Jacob choked out in a harsh whisper.

The older man's gaze softened. "I know it's hard, son. You were born with a gift that some people might also think is a curse. It could be a blessing if you let yourself find a way beyond the hurt."

"I've never allowed myself to even think about what that might look like."

"Well, maybe you should start there. Think about how much joy a lifetime of memories with Mae could bring you. Let me ask you this, would you give up one minute, one second of the wonderful memories you have with your mom and dad?"

The thunder came from his heart, pounding in his ears. A different fear, something he'd never felt before, washed over him. He'd spent so much time trying to avoid the terrible memories, he'd never thought about what it would be like to lose the good ones. Jacob replayed his conversation with Marcus and realized he could make a choice about how he wanted to feel about his memories. Jacob finally understood the traditional words of comfort Jews used when a loved one was lost. *May their memory be a blessing.*

He began to look back on the past and remembered the day his father died. While yes, the recollection was still painful, he could also wrap that memory in all the love his father had given him while he was alive.

Uncle Robert leaned forward, resting his forearms on his knees. "I want to tell you something I've never shared with anybody. When I left Colton to join the service, I left the love of my life behind. I pushed her away because I didn't want to hurt her, and I wound up hurting us both. I was a lot like you. I didn't want to make memories that would only come back to haunt me later. Mainly, I was just scared—we both were. It was the '60s, and a relationship like ours was dangerous and still illegal around here back then. At the time, I really believed I was doing the right thing. Ever since the day I came back...." His voice broke. He cleared his throat and continued. "Every day, I see her and regret those memories that we didn't get to make together. I had one perfect jewel, and I threw it away."

Jacob studied the older man and wondered, *how do you console someone for a lifetime of regret?*

"Did she marry someone else?"

"We're both still single, both still afraid. You can't let fear keep you from the person who makes you feel whole, complete. That person you can't wait to see every morning and dream about every night. Let me ask you a question. When something good or bad happens, who's the first person you want to talk to about it?"

"Mae." He didn't even have to think before her name came out of his mouth.

Uncle Robert slapped his knee. "There ain't nothin more you need from me. Now stop mopin' on my porch. Go home, think on what I've said. If you want to talk more, you know where to find me."

"Thanks."

Jacob got up and started toward his truck. Just before he got in, Uncle Robert called out, "Things are about to heat up. You let me know if you need help."

He turned and nodded. Of course, Uncle Robert was keeping track of what was going on. He would be more surprised if he wasn't.

There was no sign of Mae when he got home. Her car wasn't out front, and her apartment window was dark. He resisted the urge to go looking for her. As mad as she was at him, his hovering wasn't doing much to make amends.

Petunia was waiting for him when he got home, looking completely innocent sitting in the middle of his bed, but the unraveled roll of toilet paper strung throughout the apartment provided proof that she wasn't. Jacob heaved a sigh and started cleaning up the mess while the little cat supervised. When he finally got changed and climbed into bed, she jumped up on his chest and started her motor. Her fur was soft under his hand, and some of the tension eased out of his body while he stroked her.

He replayed his conversation with Uncle Robert, seeing the pain in the older man's eyes as he told his story. The way he clenched his hands when he talked about how their relationship would have been received, and the tremor in his voice when he spoke of regret. He didn't want to end up like Uncle Robert. Jacob looked down at the little ball of fur with a blissful look of contentment on her face and realized he'd already made a change. He'd let Petunia into his life, and despite the loss of a perfectly good roll of toilet paper, he was ready to admit he was better for it.

IT WAS early, and the park was empty when he walked toward his store with Petunia on his shoulder. He wanted to get a couple hours of work in the wood shop before he opened up the store. He was going to make something for Mae; he just didn't know what that was going to be yet. It had to be special, something that would show her that he was all-in on a relationship with her.

"Petunia, get down from there!"

He was greeted with an indignant look from the kitten, who had climbed up onto the top of a stack of pine boards he had stacked against the wall. He returned his focus to the blank sheet of paper in front of him. Forty-five minutes later, he was still trying to come up with an idea of what he wanted to make. He eyed a small piece of mahogany and his lathe, wondering if he could turn it into a pair of knitting needles as a gift for her.

There was a chuckle of laughter behind him, and Jacob spun around to see a surprising face.

"What the hell?" He checked to make sure they were alone. "What are you doing here?"

"I'm your new employee," Dan Nguyen said with a cocky smile.

Jacob frowned at the FBI agent from the Jackson office who he'd been working with since he took on the job as Rhett's handler. He'd only dealt with the agent face-to-face a handful of times, and always at the office. If Dan was here, it must be important.

The hair on the back of Jacob's neck stood up. "What's going on?"

"We're getting ready to close the operation. After the last message, the boss wants to have more assets in the area. Besides"—Dan gave him a wry smile—"you look like you could use some help." He gestured to where Petunia looked down at them from her perch.

Jacob frowned. "Okay. Do you have a place to stay?"

"Yea, I'm going to bunk with my uncle."

Dan's uncle, Minh Nguyen was a plumber who lived in Colton. When Jacob bought the hardware store, Minh started coming in for supplies, and Jacob liked him… and the tall tales he told about his fishing trips.

"Sounds good." He jerked his head toward the store. "Let me give you the tour and get you set up."

While Jacob explained how the point-of-sale system worked, Dan shared that some names on the flash drive from Rhett had some of his supervisors pretty rattled.

"The guys are nervous," Dan said with a frown. "They're worried we might have a mole in our ranks."

"I'll be honest, I've wondered about that."

"Right now, everyone is looking at everyone else with suspicion. My supervisor thought it would be better to tighten things up. All information stays between Rhett, you, and me from now on."

"There's someone else you need to know about." Jacob told Dan about Uncle Robert.

The younger agent's eyes grew wide. "Robert Ellis is a legend."

"He's one of the best men I've ever had the honor of knowing. He'll help if we need him."

Dan nodded. "Good to know."

Jacob glanced up and saw the Jewels clustered at the front door. He glanced at his watch.

"Time to get started." He gave Dan a wry smile. "Brace yourself. These first customers are going to put you through your paces."

He opened the door. "Good morning, ladies. May I introduce you to my new employee, Dan Nguyen?"

The three sisters clustered around him and began peppering him with questions while Jacob stood by watching with amusement. At one point, Dan looked at him and mouthed *Help*, but Jacob just shook his head and chuckled while he continued to restock the wall of nuts and bolts.

At the end of the day, Dan slumped against the counter, wiping his brow. "I think the whole damn town came in today."

Jacob nodded with a smile. "Folks around here get excited when they hear there's someone new in town. Between your uncle and the Jewels, everyone in Colton probably knew that you were working here before noon."

"Well, I gotta say—Ow!" Dan reached down and pulled Petunia off his pant leg.

Jacob plucked the kitten out of Dan's hand. "Sorry, she's a climber." He tucked her in the crook of his arm and jerked his head toward the door. "Come on, there's a rooftop bar in town. I'll buy you a beer."

They stopped to pick up some fried chicken to go from the Catfish on the way back to his apartment. Dan looked around Jacob's place while he grabbed a few beers out of the refrigerator.

"This is nice, man. I like how you blended the old with the new. These floors are amazing. You don't see old wood like this anymore."

"Heart pine, you don't see planks that wide anymore. We got lucky when Dax bought the place that they were still in good shape and we could salvage them."

Dan knelt down, running his hands over the boards Jacob had sanded to a satin finish. "I've always wanted to do something like this. Take an old building and fix it up."

Jacob waved his hand toward the town square. "Pick one, there's plenty around that need it."

"My life is in Jackson for the time being. I don't see myself settling down anytime soon."

Jacob put some food out for Petunia and then gathered up the chicken and beer. "Come on."

When they came out to the rooftop, Dan blew out a low whistle. "You weren't kidding about this being the best view in town."

Unfortunately, they weren't alone. Chloe and Reid were sitting on the lounge chairs Jacob had made for the rooftop deck he'd created as part of the building restoration. Market lights zigzagged across the rooftop from large wood beams that he'd cemented into large pots. He left enough room for dirt at the top, and everyone in the building pitched in to keep them filled with colorful flowers.

Chloe waved them over with a smile.

"Sorry, we didn't mean to interrupt."

"No worries. Hi, I'm Chloe. You must be Dan Nguyen. Everyone's been talking about you today," she said with a friendly smile.

"Chloe manages Taylor Colton's production office," Jacob explained as Dan shook her hand. "And this is Reid Ellis. His brother Dax owns the building. Reid decided he'd had enough of life in the DA's office in Chicago and moved back to Colton. He's learning everything he can about making whiskey over at the Buckthorn with Primus Wallace."

"Wow, my uncle Minh has brought me some of his whiskey. That man is a master distiller."

Reid nodded, shaking Dan's hand. "He is. I'm trying to soak up as much knowledge as I can. But I was just telling Chloe, I've got an offer from the county prosecutor's office, and I think I'm going to take it."

Jacob glanced at Dan. Reid could be a useful asset.

"Sorry, I can't stay," Chloe said. "Adam is taking me out to dinner tonight, and I've got to get ready."

Jacob smiled. Chloe and Taylor's apprentice, Adam Freeman, had been inseparable just about since the day they met.

Reid stood up. "I've got to get going too. Primus always appreciates the setup help before he opens. These long nights are starting to catch up with him."

As soon as they were alone, Jacob said, "Interesting about the prosecutor's office. Reid could be a helpful asset to have on the inside."

Dan rolled the beer bottle between his palms. "Maybe. I don't like the idea of bringing in someone else unless we have to. What do you know about him? Can we trust him?"

Jacob didn't hesitate. "Absolutely."

CHAPTER FOURTEEN

"EVERYONE IS so excited about the Fourth of July celebrations this year," Mae's mom said with an approving smile, handing her a glass of sweet tea.

"It's been far too long since we had fireworks in the park," her dad said.

Mae toyed with the food on her plate. She usually loved her mom's lemon chicken, but the flavor was off tonight. She set her fork down and pushed her plate away. "Besides the old town council not wanting to spend the money, I've always wondered why they stopped."

Her dad's face became stormy. "Some folks wanted to keep the celebrations segregated. When they figured out they couldn't do that back in the '70s, they stopped rather than have to open the park up to Black and White folks. That's why we haven't had any community celebrations for years." Joseph snorted a laugh. "Callie's grandfather formed the first Black Boy Scout troop in the '50s. They asked if they could be a part of the annual Christmas parade. When they were told no, Richard brought them anyway. He lined them up on the parade route and when the other troop went by, they jumped out and marched with them. Good Lord, you'd have thought they'd committed murder. They canceled the parade after that."

"Unbelievable." Mae shook her head. "I guess I'll add restarting the Christmas parade to my list."

"You have a lot on your plate, sweetheart, and there's only so much you can do while you're here."

"Your mother's right, Mae. Don't worry yourself with fireworks and small-town parades. You're destined for bigger and better things."

"Yeah, I know, Dad."

Mae winced, her tone making her sound like a sulky teenager.

Her mom gave her a worried look. "Everything okay, honey?"

"Everything is fine. I just wish... the thing is, I don't know that I want bigger or better things. I enjoy living in Colton, and I really love the work that I'm doing right now. I can see how it affects the people living here."

"But just imagine how much more you can do on a national level," her father said.

Her mom frowned. "This is about that boy, isn't it?"

"What boy?"

"You've been sneaking around with that Winters boy for months now. Did you think I didn't know? Don't let him keep you from achieving your dreams, sweetheart."

"But they aren't my dreams, they're yours." Mae took a deep breath. "I… I can't keep trying to make up for my sister disappointing you."

Ella gasped. "Is that what you think?"

"Of course it is. I've been trying my best to make up for Beth abandoning our family for years. Every time she doesn't show up when she says she will, every promise she makes, I have to make up for the hurt she causes you." Mae pounded her chest.

Her parents looked at her with twin expressions of sadness. Her mom came over and wrapped her in a hug.

"I'm so sorry, sweetheart. We never meant for you to feel that way."

Mae hugged her mom back. "It's okay. I know you weren't doing it on purpose."

Ella pulled away, wiping at her tears with her thumbs. "No, it's not okay. We need to talk about this."

"Come on, honey, let's all sit down."

They sat down at the kitchen table. Her mom grabbed a box of tissues and set it in the middle. Her dad leaned forward and clasped his hands in front of him.

"Sweetheart, we love you. We've only ever wanted the best for you and your sister. Somewhere along the line, we lost track of what you wanted."

Mae's mom reached over and put her hand on her dad's.

"You tell us what you want, and we'll listen."

Mae grabbed a tissue and dabbed at her eyes. "I like being mayor, I think I'm pretty good at it, and there's still work that I want to do. I've been thinking that when the election comes around in November, I want to run for a full term."

"What if you don't win, what happens then?" her mom asked.

"Then I want to start a consulting business, taking what I've learned here and helping other small towns that are struggling with trying to keep up with modernizing infrastructure and technology."

Joseph nodded. "That's an interesting idea, but you could also do some of those things working for one of the bigger firms in DC."

Mae sighed. "I don't want to leave Colton. I like my life here."

"And what about what your mother said, are you wanting to stay because of that Winters boy? I can't support you staying here and giving up your goals for someone else."

"I don't want to stay in Colton because of a guy. I'm not my sister. I don't chase other people's dreams. I chase my own." She took a deep breath and looked her parents in the eye. "When I make a decision about what I'm going to do next, I'll let you know, but at the end of the day, it will be my decision. I hope you can respect that."

Her parents exchanged worried looks. She realized that the unconditional support she'd always thought she had was only there as long as her goals aligned with theirs. And their reaction to Jacob surprised her. Did they really think Jacob wouldn't be a suitable partner for her? Couldn't they see how he supported her? No, they wouldn't know any of that, since they'd never seen them together other than on an occasional Sunday dinner, where he was a guest along with Callie and Dax. Her parents had never seen them as a couple, and now it was too late. Mae left her parents' house feeling exhausted. The weight of their expectations combined with her disappointment made her stomach churn.

Instead of heading home, she went out to her thinking rock. The evening air had just a slight chill to it, and Mae finally felt like she could breathe again. The water was calm and still, and the log where her turtle friends usually rested sat empty. She looked around, noticing the scent of eucalyptus in the air; she'd never noticed any plants growing nearby. The light from a fire flared from the other side of the pond, and Mae scowled, watching a group of young men pull a red cooler out of the back of a pickup truck.

She was just about to call Isiah when she caught a movement out of the corner of her eye. She jumped up when Rhett Colton walked out of a thicket of bushes, his shaggy blond hair looking almost silver in the moonlight. Gone was the little boy she used to know. His silvery-blue eyes that used to be filled with so much mischief and fun were now set in a man's face, looking angry and… haunted.

"You need to get out of here." He scowled at her.

Mae lifted her chin. "I don't have to go anywhere. Turtle Pond is as much mine as it is yours."

Rhett's eyes darted toward the group on the other side of the pond. He looked back at her. "Mae, I need you to go."

His voice had lost its hard edge, and there was just a hint of a pleading tone that made Mae pause. The air grew even heavier with the slightly minty scent of eucalyptus. Her breath was shallow against the pressure she felt against her chest. The air kept closing in around her, pushing her back. It was almost as if it was trying to keep her away from Rhett.

She glanced toward the men on the other side of the pond and said, "Yeah, okay, I'll go."

The minute the words left her mouth, Rhett gave her a slight nod and backed away. One blink and he was gone. But, walking back to her car, she had the feeling that he wasn't far off, watching her to make sure she left.

JACOB'S GUT tightened as he read the message on his phone.

"Everything okay?" Dax asked, giving him a worried look.

"Yeah, fine, just a delivery that's going to be delayed," he lied.

He checked his phone one more time before pocketing it. Rhett told him Mae was safe, and he had to trust that even though every muscle in his body screamed to go find her and make sure. Dan shot him a worried look from across the peanut-strewn table at the Buckthorn. Jacob pressed his lips together and gave a slight shake of his head.

Reid brought over a bottle and a handful of glasses. "Gentlemen, I thought you'd like to give this a try."

Everyone looked at him in surprise, seeing the clear contents of the bottle. Reid pounded each of them a glass and stood at the end of the table with his arms crossed, waiting.

"Gin? I'm surprised Mr. Wallace would allow anything other than whiskey to be made here."

"Primus was the one who suggested it. He wants me to learn about all the methods of distillation. He got ahold of some nice juniper and gave me a chance to experiment."

Jacob downed the clear liquid and nodded his appreciation. "That's real nice, Reid. You're well on your way to becoming a master distiller, if you ask me."

Dan sniffed at his glass before downing his shot. He swallowed and looked at Reid with a smile. "Really nice. What other botanicals did you use? Did you do a one-shot or two-shot production?"

Reid's eyes lit up. "Sounds like you might know a little something about distilling?"

"Just a bit. I'm more of a brewer myself. I've been messing around with making IPAs lately."

"Where are you getting your hops?"

Jacob poured himself another shot as Reid sat down next to Dan and the two launched into a discussion of beer-making techniques. This was good, the two finding common ground. It would make it easier for Dan to trust Reid as their inside man in the prosecutor's office if they got to know each other better.

Dax chuckled. "Good Lord, now there's going to be two of them talking nonstop about all things brewed and distilled."

Isiah came in, still in uniform. Based on the look on his face, it had been a long day.

Jacob poured him a shot. "Here, it looks like you could use this."

Isiah shook his head. "I'm still on duty."

Mr. Wallace appeared at their table with a cup of coffee.

"Thank you," Isiah said.

The old man patted him on the shoulder. "You're a good man, thank you."

"I'd better get back and help him." Reid turned to Dan. "You want to come along? I can give you a tour."

"You don't have to ask me twice."

Dax turned to Jacob after his brother walked away. "I've been meaning to ask—how did you end up hiring Dan to work at the store? I didn't know you were looking for anyone."

"Minh mentioned his nephew was thinking about moving to Colton, and I figured business has been good enough that I could hire someone full-time." The lie fell easily from his lips.

Jacob felt both guilty and relieved when his friend accepted his explanation without question.

He turned to Isiah. "Any trouble tonight?"

"Mostly mundane stuff, but there was a party at Turtle Pond I had to break up."

"Kids have been partying out there for as long as I can remember," Dax said with a knowing smile.

Isiah frowned. "These weren't kids. Bunch of young men. Rhett Colton was with them."

Dax sucked in his breath. "Did you have backup?"

"I didn't know what kind of party it was until I got there."

"You need to hire another deputy," Jacob said.

A knot of worry formed in Jacob's gut, recalling the conversation he had with Rhett. Isiah could have been in real trouble without backup.

Isiah scrubbed his face with his hands. "Yeah, you're right. I've been talking to Mae about it, but we haven't found the right candidate yet, not with what the town budget can afford to pay."

"The Colton Foundation can help too," Ashton Beaumont said, joining them at the table.

"Whatever it takes." Dax nodded in agreement.

"Anybody else you recognized besides Rhett?" Jacob fished for more information.

"No, there wasn't anyone else I was familiar with around here. That's the trouble these days. These guys aren't wearing white hoods anymore. They blend in, and you don't know if the guy smiling and shaking your hand really wishes you would just go back to Africa."

Ashton shook his head and sighed. "I know it's not the same, but they hate me just as much. That's part of why I don't broadcast my sexual preference. I'd like to think I can live here and not worry about my safety, but"—he shrugged—"you just never know."

Jacob clenched his fists under the table. It wasn't just Mae who was in danger from these assholes.

The mic on Isiah's shoulder came to life, and he jumped up from the table, draining the last of the coffee in his cup.

He turned and pointed to Ashton. "Tell that sister of yours to slow down. One of these days, instead of getting a ticket, she's going to end up spending some time in my jail."

"Yes, sir," Ashton said with a wry smile.

"Speaking of your sister, what in the heck is going on with her?" Dax asked. "I just about fell out of my chair when I heard she's been working as the new office manager over at Town Hall."

"You and me both. I looked out the window to see if there were any pigs flying. Mae is some kind of goddamn miracle worker as far as I'm concerned."

Jacob chuckled. He'd had a similar reaction when he heard that Mae had agreed to let Presley fill in as office manager.

Ashton sobered. "Presley said Mae was the only one around here who was willing to give her a chance to show she could change. I hate to say it, but when I thought about it, she's right. I've gotten so used to thinking of her as a nitwit, it never occurred to me she wanted to change. She'd been asking me questions about politics and stuff, and I'd just shoo her away. It never occurred to me she was askin' because she wanted to change the way she's been thinking. I give Mae a lot of credit. Most folks wouldn't have taken the time or made the effort after everything my sister's done. Most folks around here don't have a whole lot of forgiveness in their hearts where Presley's concerned."

Jacob's heart ached. He missed the caring side of Mae that he'd been lucky to be on the receiving end of. He hadn't appreciated it as much as he should have when he had it. For all of Mae's fire, she was kind and forgiving. He could only hope that when the truth came out about what he'd been doing in Colton, she'd be willing to forgive him. Glancing at his friends, Jacob wondered if they would be willing to do the same.

Would he lose his friends and Mae forever?

Chapter Fifteen

"Boy, he's got a lot to say." Callie laughed at the mockingbird perched on a branch in the ginkgo tree that had been added to the garden at Halcyon.

With Jo's arrival in Colton, they'd outgrown Callie's porch, and they started having their girls' night out in the garden at Halcyon.

What was once a patch of weeds had transformed into a beautiful oasis. The original garden design remained, with four sections divided by a brick pathway and a small fountain in the center. Yellow roses, lavender, and small boxwoods replaced the weeds that had overtaken the garden. Originally, the garden had been surrounded by a high brick wall, but Taylor and Jo had decided not to restore that detail. Restoring the walls would have hidden the beautiful garden that brought solace to Jo's ancestor Ada Mae, an enslaved woman on the plantation forced into a relationship with her master. Instead, the garden was expanded to run the length of the house, adding a large patio living space with an outdoor kitchen.

Mae frowned at the loud intruder. She couldn't help feeling like it directed its chatter at her, mocking her for being so blue. Callie was sitting on the other end of the wicker sofa Mae occupied, while Emma was curled up on a matching sofa across from them. Jo was rocking in the oversized rocker between them. Mae wasn't really in the mood for a girls' night out, but she'd never missed one, and she knew Callie would pepper her with questions if she didn't show up. After all, she'd been the instigator who started the tradition in the first place.

"Can we talk about the elephant in the room?" Jo asked, looking at Mae with a raised eyebrow.

She froze for a second. Had Jo figured out her secret?

"Presley Beaumont working as your assistant. How did that happen?" Jo asked.

Mae exhaled the breath she didn't realize she'd been holding. "We ran into each other at Turtle Pond and started talking. It turns out she's finally decided she wants to learn how to act right."

"And that's why you hired her to be your office manager?" Calle frowned. "I still don't understand why you would do that."

"I needed to hire someone after Grace left, and she volunteered." She shook her head with a laugh. "I still can't believe it, but she's actually pretty good at her job. Anyway, she's just helping until I can hire someone permanent."

"But why?" Emma asked, "I mean, does she have any office skills?"

"I know it doesn't make sense." Mae sighed. "Lord, it doesn't make sense at all, but she's trying, and if someone shows you they're trying to change, shouldn't you give them a chance?"

Mae looked at Callie. "Can you imagine what your life would be like if you hadn't gotten to know Dax for the person he is now instead of the mean little boy we grew up with?"

"I would have missed out on marrying the love of my life," Callie said, her voice trembling with emotion.

Jo looked at Callie and then Mae. "You just won your argument. I don't have the right to say anything about you hiring Presley when I gave Taylor a second and a third chance. You're doing a nice thing, Mae."

"How did this start?" Callie asked.

"It's a long story, but she and I have been talking. She's trying to learn and be something more than the empty-headed beauty queen stereotype."

"Well, I never thought I'd see the day that would happen, but I'm happy for her."

Mae thought about Presley's reaction when Isiah came into the office. "I think she's trying to make a good impression on someone. Or at least that's what ignited the spark, but once she started learning more about history and current events, she's really got into it. She genuinely wants to improve herself."

Callie lifted her eyebrow. "Any idea who inspired this change?"

"I have a good guess, but I'm not going to say. Don't start none, don't get none."

Jo nodded. "Fair point. Just promise me you won't let her make a mess of the new computer systems I designed for you."

"Believe it or not, she's taken to it like a duck to water," Mae said.

"Well, color me surprised," Emma exclaimed.

Mae giggled. "That's one way to put it. Presley has a thing for rainbows and color-coordinating."

"Ugh, don't remind me." Callie slapped her forehead. "I still have nightmares about when she and Dax's mama broke into the library and color-coordinated all the books."

"Yeah, that was pretty bad," Mae agreed. "She feels terrible about it now. Presley's said more than once that she'd like to apologize to you, but she's afraid you wouldn't accept it."

Callie's mouth turned down. "Now I feel bad."

"I guess I'd be willing to get to know this new version of Presley Beaumont, but I'd still be terrified to let her behind the counter at the pharmacy," Emma said.

"How are y'all doing at Walker's these days?" Mae asked.

She and Callie had both been eyeing Emma for any signs of physical abuse since they arrived. Mae thought she detected a shadow of a bruise on her cheek, but it was hard to tell under her makeup and in the evening light.

Callie poked Mae with her toe when Emma dropped her eyes.

"Business hasn't been very good lately," she said with a slight tremor in her voice. "Folks have been staying away since all the stuff about the town council came out." Emma looked at Mae. "Dad says it's your fault"—she swallowed—"yours and the rest of the Black folks in town. He says you all don't know your place anymore. I'm so sorry, you know that I don't feel that way, right?"

Mae got up and went over to sit next to her friend and put her arm around her. "Of course not. We all know that you're nothing like your daddy."

"I'm so sorry, Emma. Taylor and I have both been avoiding coming into your store," Jo said.

Emma shook her head, tendrils of her strawberry-blond hair brushing against her cheeks. "It's not my store. It's not really my father's either. Walker's passed down through my mother's family. Dad took my mother's name and kept the store name. He wanted to keep it since it had such a good reputation back then." She sighed. "He's ruined that now. It was pure greed. He would do anything for money."

Mae took Emma's hand in hers. "Em, we've been friends since we were five. What can I do to help?"

"There's nothing you can do. He's so angry about not being on the town council anymore. I just wish his trial for embezzling town funds would happen already. It keeps getting delayed, and every time it does, he gets more confident that he's going to get the charges dropped. He's my dad, but I don't want him to get away with what he's done."

"Taylor and I would be happy to have you come stay at Halcyon," Jo offered.

Emma's eyes brightened for a second, and then her face fell.

"I don't have any money, and I can't afford to leave."

Mae frowned. "I thought pharmacists made a pretty good salary. Is your dad not paying you enough?"

"I… Dad doesn't pay me a salary, just an allowance."

"What do you mean, he doesn't pay you?"

"He says the store doesn't make enough to pay me. I only get enough money to pay for new clothes every once in a while. I shop secondhand and squirrel away as much as I can."

"That's ridiculous. I know for a fact your daddy has plenty of money still stashed away. The state is still trying to recover the funds he embezzled from the town."

"I know about the money," Emma said in a hushed voice. "I… I've been working with the prosecutor to help find it." She looked up at them with fear in her eyes. "You can't say a word. He would kill me if he found out."

Callie came over to sit on Emma's other side and took her hands in hers. "This stays between us."

Emma looked at Mae again. "Just be careful, please. Dad has said some really ugly things about you."

"What about tonight? Will he say anything about you being here with us?" Jo asked.

"I said I was going to the movies in Wynona," Emma said.

Mae sighed. "I hate the idea of you living under his roof."

"He'll go to jail soon… I hope."

"Emma, promise you'll let me know if you need help."

"You let any of us know," Callie added.

Emma glanced at her watch. "I'd better get going."

As soon as Emma left, Jo looked at Mae and Callie, wide-eyed.

"That was some heavy shit."

"Emma's dad has always been a mean son of a bitch," Mae said.

Callie frowned. "Emma's stepmom took off the second she realized how much trouble her husband was in. Now it's just the two of them in that house."

"Good gravy," Jo muttered.

Mae's lip curled up. Jo was becoming more of a Southerner every day.

"We need to keep an eye on Emma. She may not be related by blood, but she's family. We can't let her get hurt." Callie gave Mae a stern look. "The same goes for you," she said, pointing at her.

"Pssh"—Mae waved her hand—"I'm fine."

"We know you are, that's not what we're worried about. There are a lot of folks around here who don't know how to act right. Did you hear we had a group from the Daughters of the Confederacy show up here trying to present Taylor with a Confederate flag?" Jo said.

Mae sat up straight. "Good Lord, are you kidding me?"

Jo shook her head. "Nope."

"What did Taylor do?" Callie asked.

"You should have seen him. He went full-on Rhett Butler. You've never heard so many insults said with a charming smile."

Mae laughed. "I would have bought a ticket and brought my lawn chair to see that show."

"The looks on their faces"—Jo bit her lip trying not to laugh—"I'll never forget it as long as I live. We should have invited them to the wedding. Now that would have been something."

Mae thought for a minute before voicing out loud something she'd been wondering about for a while. "Can I ask you a question?"

"Sure," Jo said.

"Were your parents okay with you marrying Taylor? I mean… did they have any objection to you marrying a White boy?"

Jo cocked her head, looking at her thoughtfully for a minute. "No, not really. They weren't worried about us being together, but they were concerned about us living in the South."

Callie nodded. "Some old prejudices are hard to die."

"I did a little research, and it's still something like only three percent of interracial couples down here," Jo said.

Mae was surprised. "Wow, I thought it was more than that."

"Are you worried people would have a problem if you and Jacob were together?" Callie asked.

Jo's eyes widened in surprise. Her mouth formed an *O* before she snapped it closed.

Callie winced. "Sorry, I didn't mean to share your secret like that."

"It's okay." Mae reached for Callie's hand with a smile. "No, I'm not really worried about what people will think, and it doesn't matter now."

Jo came over and sat down next to her, wrapping her arm around Mae's shoulder. "Breakups are hard, relationships are hard. You know the challenges Taylor and I faced. I'm here for you anytime you want to talk."

Callie nodded in agreement. Mae wasn't even sure why she was asking. It wasn't like she and Jacob were going to get back together. But if they did… she wasn't worried about how folks around town would react, but she was just a tiny bit worried about her parents. She'd never brought home a White boyfriend before.

Mae hung out with Callie and Jo, enjoying some quality girl time that was long overdue. She lingered in the garden, the sweet scent of roses and conversation flowing around her, only interrupted by an occasional high-pitched trill from the mockingbird that continued to keep watch over their meeting. Eventually the long day of work caught up with Mae. Her second yawn gave her away.

"You're worn out," Callie said.

"Yeah, I guess so. Sorry to break up the party, but I think it's time for me to head home."

She said her goodbyes and climbed into her Jeep, ready for a cup of tea and a warm bed. A wave of exhaustion made the staircase up to her apartment seem like an impossible climb. When she reached the hallway, Mae paused in front of Jacob's door and lifted her hand to knock, and then let it fall back to her side again. She listened to Jacob talking low and sweet to the little cat he'd adopted, and her heart broke just a little more.

With a heavy sigh, she turned her back on Jacob and went into her apartment. She changed into a pair of leggings and a tank top. She eyed one of Jacob's flannel shirts that hung on her closet doorknob. He'd left it behind, and she'd started wearing it as a robe. He'd teased her about it, the way it was so big on her she could wrap it around herself twice. That's what she loved about it. She could wrap herself in Jacob when he wasn't around. Giving into temptation, she pulled it off the knob and slipped into it. Fingering the frayed hem and the spot where the black and blue threads intersected with white, creating the exact shade of blue as

Jacob's eyes. She blinked back yet another round of tears as she wrapped it around herself.

Jacob was right; she could wrap it around herself twice.

Mae wandered into the kitchen and put the kettle on, rummaging through the cabinets for some chamomile tea while she waited for the water to boil. She was dunking the tea bag into the boiling water, watching it change from clear to pale gold and inhaling the fragrant steam rising from the cup, when she heard a bang and the horrifying sound of one of her windowpanes shattering and crashing to the floor.

CHAPTER SIXTEEN

IT WAS the gunshot that made him jump out of his chair. The sound of breaking glass had him running toward Mae's apartment a second later. He didn't bother to see if the door was unlocked, ramming his shoulder against the wood.

Mae was standing in her kitchen, staring at the window with wide eyes.

"Get down!" he shouted, charging toward her. He pulled her to the ground just as another shot rang out. "Stay down," he ordered.

His senses heightened, his ears straining, he listened for another shot as he crawled to the light switch and plunged the room into darkness. Moving back to Mae, he grabbed her and held her against his chest, shielding her with his body while he slid them both across the floor to the door and out of her apartment into the hall. Her entire body trembled against his as he pulled her into his lap, checking her over for any sign that she'd been injured.

Reid came flying down from the top floor. "Are you okay?"

"Can you grab a blanket?"

Reid nodded and started back toward the stairs.

"And call Isiah," Jacob called out.

"Got it."

Jacob turned his attention back to Mae. "Are you hurt anywhere, baby?"

"I... I...." She looked at him with wide eyes, her lips pale.

He rubbed her arms. "You're in shock."

Reid came back with a blanket and tucked it around Mae. That's when Jacob noticed she was wearing his shirt. He fingered the worn flannel, somehow grateful that she was wearing it, as if it protected her when he wasn't there. He closed his eyes for a second, taking a deep breath, refusing to think about what could have happened if he hadn't been there or worse, if he hadn't gotten to her in time.

"I was just making dinner. I heard the window break, and then I saw a bullet hole in the cabinet." She shuddered and buried her face in his chest.

Petunia poked her head out of Jacob's apartment and crept down the hall toward them. She climbed into Mae's lap, forcing her head under her hand. Before he could shoo her away, Mae petted her and sighed. Her trembling body relaxed just a bit. *Good job, Petunia*, he thought.

When he heard sirens in the distance, he jerked his chin toward Reid. "Go downstairs and open the door for them, will you?"

Reid ran down the stairs, and a few seconds later, Nate rushed down the hall carrying his kit.

"Any injuries?"

"I don't think so, just mild shock."

Nate gently took Mae's arm and started taking her pulse. "Isiah should be here any minute. He called me while he was on his way."

Before Nate finished, Isiah reached the top of the stairs.

"Two shots fired. Check the kitchen cabinet for one bullet," Jacob said.

Isiah nodded and stepped over them into Mae's apartment.

Mae sat up with a gasp. "Is it safe? Isiah, get out," she shouted, struggling to get up.

"It's okay, sweetheart, let him do his job," he said, pulling her back down into his lap.

She watched anxiously while Isiah searched her apartment.

"I'm sure whoever it was is long gone. There are too many people around now. Isiah will be okay," Jacob reassured her.

He knew the moment the shock had worn off when she stiffened in his arms and then stood up, holding Petunia out to him. He took the cat and shut her in his apartment.

Chloe and Adam came up the stairs. "What's going on? I saw Isiah drive up?"

"Someone shot through my window," Mae said.

Chloe gasped while Adam wrapped a protective arm around her.

"Oh my God, Mae, are you okay?" Chloe asked.

"I'm fine, but I think for tonight, it would be best if you didn't stay here."

"She'll come and stay at Halcyon with me," Adam said.

"Good. I think since your apartment is on the other side of the building, it's probably safe to go in and pack a bag," Mae said, looking at Jacob for confirmation.

Jacob nodded. "Let me go in and do a quick check before you go in."

Chloe and Adam followed him down the hall and waited outside while Jacob slowly cracked open the door and checked for any signs of damage. He wasn't too worried. He knew in his gut that Mae was the target and no one else. He gave the all-clear, and Chloe grabbed her things. Based on the way Adam stayed by her side, she'd be all right. Jacob watched with envy the way Adam cared for his girlfriend. He wanted to do the same for Mae, but he knew she'd already taken as much comfort as she would allow herself from him.

With Chloe in good hands, Jacob went back down the hall to where Isiah and Reid were huddled with Mae.

"You can't stay here tonight," Isiah said.

"You can stay with me."

Mae rolled her eyes at Jacob's suggestion. He knew she wouldn't agree the minute the words left his mouth.

"Do you want me to take you to your parents' house?" Isiah asked.

Mae pressed her lips together and shook her head. "No, they'll freak out if I pull up with the sheriff this late at night."

"Mae can come stay with us," Dax said, walking down the hall toward them with Callie.

Callie pushed past her husband and rushed toward Mae, gathering her in her arms.

"Reid called," Dax said with a nod toward his brother.

Callie led Mae toward her apartment. "Come on, let's get some clothes packed, and I'll take you home."

Jacob moved into their path. "You two stay out here. I'll go in."

"I thought you said whoever fired the shots is probably gone," Mae said.

"Stay here," Jacob ordered with a stern look.

Mae opened her mouth and snapped it shut again. "Fine, just grab me some sweats out of my dresser drawer, please."

Jacob went into the apartment. Seeing the shattered window set his teeth on edge. As soon as he could get everyone cleared out, he needed to get ahold of Dan. He found a tote bag in Mae's closet, grabbed it, and started throwing in anything she might need. Along with sweats, he grabbed clean underwear, a pair of jeans, and a clean T-shirt for in the morning. In her bathroom, he grabbed a few toiletries, the obvious things like deodorant and a toothbrush and toothpaste, adding it all to the bag. He did one last look around for anything else she might need and grabbed her messenger bag with her laptop on his way out. Just as he was about to leave, he saw the balls of blue yarn on her coffee table, recognizing it from the sweater she'd been knitting for him. He remembered her hands on his shoulders while she took his measurements and asked him what his favorite color was. The way her breath felt against his neck when she laughed and asked why all guys liked the color blue. He sucked in his breath, reminding himself that it was for the best. But he hated the empty feeling knowing that Mae had started to unravel him from her heart.

He handed Mae's bag to Callie. "I'll get the glass cleaned up as soon as Isiah gives the all-clear."

Mae left Callie's side and came toward him. She stopped just out of arm's reach and said, "Thank you, Jacob, I...." Her voice trembled.

He closed the distance between them and pulled her into a hug. "I'll always be here for you, Pixie. I'm not going anywhere. You're my whole world, and I don't want to hide it anymore."

She let out a soft gasp and pulled out of his arms. Her eyes locked with his for a moment before she backed away, shaking her head. "It's late. I have to go."

He narrowed his eyes, watching her turn and walk away. Was she really saying it was too late for the two of them?

As soon as Callie and Mae were out of earshot, Dax turned to the other three of them. "There's no way that was an accident."

Jacob gave a slight shake of his head when Reid glanced at him.

Isiah frowned. "No, I don't think so."

"Damn it, I've been worried about this. I'll go downstairs and check footage from the video cameras," Dax said.

"I found both the bullets. I'll be sending them into the state lab first thing in the morning." Isiah turned to Dax. "Mind if I come look at that footage with you?"

"Let's talk in here," Jacob said to Reid, jerking his head toward his apartment when Dax and Isiah went downstairs.

"You doing okay?" Reid asked.

Jacob ran a hand over his face, the adrenaline finally seeping from his body. "Since our local Klan boys showed up at the Buckthorn, I've been waiting for something to happen. I'm surprised they'd pull such an obvious attack on Mae."

Reid shook his head. "I've got to tell you, in the short time since I took the job at the prosecutor's office—" Reid inhaled, his expression grim. "Some of the stuff I'm seeing in the office turns my stomach."

"It's hard, I'm sure. Can you stay with Isiah and Dax while I get some plywood from the store and take care of Mae's window?"

Reid nodded. "I'll give you a heads-up when they're ready to leave." He sighed. "I wish I could do more to keep Mae, and everyone else in Colton, safe from the assholes who think they won the Civil War."

Jacob had to put pressure on the higher ups to bring Reid into the operation as soon as possible. They needed all the help they could get. Another battle was coming and this time they were fighting for the town, their families, and Jacob was going to fight for the woman he loved. That was a sacrifice he was willing to make. How much was Reid willing to risk?

BROKEN GLASS scraped across the floor underneath the bristles of the broom. With each pass, Jacob's anger increased, along with the tension banded around his chest. By the time he fitted the piece of plywood over the opening, he could barely breathe. The burner phone he kept with him at all times vibrated with a message just as he closed the door to Mae's apartment. He looked down at the splintered lock. He'd have to replace the doorjamb and the lockset tomorrow. Looking down at his phone, he frowned.

"Everything okay?" Reid asked, coming back upstairs.

"I've got to go."

Reid nodded. "Dax and Isiah just left. Dax wanted me to let you know he'll stop by the store tomorrow."

"Thanks."

"Just let me know what I can do to help."

"I will."

Jacob grabbed his keys and headed downstairs and out of the building.

Rhett wasn't there when Jacob and Dan reached the clearing, but they only had to wait a few minutes before he appeared. His face was haggard and pale when he arrived. When he saw Dan, he hesitated for a moment, his eyes darting around the clearing before he moved forward.

"It wasn't one of ours," he said without any preamble. "I don't know who's behind it. Our group is pissed because they don't want anyone to steal their thunder. That's all I've got."

"Rhett, this is Dan Nguyen."

"I know who he is. Heard you're Jacob's new employee."

Dan nodded.

"It helps, everyone thinks Jacob is a ni—" Rhett sucked in his breath. "Sorry, it's hard to switch gears sometimes."

Jacob gave him a sympathetic look.

"They think Jacob here is a liberal Jew. Hiring you just confirms what they believe. They won't suspect you."

"We've got someone in the county prosecutor's office now too," Dan said.

"Good, that's good. I'm doin' everything I can to put myself in a position where I'll be a part of whatever they've got planned. Whatever it is, it's gonna be on or around the Fourth of July." Rhett scowled. "They want everyone to know how patriotic they are."

"Just be careful. If you need extraction, you know what to do."

Rhett nodded and started backing away. "This will be the last time I can meet in person. I can't do anything that will raise suspicions. The closer we get to the Fourth, the more skittish these guys are getting. I'm ditching the burner phone tonight. If I need to make contact, I'll text from this." He held up his wrist, where a smartwatch glinted in the moonlight. "The message will come from an encrypted account. They won't be able to trace it back to me."

Dan nodded. "Got it."

"We're thankful for the sacrifice you're making, Rhett," Jacob added.

Rhett nodded before turning away and disappearing back into the woods.

"I'M WORRIED about him," Jacob said as they drove away.

"He looks like shit," Dan said.

"It's worse every time I see him."

"He knew what he was signing up for."

"Did he? Do any of us really know the toll this job is going to take on us?" Jacob gripped the steering wheel tightly, peering into the darkness. He wouldn't use headlights until they were back on the main road. "We all come in thinking we can handle it, but none of us are really prepared for the sacrifices we might end up making."

"This hasn't been easy on you either," Dan said quietly.

"I hate lying to everyone. I wouldn't be human if I didn't. I was happy to take this job, to get to make sure that my friends have a safe place to live."

"You didn't expect to fall in love, did you?"

Jacob jerked his head. "What?"

"You didn't expect to fall in love with Colton, to want to put down roots here. You weren't planning on buying the hardware store, were you?"

Jacob relaxed just a fraction when he understood Dan wasn't talking about Mae. "I'll admit it was an impulse. I guess it runs in my blood," Jacob said with a wry smile. "My grandfather and great-grandfather ran a general store back home. Papa always wanted my dad to keep the family tradition going, but my dad couldn't stand being in one place all day. When he realized Dad would never take over, he sold the business." Jacob described the hardware store he remembered visiting when he was a little boy.

"Your memory is amazing," Dan said with awe.

"It's a blessing and a curse," Jacob said.

CHAPTER SEVENTEEN

CALLIE HAD forced a cup of tea and some cake on her, insisting she needed the sugar to help with the shock. She didn't want to admit that the numbness that washed over her when she heard the glass shatter as she stood in her kitchen still hadn't worn off. As much as she appreciated her best friend's care, it wasn't as comforting as being held by Jacob.

Now she was tucked into the corner of the sofa in Callie and Dax's living room with a quilt wrapped around her. Callie perched next to her, watching her anxiously.

Callie pointed at the cup of tea she had clutched in her hand. "Do you want something stronger?"

Mae wrinkled her nose. The thought of anything other than tea made her want to gag. "No, this is good."

Dax came in looking grim.

"Was there anything on the security camera?" Callie asked.

"There was a truck on the other side of the park, but the trees obscured it, and we couldn't get a number off the plate. Isiah sent it to some buddies who work in analytics at the Bureau to see if they can get a make and model." Dax came over and sat on the coffee table in front of her. "Are you doing okay?"

Mae nodded. "I'm okay, shaken, but okay. The whole thing seems so surreal, I'm having a hard time wrapping my brain around what happened. It seems fuzzy now."

"Understandable." Dax patted her knee. "If you want to know what happened, Jacob can fill in the blanks for you. He'll remember every detail."

"Jacob may have a good memory, but everything happened so fast, he probably doesn't remember much more than I do." Mae wrinkled her forehead when Dax huffed a laugh. "What's so funny about that?"

"Jacob has more than just a good memory. He has a photographic memory that's above average. More than that, very few people have the amount of recall Jacob does. He's one of the rare cases who can recall every detail of every day of his life since he was about three years old."

Mae's eyes grew wide. "Holy shit, that's amazing."

Suddenly another piece of the puzzle that was Jacob Winters clicked into place. No wonder he always seemed so... burdened. It couldn't be easy to carry all of those memories with him every day. Once again, she got the urge to go to him, wanting to comfort him as much as she needed him to comfort her.

"I'm going to have all the windows in the building replaced with safety glass."

"That's going to cost a fortune and is totally unnecessary," Mae said.

"I care about everyone who lives in my building." He gave her a warm smile. "You're family to me, and I'm going to do whatever I need to do to protect my family."

Tears pricked at the back of her eyes. A lot of time had passed since she'd considered Dax her childhood nemesis, and now she considered him the brother she never had. She loved him because he loved her best friend and made her happy.

She sat up and gave Dax a hug. "Thank you. I'm glad you came back and gave Colton another chance."

"It was you who gave me the chance."

Mae couldn't fight back the tears this time. When she let go of Dax, they were running down her face.

"Oh, honey." Callie put her arm around her.

"I think everything has just caught up with me," she said with a watery laugh.

"It's been a long night, and I expect all hell's gonna break loose when word gets out tomorrow."

"Oh no"—Mae gasped—"I've got to let my parents know what happened, or they'll have a conniption fit."

"Do you want to head over and tell them now?" Dax said.

Mae blew out a shaky breath. "I don't want them up all night worrying. We'll go over early in the morning."

Callie rubbed her back. "Do you think you could try to get some sleep?"

Mae shrugged. "Probably not, but I'll try."

By the time she climbed under the covers in the guest room, she was more exhausted than she realized. She could have sworn she'd just closed her eyes when Callie gently shook her awake.

HER MOTHER was just coming down the hall from the bedroom, still in her robe with a scarf on her head, when Mae walked in with Callie and Dax.

Her mom drew up short. "Sweetheart, what are you doing here so early? What's wrong? Callie, Dax, what are you doing here?" She turned and yelled down the hall. "Joseph, come here, something's wrong."

Joseph came out of the bedroom, tying the belt of his red plaid flannel robe at his waist with a furrowed brow. "Baby girl, what's going on?"

"Come on, let's sit at the kitchen table," Mae said.

"I'll get some coffee going," Callie offered.

Once they were settled around the table, Mae didn't know how to tell her parents what happened. There was no way she could do it without upsetting them.

She took a deep breath and began. "Last night"—she cleared her throat—"someone shot at me though my apartment window."

Mae's mom gasped and began to shake. Her dad pressed his lips together, fisting his hands on the table.

"Isiah is investigating, and we'll do everything we can to find out who's behind it," Dax said.

Mae looked over at her dad. His hands were clenched so tightly the skin was pulled taut over his knuckles.

"Dad, are you okay?"

He cleared his throat twice before he spoke. "You know, they ran Callie's grandfather out of Colton for a few years in the '50s. He was working with Medgar Evers over at the Greenwood NAACP office. He begged Medgar to leave with him, but he stayed." Joseph looked at Callie. "Your grandfather never forgave himself for leaving."

"I didn't know that," Callie said.

Her dad grasped Mae's hand. "Richard shouldn't have felt guilty for leaving. He saved his family's life. He tried to save Medgar's too. If you want to leave, you have nothing to feel bad about."

Mae shook her head. "I'm not going anywhere."

Her mother let out a soft sob, and Mae put her arm around her but looked at her father. "Richard Colton was on his own back in those days, and people were afraid. I'm not afraid, and I know I've got an entire community who wants Colton to be a safe place to live. It doesn't matter who you love, what color your skin is, where you come from, or what God you pray to. I want everyone who loves Colton as much as I do to be safe and feel included… to know that they are welcomed and loved in this community. I'm not going anywhere."

"I'll always be here for you, Pixie, I'm not going anywhere…."

She took a deep breath. She needed to see Jacob. She'd been avoiding him for too long. If she was willing to fight for Colton, shouldn't she be willing to fight for a relationship with Jacob?

"Dad, are you going to be okay?" she asked.

"Don't ask me that right now, baby girl. Right now, I'm so mad I can barely see straight." His lips trembled. "I'm proud of you."

She sniffed, swallowing back her tears. "Mom, I know this is hard, but I'll be okay, I promise."

Ella pressed her head against hers. Mae breathed in the gardenia and clove scent of her perfume that clung to the silk wrapped around her head. She didn't speak, but she could feel her mom's strength flow into her. After a few moments, she sighed and pushed herself up from the table.

"You're gonna need a hearty breakfast," her mom said. "You know how folks around here are. Every chatterbox in town is going to be beating a path to your office wanting to hear about what happened." Ella started pulling eggs out of the refrigerator, muttering, "Some of those old biddies live for nothing more than spreadin' twallop."

Mae's dad moved over to the seat her mom vacated. While Ella and Callie started making breakfast, he sat holding Mae's hand and asked Dax what they could do to increase security around the Barton Building.

After an enormous breakfast that her mother forced her to eat despite her rolling stomach, both her parents insisted on driving her into town and walking her up the steps of Town Hall.

Presley jumped up from behind her desk when they came in. "Mrs. Colton, Mr. Colton." Her administrative assistant greeted Mae's parents with something between a curtsy and a wobbly bow.

Mae elbowed her father in the ribs when he chuckled. He put his hand to his mouth and coughed to hide his laugh.

"Thank you, Presley. I've heard that you have been quite a help to Mae," her mom said, using what Mae always thought of as her presidential voice.

Presley looked at Mae with wide eyes. "I heard what happened. The phone's been ringin' off the hook all morning. Daddy, I mean Judge Beaumont, wanted me to let him know as soon as y'all got in."

"Thanks, Presley." Mae turned to her parents. "I've got it from here."

They both frowned at her, clearly reluctant to leave.

Presley piped up. "Mrs. Colton, Mr. Colton, y'all don't worry. Everyone at Town Hall is gonna make sure she stays safe."

Now it was Mae's turn to hide her laugh. Her mother's eyebrows rose up so high she thought they might disappear altogether. You could have knocked her over with a feather at Presley being so bold.

Her dad put his arm around her mom. "Come on, Ella, let's let our girl get to work."

She gave her parents a hug and watched from the window as they talked on the sidewalk for a minute before her dad headed toward Hank's and her mom started walking toward the Jewels' house.

"Mae, are y'all okay?" Presley asked in a shaky voice.

She let out a long breath. "Yeah, I'm fine."

She noticed folks gathering in the park, pointing at her boarded-up window, and others heading toward Town Hall. "Brace yourself. It's going to be a long day."

SOME DAYS were longer than others, and this one seemed to go on forever. Jacob spent most of it listening to everyone gossip and speculate about what happened with one ear, while he kept an eye on everyone coming in and going out of Town Hall. He was grateful that the store was located at the end of the block on the opposite corner, giving him a perfect view. It was the only thing keeping him sane and from going over there to check on Mae in person.

He rubbed his eyes with the heels of his hands. Even though he knew she was safe with Dax and Callie, he couldn't sleep last night, unable to stop replaying every detail of what happened. He'd written it all down, and Dan had submitted his report to their boss that morning.

"How you holding up?" Dan came over to the front window Jacob had returned to time and time again throughout the course of the day.

"I'm tired of people."

"If you want to head out, I can take care of things until closing," Dan said, jerking his head toward Town Hall.

"I'll wait."

There was no point going over there. Mae wasn't going to let him do anything to help her.

The bell over the door jangled, announcing another customer. Jacob looked over and watched Joseph Colton coming toward him.

"Jacob." Joseph held out his hand.

"Mr. Colton"—he shook his hand—"what can I do for you today?"

"I heard from Isiah what you did for my Mae last night. I wanted to come by and thank you in person."

"I'm glad I was home and there to help."

Joseph glanced toward Dan. "I wanted to talk to you about what else we can do to make sure Mae doesn't get hurt."

"I don't think you've met Minh's nephew, Dan. Anything you want to talk to me about, you can say in front of him."

Joseph shook Dan's hand with a nod and then turned back to Jacob. "I know my daughter, and she's going to want to go back to her apartment even if her mother and I would feel better if she moved back home with us for a while."

"Yeah, I kind of figured that as well."

"I'd like to ask if you'd keep an eye on her for us since you're right across the hall."

"Of course."

Joseph put his hand on Jacob's shoulder. "We haven't seen you at Sunday dinner in a while. Why don't you come by this weekend?" He smiled at Dan. "You too. As a matter of fact, I think we'll have everyone over for barbecue to show those bastards we aren't afraid."

"Thanks, I'll have Uncle Minh bring some catfish."

"Well, now it's a party," Joseph said with a smile.

The store stayed busy for the rest of the afternoon, which was both a blessing and a curse. If one more person asked him if he'd heard about what happened to Mae, he was going to need to break something.

"Oh, what a sweetheart," Ms. June exclaimed, coming up to the counter with a case of canning jars.

She set the jars down and scooped up Petunia, cradling her in her arms as if she were a baby. Petunia was not as impressed with Ms. June. With a strangled yowl, she jumped out of her arms and up onto Jacob's shoulder.

"Sorry about that," Jacob said.

"That's quite all right, dear. She's clearly loyal to her owner."

"Will this be all for you today?"

"Yes, dear, I think so, unless"—she looked over her shoulder, scanning the shelves—"no, I think this will be enough for now."

Jacob braced himself as she leaned forward conspiratorially. "I'm sure you've heard about what happened to Mayor Colton by now. Everybody's been talking about it." She frowned. "I was over at the pharmacy and that Clyde Walker was saying how disappointed he was that the shot missed. Can you believe that? Poor Emma was shaking like a leaf as he ranted on and on. If it weren't for folks feeling sorry for Emma, I don't think anyone would ever shop there again. I wish my Douglas was still alive. He would have given that man a stern talking-to."

Jacob schooled his expression, making brief eye contact with Dan who moved closer, pretending to rearrange the other shelves while Ms. June was talking.

"Considering Clyde is already in trouble with the law, that's pretty ballsy of him," Jacob said.

"That's exactly what I thought, but he seems pretty confident that nothing's going to happen to him. I just feel sorry for Emma. You know, her mother and I were friends when we first moved here. She was a lovely woman, and she'd be heartbroken to see what's happened to Emma. I tried to stay in touch with her after her mother died, but that evil stepmother of hers wouldn't even let me in the yard."

"That's unfortunate," Jacob murmured, ringing up Ms. June's purchase. "I wonder why Clyde thinks he's going to get rid of the charges against him. I heard they had a pretty excellent case."

"I don't know, but I hope it's not true." Ms. June frowned.

She collected her jars and headed out. As soon as the door closed behind her, Petunia jumped off his shoulder and ran off, chasing a dust bunny.

"Did you get all of that?" Jacob asked.

Dan pulled out his phone and played back the recording he'd made. "I think so. Anything we missed, you can fill in the blanks. Tell me about Emma Walker."

"Honestly, she's so dang shy and quiet half the time, I hardly notice her. She's been friends with Mae and Callie since they were little, but from what I understand, she has to sneak around to see them."

"If Emma's as shy as you say, maybe you should try to talk to her since she already knows you. Her father's name has come up more than once in the reports we've gotten from Rhett."

Jacob nodded. "Folks have said he's meaner than a snake. I'll see what I can find out...." His words trailed off as he noticed Mae at the top of the town hall steps.

"Go," Dan said, following Jacob's gaze. "I've got it covered here."

Jacob scooped up Petunia and moved like a guided missile out of the store toward Mae. He jogged up the steps, meeting her halfway.

"Hey, Pixie, how was it today?"

She looked like she'd been through the wringer, with circles under her eyes and her shoulders slumped.

She gave him a tired smile. "It was a long ass day."

"Will you let me buy you dinner?"

She glanced toward the Catfish. "I don't think I can handle being whispered about any more today."

"Can we make you dinner?"

Mae looked at the little cat in his arms and reached out to scratch her between the ears before glancing up at him. "I think I'd like that."

Chapter Eighteen

Mae sat at Jacob's kitchen island with Jacob's cat sitting in her lap, both of them watching Jacob as he prepared chicken fettuccini.

He leaned across the island with a dish towel over one shoulder, looking way sexier than she wanted him to be. "What would you like to drink? I've got a bottle of wine that I think is still drinkable in the fridge, or there's whiskey."

"I think I'd just like some water. I'm so worn out, any alcohol will knock me out."

He frowned at her for a minute before getting her a glass. He came back with a plate piled high with creamy pasta. Mae inhaled the scent of Parmesan and chicken with fresh basil.

"This smells amazing, but I don't think I'll be able to finish all of this."

Jacob had his back to her, filling his own plate. "Eat as much as you can. You've lost weight."

Mae put Petunia on the floor just as one of her paws snaked out in an attempt to steal a piece of chicken. Mae chuckled and picked up her fork, watching the cat stalk over to her full bowl of food and sit next to it, glaring at her.

Jacob sat down next to her, and they both focused on their food for a few minutes before Mae set her fork down and turned to him, resting her head on her palm.

"Tell me about Petunia," she said.

He hesitated for a moment before pushing his plate away and turning toward her.

"It wasn't intentional. I wasn't committing to anything," he said, repeating what she had accused him of when she first saw the cat.

"I shouldn't have said what I did that day."

"You were mad and hurt."

Her stomach was full, and for the first time in twenty-four hours she felt relaxed. Her eyes drifted closed and she didn't have the energy to fight it. Mae felt herself being lifted and laid down on the bed. She sighed, taking in the smell of citrus and pine on the sheets; they smelled like Jacob. She must have said it out loud because she heard his low, deep chuckle. Jacob pulled her shoes off and tucked her under the covers. A moment later the bed dipped, and even though she was half asleep, her body knew where it wanted to be. She rolled over, tucked herself into Jacob's side, and let out a contented sigh.

"Tell me about Petunia," she asked again.

Jacob pulled her closer, wrapping her in his arms as he told her about how the little kitten climbed up his leg and settled itself in the crook of his neck. How did she not know about his memory, she wondered, listening to the way he described every detail?

She yawned and asked sleepily, "What made you pick the name Petunia?"

"It was my mother's favorite flower. She planted them in the window boxes at our house in Staten Island."

Mae lay perfectly still, afraid to breathe. It was the first time he'd ever told her anything about his family.

"She always said their fragility made them beautiful and their beauty gave them strength."

Her breath hitched when he continued. "But she was wrong. Their fragility isn't what made them beautiful"—his voice dropped to a whisper—"it's their strength… just like yours." He kissed her temple and tucked the covers over her. "Go to sleep. We'll talk in the morning."

She wanted to keep talking, but she couldn't fight her body's need for sleep any longer.

JACOB WATCHED Mae sleep until his eyes began to burn and grow heavy. He changed into a pair of pajama bottoms and a T-shirt and climbed back into bed, gathering Mae into his arms.

She sighed and wiggled closer to him, mumbling "Missed this" in her sleep.

"I missed you too," he whispered.

It was so much more than that. His memory couldn't recreate this, holding Mae, her smell, her taste, or the feel of her skin under his fingertips. He closed his eyes and reveled in the feel of her body pressed against his, taking deep breaths, trying to imprint her scent.

The dream began with a noise. Jacob heard a rustling sound and opened his eyes to see an old Black woman standing at the foot of his bed. She was so vivid and real in his dream, he could smell the eucalyptus that wafted toward him when her skirts moved.

"Who are you?"

The woman pointed at Mae. "*She is the daughter of my hopes and dreams. I am the mother of her history. I am the memory of all three of my girls, Callie, Josephine, and Mae.*"

"You're Ada Mae?"

The woman nodded. "*You must learn that you cannot go beyond the past unless you embrace your memories, both the good and the bad.*" She smiled at him with love in her eyes. "*You have so much good ahead. Your children will bring you so much happiness, and sadness. It's the combination that makes a full life.*"

"I'm scared. I want to, but if I don't keep her safe, I'll never forgive myself. I can't take that risk."

The woman's smile fell, and her eyes glittered with unshed tears. "*Then you aren't as strong as I thought you were. You cannot keep her if you cannot love her and cherish every memory you make with her.*" She sighed. "*You will lose your family.*"

Her words hit him like a punch in the gut.

"I won't let anything bad happen to her. I can keep her safe."

She shook her head sadly and spread her hands out in a helpless gesture. "*I will give her all the strength I can, but the loss will be great.*"

"What do you mean?"

"*If this is the path that you choose, the life that she carries will no longer burn bright.*"

Jacob called out, reaching for the woman as she faded away.

"Jacob?"

He blinked, the dream fading away to find Mae looking down at him, gently shaking him. He reached up and pressed his palm to her cheek.

"I will never let anything bad happen to you."

"I'm fine, Jacob. You were having a bad dream."

He shook his head and pulled her against him, banding his arms around her. "I'm so sorry I pushed you away. I wish I could give you everything you want, but... I—"

Mae pushed herself up and put a finger to his lips. "It's okay." She sighed. "I don't understand, but I knew you didn't want a commitment. Maybe in time I'll be able to move beyond this and start over with someone new, but it will never be the same. I gave you a part of my heart I won't get back."

"I can't stand by and watch you make a life with someone else."

Mae sat up and drew her knees up to her chest. "I'm sorry, Jacob, but you can't have it both ways."

Jacob sat up, and Petunia jumped off and stalked over to her cat bed in the corner and resettled herself. He moved so that he was sitting across from Mae. "You need to let me finish. What I wanted to say is that I'm scared that I won't be able to give you everything you want. I don't want to hold you back, keep you from achieving your goals, working in Washington—"

"Why does everyone think they know what I want?" She pounded the mattress. "Just once, I would like someone to ask me instead of assuming they know what my future is going to look like."

Jacob's lips twitched as he fought back a smile. There was the fire and the passion that he'd missed so much.

"You're right, I shouldn't have assumed what you want. What do you want to do?"

She blew out a shaky breath. "I don't know. I don't want to go to Washington, at least not right now. I like what I'm doing here. I think I'd be good working as a consultant for other small-town administrators who are facing some of the same challenges we have here."

"I think you would be great at that."

She looked at him. "And I want to live here in Colton with my family and friends and... you." His mind was spinning with a crazy mixture of hope and fear. "We don't have to get married or anything. I just want to be with you."

Could he do this? Could he make a compromise and give Mae what she wanted? He sucked in his breath, realizing he was wrong. This wasn't about making a compromise; it was about allowing himself to be happy. Was there anyone else he could ever imagine being happy with? No, only Mae, it would always be her.

He reached out, linking his pinkie with hers. "Would you be willing to give a grumpy lumberjack another chance?" He gave her a wry smile.

"We kind of skipped the dating part. What if we start over and I try to learn how to be a proper boyfriend?"

Mae's eyes grew wide. "Is that really something you'd like to do?"

He nodded. "I do."

Her face fell. "What if it doesn't work, if we don't work that way?"

"We already know we work, Pixie. We just have to get beyond what we think we're supposed to do or what we think other people want us to be and just... I don't know, be us."

"I like that idea, of just being us."

"Come here, Pixie."

She didn't hesitate when he held open his arms for her.

"I hated not seeing you today. I worried about you every minute I couldn't see you," he confessed.

"I wanted you with me too. Last night was.... I still can't believe someone shot at me. I don't want to think about what would have happened if you hadn't been there." She buried her face in his shoulder and shuddered. "When you said I could have stayed with you last night, I wanted to say yes. I always feel safe with you."

"Oh, Pixie, how are we going to figure out how to stop being so stubborn? I couldn't sleep last night. I almost got up and drove over to Dax and Callie's to bring you back."

She reached down and linked her fingers with his. "I wish you would have, but I would have been too stubborn to go if you had."

"Will you stay now?"

"I will. I'd rather be here with you than back in my apartment."

Relief washed over him. "I would have gone crazy with you there by yourself."

She nodded against his chest.

They sat like that for a while until he felt her relax against him.

"Come on, let's get back under the covers."

Mae yawned and sat up. "I need to use the bathroom."

His body immediately missed her warmth when she left his lap. As soon as he straightened the covers and fluffed the pillows, Petunia jumped back on the bed and stalked toward his pillow and curled up on it, giving him the stink-eye. Mae came out with a sleepy smile as she climbed back under the covers, giving the kitten a little pat on the head. Jacob took his turn in the bathroom and then climbed under the covers with her.

"Jacob," she whispered as he settled her so that she spooned against him.

"What, Pixie?"

"I… I don't want to jump back into bed with you… I mean the sex part."

He kissed her head and then nuzzled his cheek against it, loving the feel of her short soft curls against his skin. "Nope, we're going to go on at least three dates first."

"Well, let's not get too crazy about this whole boyfriend/girlfriend thing."

He chuckled. "I never said the dates couldn't happen all on the same day."

She reached over for his hand and drew it against her chest. "That would work."

A few minutes later, her breathing evened out. Jacob pressed his lips against her shoulder. He had a second chance, and he wasn't going to make any mistakes this time.

CHAPTER NINETEEN

"MORNING, MADAM Mayor," Tillie said, pouring her a cup of coffee.

"Tillie, I thought we agreed that you were going to keep calling me Mae the way you always have."

Tillie put her hand on her hip. "Absolutely not." She glanced around the café. "Everyone needs to hear it, especially after what happened the other night. I'm proud of our mayor," she said loud enough for everyone to hear.

Mae hid her smile, taking a sip of the piping hot coffee. She set the cup down with a frown.

"Tillie, I usually love your coffee, but do you think I could have some tea instead, maybe chamomile?"

"Sure, honey." Tillie patted her hand. "What can I get you for breakfast?"

"I'd love some scrambled eggs and toast, please."

"Coming right up."

Mae looked around the café, nodding and smiling to folks. Some smiled back, a few glared and turned away. It wasn't a surprise; she knew she wouldn't be able to win everyone over when she accepted the position. The question was, how many folks in town would vote for her if she ran for another term?

Tillie returned with her order and a cup of tea. As she slipped the plate in front of her, she leaned against the counter and said in a hushed voice, "I gotta ask, I heard you let Presley Beaumont help in the office. What in good graces is going on with that?"

"I know everyone thinks I've lost my mind, but she's been doing a good job helping until I can find a replacement for Grace."

"That one"—Tillie rolled her eyes—"I'm amazed she lasted as long as she did."

Mae leaned forward. "I'm not gonna lie, I wasn't sorry to see her go."

"Just be careful, honey. Now that shots have been fired, things might escalate."

Mae took a whiff of the eggs on her plate and settled for a bite of toast instead, hoping it would calm her nervous stomach. "I'm not going to let anyone run me off, Tillie."

Tillie grabbed Mae's arm, her face a mask of worry. "Some of these folks are willing to do real harm to make their point. You be careful."

Colton was home, and home wasn't a place where you felt threatened. She thought about Emma and realized that thinking that way was a privilege everyone didn't have. Tillie and Jacob were both right. She should be more careful going forward.

"I will, I promise."

"Now eat up, honey, you've barely touched your food."

PRESLEY WAS already at her desk when Mae arrived at her office after breakfast. She had to give her credit. Presley hadn't been late once since she started.

"Morning, Presley. Anything urgent I need to know about?"

She nodded and handed Mae a stack of messages. "I hate to tell y'all, but the county planner called, and he said there's gonna be a delay gettin' the new main lines installed."

Mae groaned and took the stack of messages. "Thanks."

She shut herself in her office, and the next few hours flew by while she argued with the county planner and the civil engineer, trying to come up with a plan to replace the ancient plumbing in town.

There was a knock on her door, and Presley popped her head in.

"Can I get you anything?" she asked.

"No"—she sighed—"thanks for asking, but I'm fine."

Presley wrinkled her forehead and started to say something, but she just shook her head, closing the door again.

Mae spent a few hours pretending to work, but really she just sat at her desk, staring off into space daydreaming about Jacob and their date.

There was another knock on her door, and Presley came in with a takeout box.

"It's past lunch, and you haven't eaten. I went ahead and got you something from the Catfish. It's just a sandwich and some sweet tea."

"I appreciate it, but food just doesn't sound appealing right now. I think I might be coming down with the flu or something."

"You gotta eat, Mae."

Mae waved her off. "Missing a meal won't hurt."

Presley wrinkled her forehead. She looked over her shoulder and then went over and closed the door.

"Mae"—she turned back to her, twisting her hands in front of her—"you... you need to eat. It's not good for—"

"Good for what?"

Presley just stood there, chewing on her lip.

"Spit it out," Mae ordered.

"Don't be mad, okay? I... is there any chance you might be pregnant?"

"What in the—" she started to exclaim and then snapped her mouth shut. "Why would you think that?"

"You mentioned how the coffee tasted bad the other day, and you've been kind of emotional lately. It just made me wonder. You remind me of some of my friends when they're pregnant."

Was she pregnant? How could she have missed the signs? But with each passing moment, they became clear as day. She looked down at her planner and flipped through the pages. She'd missed her period, but she'd always had erratic periods, so that wasn't something she would necessarily be alarmed about. Now it made sense that Tillie's catfish, which she'd always loved, turned her stomach.

Mae jumped up from her desk. "I think I'm going to be sick."

Presley jumped back and opened her office door as Mae ran past. She made it to the ladies' room just in time to revisit her breakfast in the most unpleasant way.

She looked at her reflection in the mirror while she washed her hands. She looked like hell. How long had she been walking around with dark circles under her eyes like that?

"In the sisterhood of women, someone should have said something instead of letting me walk around lookin' like this," she muttered to herself.

She put her hands on the counter and took a deep breath. Presley couldn't be right. But as she ticked the days off in her head since she should have had her period, she knew she was. It didn't matter how long she hid in the bathroom; she wasn't going to be able to compose herself, not really.

Straightening her shoulders, Mae left the bathroom and walked back to her office. Pregnant or not, there was still work to do. She'd rather work than face the reality that she may have just completely ruined her life.

"Oh, hello dear." Ms. June jumped up when she walked in.

Aw hell, she'd forgotten it was Tuesday, Mae suppressed the urge to yell or cry. She wasn't sure which would make her feel better.

Presley gave her a sympathetic look as Ms. June followed her into her office, already babbling about her latest ideas for town improvements.

Mae sat numbly, her mind spinning, while the older woman talked about how the town needed a free tool library.

She wasn't supposed to be a mother. She always pictured herself being the cool auntie, never as one of the mothers in the park watching their children running around or taking them to story time at the library. Callie was the one who was supposed to have kids. She was the motherly type.

"So what do you think?" Ms. June interrupted her thoughts.

"I, uh, I'll give it careful consideration." Mae managed to give her standard answer for all Ms. June's requests.

The door opened, and Presley popped her head in. "I just wanted to remind you about that meetin' y'all have."

Ms. June got up. "I've taken enough of your time. We can continue this next week."

"Yes, ma'am, thank you."

"Come with me, Ms. June, I'll make sure to put you on the schedule. Let's set you up for a weekly meeting with the mayor. I've got the schedule color-coded. What color would y'all like to be?" Presley said.

The two of them walked out of Mae's office discussing shades of green, leaving Mae blissfully alone. She dropped her head in her hands and exhaled. How did her life go from being so full of possibility to this?

Presley came back in, closing the door behind her, and dropped down in the chair across from her. "I'm really sorry. I shouldn't have said anything."

"No, I guess I'm glad you did... or not"—she sighed—"I don't know."

"What are you gonna do now?"

"Drive over to Greenwood and buy a pregnancy test, I guess."

"Hold on." Presley jumped up and came back with her purse and began rummaging through it before pulling out a small rectangular object wrapped in plastic and holding it out to her.

Mae took it and looked back at Presley with wide eyes. "Do I want to know why you have a pregnancy test in your purse?"

Presley shrugged. "It's just kinda somethin' we do. It seems like there's always someone in the bathroom at church who thinks they need to take a test."

"What the hell kind of church do you go to?"

"The kind where a lot of girls want to get married and have babies."

Mae shook her head, looking down at the test.

"You don't have to do it now if you don't want to."

The plastic crinkled as Mae turned the test over in her hand. "I don't think I'm ready for this yet."

"Well, now y'all can get married."

Mae shook her head. "No, that's not going to happen."

"But isn't that what you want, a husband and a family? That's all I've ever wanted," she said with a dreamy smile.

"I always thought I'd be the cool auntie, not a mom. But I guess dreams and goals change, sometimes when we put the work into making it happen, and sometimes because life sends you an unexpected curve ball. Good Lord"—Mae dropped her head in her hands—"I sound so rational."

"That's what happened to me. I didn't even know I needed to change until somethin' happened that made me realize I haven't been very… good."

"Something or someone?"

Presley turned bright pink.

"Honestly, Presley, I never thought you'd change, and I'm glad to see you trying, but if I can give you a piece of advice, don't do it for someone. Do it for yourself. If you're just trying to impress someone, none of what you're doing will matter." Mae pressed her hand to her heart. "You have to want to change in here, for you, and not to impress some guy. As for helping out here, you've done a good job so far, so I think we should make your employment here official."

Presley's face split into a wide grin. "Really? I'd love to keep working with y'all. I promise I won't make any more mistakes."

"Let's not get overly confident. We all make mistakes. I'm just asking that you learn from them."

"Yes, ma'am."

"I've got to be honest with you and say this conversation has drained me. I am worn out, but I've got one more thing I need to talk to you about. I'm going to ask you to keep what happened here today to yourself. You don't say one word to anybody, you hear me?" Mae waggled her finger at her.

Presley shook her head. "I won't say a word, I swear."

"I'd appreciate it, thanks. Now, let's get back to work. I'll take that file for the sewage grant proposal when you can."

Presley nodded and went back out to her desk. Mae's shoulders slumped. She blew out a shaky breath and closed her eyes for a minute. She opened them again and eyed the pregnancy test on her desk. What would Jacob say if she was pregnant? It didn't matter, she didn't need him. Raising a baby alone wasn't her first choice. Having a baby at all wasn't something she'd ever thought she'd want to do. Her hands shook as she pulled out her phone to call her gynecologist's office.

Relieved she was able to get an appointment for the next morning, Mae tucked the pregnancy test that Presley gave her into her handbag for when she got home. By the time five o'clock rolled around, Mae was beyond done for the day. She was thankful for Presley, who took charge of keeping her organized through the rest of the day; Mae wouldn't have been as productive as she had been without Presley keeping her on track with the files and reports she needed.

"See you tomorrow afternoon," Mae said as she stood on the top of the town hall steps.

"I'll take care of everything until you get in."

"Just call if anything comes up. I should be in before noon."

"If you need anything, you can call me too. Not just for work stuff, but if you want company or something...." Presley trailed off with a shrug.

"I'll keep that in mind, thanks."

As she walked across the park toward the Barton Building, Mae couldn't help wondering how the world had turned upside down so much that Presley Beaumont had become her confidant. A breeze picked up, and somewhere in the trees, she could have sworn she heard laughter.

CHAPTER TWENTY

INSTEAD OF waiting for her appointment with the gynecologist the next day, Mae drove three towns over to buy a pregnancy test. She bought one of each brand and then spent the rest of the evening staring at different versions of the same result. Two blue lines. Two pink lines. A plus sign. They all said the same thing—she was pregnant.

No, she wasn't just pregnant; she was also a coward. It had been three days since she'd taken the tests, and she still hadn't said anything to Jacob. Her gynecologist confirmed it the next morning after Presley confronted her. She pressed her hand to her flat stomach. Since then, she'd gone through every emotion possible. She'd never been a fan of roller coasters, and she really didn't like the ride life had taken her on now.

JACOB MADE her a candlelit dinner on the roof deck for their first date, and she barely remembered any of it, she'd been so distracted. Her mind was a whirlwind trying to process her new reality.

"Hey, are you all right?" Jacob asked. They were sitting on the sofa in his apartment, where they had just finished watching a movie. "I was asking what you thought of the movie?"

"Oh, it was good."

Mae had no idea what it was about, she'd been so distracted by her thoughts.

Jacob narrowed his eyes. "What's going on, Pixie?"

This was it. She needed to tell him.

"I'm just distracted with all the details for the Fourth of July celebrations," she lied.

A shadow of worry passed over Jacob's face, and then he smiled and kissed her temple. "I'm sure everything will work out just fine."

Would it? Jacob had just come around to the idea of a committed relationship. How was he going to feel about becoming a father? Not wanting kids was one of the few things they didn't argue about. They had talked about how neither of them wanted children, agreeing that neither of them were white-picket-fence people.

Of course, she'd come up with all of her reasons before she met Jacob. Now, the idea of having a piece of him with her, a little boy or girl with his smile, made her happy. Scared shitless and totally freaked out, but underneath all of that, she already cherished the tiny life she carried.

"I was thinking I might spend the night in my apartment tonight now that the windows have been replaced," she said.

Jacob frowned. "Why, what's wrong?"

"Nothing's wrong. I just want to be back in my own place. It's been so crazy since the shooting and the two of us, I could use a little alone time."

He sighed. "I don't like it, but I understand."

"Tomorrow's Friday. How about we have a picnic after work?"

"I like that idea," he said with a wolfish grin.

That night, Mae lay in her own bed staring at the ceiling. She'd tell him tomorrow. Squeezing her eyes shut, she sent up a silent prayer that everything would be okay.

JACOB DID a double-take when Presley Beaumont walked into the hardware store Friday morning looking like a younger version of Dax's mother, Dorothy Ellis. Wearing a pale lavender suit with beige heels, she even had a string of pearls around her neck, just like Dorothy used to wear.

Presley's eyes darted toward Dan and then returned to Jacob. "I was wonderin' if I can talk to you."

"What do you want, Presley?"

"I, um"—her eyes darted toward Dan again—"it's kind of private."

Jacob sighed and stepped out from behind the counter and waved Presley toward his workroom in the back. He raised an eyebrow when Presley pulled the large barn door separating the two spaces closed behind them. She shifted from foot to foot, chewing her lip.

"Spit it out," he ordered.

"I went to see Ms. Ellis today."

"And this matters because?"

"Because she said somethin', and I… I think you should know."

"What could she have said that you think I should know about?"

Presley twisted her hands in front of her. She looked over her shoulder as if she was checking to make sure no one was listening.

"I tried to tell Isiah, but he wouldn't listen, and since... well, you know."

"No, I don't know." Jacob tried to keep his impatience out of his voice.

Whatever it was that Presley wanted to tell him, it must be important. He didn't have much of a relationship with Presley. Their paths didn't cross very often, so he was surprised to see her looking so nervous and anxious. Whatever it was, he didn't know why she'd come to him of all people. He looked at her again, and there was something about the way she was standing in front of him now that raised alarm bells in the back of his head, so he took a deep breath and waited for her to explain.

She blew out a shaky breath. "I figured since y'all were a couple. and with the baby and all—"

"Wait, what baby?"

Presley's eyes grew wide. "Oh, Lord have mercy. I—I thought you knew." Her chin began to tremble, and her eyes grew bright. "I did it again. I can't seem to do anything right. Lord a'mighty, I wanted to do better."

While Presley admonished herself, Jacob fought to breathe. Was Mae pregnant? He reached out for the workbench next to him to steady himself. He shoved his own feelings aside and focused on getting the information he needed.

"Presley, I need you to explain what's going on."

Presley nodded. "Sometimes I go to visit Ms. Ellis. Daddy would have my hide if he knew. She should be in jail for stealing all that money from the town and trying to kill someone, but I felt sorry for her sittin' in that prison cell. I know what she did was bad, but she's old, and I just...." She shrugged. "She's not sorry for tryin' to kill Callie or Reid. I thought maybe she'd see what she did was wrong, but she's holding fast to what she believes. She was in a rare mood when I visited her this morning, and she kept talking about how she had friends who were going to make sure Colton didn't get corrupted having... having Mae as the mayor and Isiah for a sheriff."

"I'm guessing that's not the language she used, was it?"

"No, sir," Presley said in a shaky voice.

"Did she mention any names?"

Presley hesitated. "She said she was happy Mr. Walker was goin' to get the charges against him dropped because he had friends in the right places who could help."

"Okay. Now, explain to me what you meant about the baby?"

She took a step back, shaking her head. "I shouldn't have said anything. I might be wrong. I've just seen so many of my girlfriends... well, most of my friends want to get married and start a family right away, and so I, I guess I've just gotten kind of good at reading the symptoms and—"

"Get to the point," Jacob barked. Presley jumped and took another step back with fear in her eyes. "Sorry." He grimaced. "Can you please just tell me what you mean?"

"She wasn't eating, and we were at the library during story time, and she started to cry. She fell asleep at her desk the other day. I asked her a few days ago if she might be pregnant, and I just figured she told you."

Jacob fought the rising panic that threatened to engulf him. This couldn't be happening. How could she have known and not told him yet? Anger began to simmer just under the surface.

"Jacob, are you okay? You kind of look like you're gonna pass out."

He straightened up and cleared his throat. "I'm fine. You did the right thing coming to me. I want you to do me a favor and keep this to yourself. Can you do that for me?" he asked, giving her a stern look.

She nodded. "I can do that, but can you tell Isiah that I was just tryin' to help?" Her voice dropped to a whisper. "I just didn't want anything to happen to him."

Jacob hid his surprise. This was an unexpected revelation. Presley might be annoying as hell, but he had seen an improvement lately. In her own way, she was trying.

"If you hear anything else, you come to me, okay?"

"Yes, sir." She chewed on her lip for a moment. "Please don't tell Mae it was me that told y'all about the baby. She'll have my hide."

"Yeah, I can do that. Are you sure she's pregnant?" *Please be wrong, please be wrong.* "I don't think it would be a good idea to upset Mae or start any rumors."

"I'm pretty sure. I'm really sorry. I'm trying to be better. Mae's been nice to me, and I don't want to do anything to make her mad."

"I believe you, Presley, and I won't say anything."

On shaky legs, he walked over to the door and opened it, revealing a few customers milling about, looking toward the two of them with curious eyes.

He had to give Presley credit for her quick thinking when she said, loud enough for everyone to hear, "Don't forget the cigar box is a surprise for Daddy for his birthday."

She gave him a quick wink and scurried out of the store.

He paced in his workroom, his mind reeling with what Presley had just told him. He needed to stay calm and think. Which is exactly what he didn't do.

"I'll be gone for the rest of the day," he barked at Dan on his way out the door.

MAE WAS nowhere ready to give up, but another minute on the phone with the county waste management manager might just kill her. How was she to know that the old town council had let the contract lapse, and they were using a private contractor at a lower cost? Of course, that contractor had been disposing of waste improperly, and the city was facing a huge fine.

"Bastards." Mae hung up the phone, pressing her palms against her eyes. "I'm not going to cry," she whispered to herself. She'd never been a cryer before, but now she teared up at the drop of a hat. "I will not be a hot mess for the next seven months."

She'd been shocked when the doctor told her she was almost eight weeks along. It had happened the night of Taylor and Jo's wedding.

She was so caught up in her own musings, she wasn't paying attention to the disruption outside her office until the door flew open and Jacob strode in, his eyes laser-focused on her.

"Jacob, what—"

Before she could ask what the hell he was doing, he swept her into his arms and carried her out of the office, past where Presley stood by looking frantic, twisting her fingers into knots.

"You put me down right now, Jacob Winters," she yelled.

His face was grim and his jaw clenched as he carried her down the hall and up the stairs into Judge Beaumont's office, where he gently set her on her feet.

"What the hell is wrong with you?"

Jacob turned to the judge. "I need you to marry us right now."

"Have you lost your mother-loving mind?" Mae glared at him.

Jacob stepped forward until their chests were almost touching. "Listen, Pixie, my child will not be born a bastard."

Mae's mouth dropped open, and her heart stuttered in her chest.

Judge Beaumont was never a man who reacted impulsively, and he didn't change course now. He peered at them over the top of his glasses for a moment before slowly standing up and moving out from behind his desk.

"I'll just give you two a moment," he said before slipping out the door.

"What," Mae croaked, "what did you say?"

"We have to get married."

Mae sank down into the chair in front of the judge's desk. This wasn't how she'd planned on this conversation going. She held her hand up when he started to speak again.

"Hold up, I need you to stop acting like a Neanderthal and give me a minute to think."

She blew out a shaky breath and looked up at Jacob, who looked at her with wild eyes. Okay, now was not the time to panic. It looked like he was panicked enough for both of them.

Folding her hands in her lap, she gestured to the chair across from her. "Sit down, Jacob."

He dropped into the chair with a frustrated huff.

She took a deep steadying breath, ignoring the fact that it didn't do a damn thing to steady her racing heartbeat. "First of all, I'm not going to marry you."

"Mae—"

She held her hand up again. "Jacob, I won't argue about this with you. I will not marry you." She sighed. There was no point trying to pretend anymore. "A baby doesn't make a marriage. We're going to take this one step at a time."

"How long have you known?"

"Just a few days. I was planning on telling you. I just hadn't figured out how I was going to do it yet."

Jacob leaned forward and ran his hands over his face. "I... how could this have happened?"

"The condom must have broken."

"Hell," Jacob muttered.

Mae glanced toward the door. "We can talk about this more later. I'm sure Judge Beaumont would like his office back." She stood up. "Come on, we can continue this back at the apartment."

Jacob jumped out of his seat and grasped her arm and began leading her out of the office. She gently pulled herself out of his grip and shot him a warning look. His overprotectiveness was grating on her already frazzled nerves.

"I need to grab my things and let Presley know that I'll be gone for the rest of the day."

"I'll wait," he growled.

"Yes, you will. You can wait for me back at the hardware store, and I'll stop by when I'm ready."

His nostrils flared, and he frowned at her for a minute before nodding. He hovered at her side as they made their way down the stairs and hesitated at the doorway to the lobby of her office for a moment before he stalked away. On shaky legs, Mae walked in to find Presley sitting with her father in the reception area, talking quietly.

When she came in, Presley jumped up, her voice shaking. "Can I get you anything? Mae, I'm so sorry. I didn't mean to say anything. I thought he knew, and if I had known, I would never have said anything." Her eyes filled with tears. "Please don't be mad. I honestly didn't mean to…. Oh hell, I just can't do anything right."

Mae took a deep breath. "Okay, I'm not sure what's going on here, and I don't know what you've said to whom, but here's what I need you to do now. Please cancel my appointments for the rest of the day." She waggled her finger at Presley. "Do. Not. Say. A. Word. To. Anyone about this. Am I clear?"

"Yes, ma'am."

Judge Beaumont came over and rested his hands on Mae's shoulders, looking at her with a fatherly concern that had her fighting back the urge to cry.

"Are you okay?"

She bit her lip and nodded.

"You tell me what you need, and I'll make sure you get it."

"Thank you," she managed to choke out.

The judge left, and Presley hovered while she gathered up her things.

"Are you sure you're okay?" Presley said after a few minutes.

Mae continued shoving her things into her handbag. "I suppose so."

"I... can I just...." Presley came over and wrapped her arms around Mae.

She sniffed and tried to blink back a fresh round of tears. "This is not how I pictured telling Jacob about the baby." She pulled back, looking at Presley, and a bubble of hysterical laughter burst out of her. "And the worst part is, you're the only one I can talk to about this."

Presley's face fell, and Mae innately felt bad. "My filter is.... Today's not my best day, okay? I just can't talk to Callie or Emma about this." She buried her face in her hands. "I am so frickin' embarrassed."

"It's okay, I understand. I mean, I don't understand, I mean, I don't want y'all thinkin' I'm, what's it called... appropriatin' y'all's experience. Oh hell, I'm fixin' to make a mess of this again, aren't I? I just... if you need to talk or anything, well... you've been a good friend to me, nicer than I deserve, and I just want to make sure I'm a good friend to you."

"That's not what appropriation means, Presley, but I understand what you're trying to say, and I appreciate that you're trying to sympathize with what I'm going through," she said with a watery laugh. Mae wiped her eyes with the back of her hand and smiled. "I appreciate that, I really do. Right now...." Oh hell, she was going to start crying again. Presley's solidarity was sweet, and Mae appreciated it more than she ever thought she would.

She took the tissue Presley offered her and blew her nose. "I'd better get the lead out. I expect Jacob's patience is worn pretty thin at this point," Mae said with a watery laugh.

Presley nodded. "Y'all go. I've got everything handled here."

Mae turned to go just as Ms. June poked her head in her office.

"Oh, there you are, dear. I made a new batch of kombucha that I thought you might enjoy. I have so many new ideas, I couldn't wait until next week to talk to you."

"Oh, Ms. June, I am so sorry. Mayor Colton has an emergency meetin' she's got to get to," Presley said, pushing Mae toward the door. "But I'm so glad you're here. I was hoping you could give me your opinion on the new recycling bins we're going to be orderin' for the park."

Ms. June's eyes lit up, and she clapped her hands. "Oh, how wonderful."

Presley turned to Mae and mouthed *Go*.

With a grateful smile, Mae headed out of her office. She didn't have to walk the block to the hardware store. Jacob was pacing out front when she walked out the door.

He stopped, his gaze zeroing in on her as she came down the stairs. "Took you long enough."

"Don't you dare get snippy with me. This is all your fault, anyway."

His nostrils flared, and his mouth flattened into a thin line. Instead of arguing with her, he fell in step next to her as they walked across the park.

CHAPTER TWENTY-ONE

SHIT.

Nothing about this day was going right. He was supposed to be married by now. Yeah, okay, so that might not be the best idea he'd ever had, but if he was going to be a father, he might as well be a husband. And there was no way he was going to let his child grow up without a father. The few years he had with his weren't nearly enough.

"Look, I know you don't love me." She shook her head with a sad smile. "I've said it twice now, and you haven't said it back, so I get the message."

Jacob stopped pacing and looked at her. "You think I don't love you? Jesus, Mae, of course I love you. I broke my biggest rule for you. I've compromised my mission for you."

His breath hitched when he realized he'd just blurted out what he'd intended to tell Mae in a much calmer way.

Mae froze. "Wait, what mission?"

"Shit." He gently grasped her arms and guided her over to the sofa. "You're going to want to sit down for this."

He stopped and sat down next to her and jumped up again. This wouldn't work; he needed to look her in the eye. He sat down on the coffee table in front of her and took her hands in his.

"Dax and I served in the Army together, and he wanted me to come here after we received our discharge." He got up and started pacing again. "I didn't come here just because Dax invited me. I came here on assignment."

Mae was looking at him with a furrowed brow. "Are you still in the Army?"

"No, I'm with the FBI."

"What are you doing with the FBI?"

"There's a White supremacist group active in the area, and we have an agent working undercover embedded in the group. I'm his handler."

"Who? Does this have anything to do with my getting shot at?"

"I can't give you those details."

"That's ridiculous, this is my life we're talking about. I have a right to know."

Jacob hesitated, choosing his words carefully. "I can't tell you who's undercover, but I can tell you that there is a group active in the area who have made a direct threat against you. From what we understand, they aren't the ones who shot at you. Our person on the inside told us his group was upset that you were attacked, they—" His breath hitched again. "—they want to be the ones who get credit for hurting you."

Mae's eyes grew wide. "That's sick."

Jacob sat back down. "I'm going to do everything I can to keep you safe." He swallowed. "Both of you."

Mae frowned. "So, you came here for a job. What were you going to do when your assignment was over?"

"I wasn't sure. I hadn't planned on putting down roots, but this town... you, got a hold of me. I never thought I'd find a place that felt like home again."

"Is that why you pushed me away, because you didn't think you were going to stay here?" she asked.

Jacob nodded. "That was part of it. My dad died in the first tower on 9/11. And then my mom... she was diagnosed with cancer a few years later. She died during my senior year of high school. I...I didn't want to feel that pain again."

"I know about your parents," Mae said, her eyes bright with unshed tears.

"You do?"

"You let it slip once." She shook her head with a sad smile. "The thing is, Jacob, you've been giving me small pieces of yourself, your past, this whole time. That's why it hurts so much that you couldn't give me just a little piece of your heart."

Jacob sat down again and took her hands in his. "I'm sorry. Don't think you don't have my heart, Mae, because you stole it the first time we met."

"Then why?" she asked, her lips trembling as she looked down at their joined hands.

"Because the day I buried my mother, I made a promise to myself that I wouldn't let myself love anyone the way I love my parents and the way they loved each other. Without my dad, my mom just... faded away. She didn't even try to fight the cancer. I felt so helpless, it just...

tore my heart out. I have an eidetic memory, so I can't just forget. I can remember every moment of the day they died, what Father was wearing when he left the house to start his shift the night before, looking down at my mother's hand in mine when she slipped away. The way she took her last breath.

"It was bad enough with my parents. I couldn't imagine what it would be like if I lost someone I loved and would have to live the rest of my life with that memory. I thought it would be better to shut down and not allow myself to care about anybody. But it didn't work because I met you, and I don't want to forget a single moment of my time with you."

By the time he finished he'd slipped to his knees, resting his head in Mae's lap, pressed against her belly as if he were telling their child as much as he was telling Mae.

She cradled his head in her lap, stroking his hair. The same way his mother did when he was a child.

"I'm so sorry, Jacob. It must have been terrible losing your parents when you were young and having those memories. But Jacob, not allowing yourself to care means you aren't remembering the good times, and those memories can be much more powerful if you let them." Mae tilted his head so that he was looking up at her. "Jacob, trying to run away from making memories isn't any way to live. Things happen, good, bad, ugly, and beautiful. Think of this baby—" She smiled. "You didn't plan for a broken condom, but something beautiful is going to come out of it, and there are going to be so many wonderful memories that you won't want to miss out on."

Jacob looked up into Mae's dark luminous eyes, filled with so much love, and shuddered. "I'm scared," he confessed.

"I know, so am I."

"I'm afraid I can't keep you safe."

"You can't, Jacob, that's not your job."

He sat up and sat back down in the chair. He had to keep going and tell her everything. "You have to be careful, Mae, even more now. This threat against you is serious. The agent working undercover is really worried."

Mae narrowed her eyes. "Was this about the same time you started spying on me?"

"I wasn't spying. I was just trying to keep you safe."

She jumped up with her hands clenched. "You should have told me."

Jacob stood and grasped her shoulders gently. "I couldn't. I shouldn't have told you now. This is an active investigation, and there's a lot at stake. If everything goes well, we'll have enough evidence to bring down not just one group but several in the region."

"I can't believe you thought you couldn't trust me."

"It's not about trust. We've kept a tight lid on this. There's only four people in town who know."

Mae stomped her foot. "But it's my life." She pulled out of his grasp and wrapped her arms around herself. "You're keeping secrets from me, everyone thinks they know what I want to do with my life and they're wrong, and now I'm having a baby and I didn't think I ever wanted to have kids in the first place. Everything is spiraling out of control, and I hate it."

"Sweetheart." Jacob wrapped his arms around her. She stood stiffly in his arms, but she didn't pull away.

"There's too much going on, and I don't have a handle on any of it." She sniffed.

"I know, Pixie. It's gonna be okay. I'm gonna take care of you, both of you."

She jerked her head up and pushed him away.

"You big, stupid, lumberjack. I don't want to be taken care of. You don't keep secrets from the person you love."

Jacob threw his arms up and shouted, "Well, I've never loved anyone before, so I didn't know."

"We're a pair, aren't we?" she said with a shaky laugh.

"I just… I didn't want you to go off half-cocked."

Mae raised an eyebrow, and her cheeks flushed deep pink. Oh hell, that was the wrong thing to say. He replayed the memory of telling Mae she should never play poker because her face gave away everything she was thinking. Right now, she was thinking about turning him from a rooster to a hen if he didn't act quick.

He held up his hands. "I shouldn't have said that. What I meant is that you're a fighter, and I knew you'd want to defend Colton against anyone who threatened our community. But this time you can't do that."

"I know that. I'll admit I can get carried away when I'm passionate about something, but I'm not about to go off half-cocked against the Klan or whoever it is."

"I'm sorry."

"So am I. Can I blame it on the pregnancy hormones?"

Jacob swept her into his arms again. "You can blame it on anything you want."

She sighed and wrapped her arms around his neck.

"We have a lot of things we need to work out."

"Yes, we do, but can we just... be for a little bit?" she said, resting her cheek on his chest.

Jacob glanced out the window and realized how late it had gotten.

"Are you hungry? You must be, it's late."

Mae put her hand to her stomach. "Food and I haven't had the best relationship lately."

He insisted Mae put her feet up while he made her a cup of tea. Before the water finished boiling, he glanced over and saw her fast asleep in the big leather chair in the corner of his apartment with Petunia curled up in her lap. His mind was reeling, replaying their conversation over and over again.

He went ahead and started making some dinner just in case Mae would be hungry later. Plus, he needed something to keep himself busy so he didn't freak out. *Baby, they were going to have a baby*, he kept repeating while he cooked. Yes, he was freaked out, but there was also something else. He'd never pictured his life with a child, and now that it had happened, excitement along with a healthy dose of fear coursed through him at the thought of becoming a family with Mae and a baby. They weren't going to be perfect parents, but their child would never question if it was loved.

He needed to let Dan know that Mae knew about his assignment. He'd hoped that he could keep Mae from knowing about the threat, but after the shooting, he realized that wasn't a realistic option. It was only a matter of time before he had to tell her. In some ways, it was a relief to not have to keep the secret anymore.

Mae stirred and gave him a tired smile. "Sorry, I didn't mean to fall asleep."

Jacob went over and sat on the footstool in front of her. "You're working too hard. You've got to slow down."

"Oh God, you're going to hover all the time now, aren't you?"

"I'm not hovering." He snapped his mouth shut and exhaled. "Okay, maybe I'm going to hover just a little. Bear with me, Mae, I've never been in a situation like this."

"And I have? Look, Jacob, this is new territory for both of us. All I'm asking is that you listen to me and we work together, okay?"

"Yeah, okay. But bear with me if I forget sometimes."

She smiled and leaned forward, pressing her forehead against his. "I think I can put up with you if you can put up with me."

"Are you ready for some dinner?"

"No"—she said, reaching up to cup his neck—"I think I'd like dessert first."

Jacob grinned and pulled her closer. "I think I can make that happen."

His mouth captured hers in a deep kiss. She moaned and straddled his lap.

Her eyes were bright with desire when they broke apart. "Take me to bed," she said in a breathy whisper.

She let out a small yelp when he picked her up and carried her across the room and into his bedroom.

He hesitated when he laid her down on the bed. "I don't want to hurt you."

She shook her head. "You won't. I'm not fragile, Jacob. I won't break."

He lifted her shirt and placed a kiss on her stomach. She wiggled under him and pulled her shirt off, revealing a deep purple lace bra. "Beautiful," he murmured, admiring the way the color enhanced the glow of her dark skin. He made a trail of kisses up her stomach and on her breastbone before capturing her lips again.

She grabbed at the back of his shirt, tugging at it. With a grunt of annoyance, he pulled it over his head and threw it in the corner. He popped the button on her jeans and let out a moan of appreciation when he pulled them over her hips to reveal panties in the same color as her bra. He took in every inch of her, pressing his lips to hers as he reveled in her softness against him. How could he have thought he would have any kind of life without Mae in his arms every night?

He pushed himself up, hovering over her just enough so he could see her eyes. "I love you."

Mae reached up and grasped his neck, pulling him down until his lips were against hers. "I love you."

He returned the kiss with a sigh of relief.

He couldn't help asking her to marry him again after they'd made love and he was holding Mae, his arm curled around her middle with his hand on her stomach. Happiness coursed through him. They were having a baby.

She sighed and threw her legs over his, resting her head on his shoulder. "No more secrets, Jacob. We're a team now."

He took her hand, linking her fingers with his. "So does that mean you'll marry me?"

Jacob grunted with displeasure when she pulled out of his arms and sat up against the headboard.

"Someday, maybe yes, but not now."

He sat up next to her. With a little chirp, Petunia jumped up on the bed and into his lap. He frowned, staring down at the kitten while she butted his hand with her head.

Mae sighed and grasped his chin, tuning his head until his eyes met hers.

"Our baby will have two parents that love him or her or whatever our child chooses to be. We don't have to be married to love this child. But what we need to do is figure out a way to live together and communicate. We're both going to have to work on our trust issues and learn to compromise."

Mae let go of his hand and placed hers on her stomach. "This little filbert is going to need both of us to guide it."

Jacob wrinkled his forehead. "What kind of nickname is filbert?"

Mae laughed softly, and another band around his heart loosened.

"I forget you city boys call them hazelnuts. I don't know why, I just think of this tiny one as a little nut."

"Filbert." He smiled. "If it's a boy, we could name him Phillip."

"And if it's a girl?"

"Philliphina?"

Mae scrunched up her nose. "I don't think that's a real name."

"It can be whatever we want it to be."

"I suppose so."

"If I asked you to marry me again, you wouldn't say yes, would you?"

She pulled herself up and took his face between her hands. "No," she said, pressing her lips to his forehead.

He sighed. "If I keep asking, will you think about saying yes someday?"

She nuzzled his nose, her lips caressing a trail to his mouth. It was a kiss filled with promise.

CHAPTER TWENTY-TWO

JACOB'S QUEST for peace and quiet was thwarted when he found Reid and Chloe sitting together on the rooftop deck, deep in conversation. He'd come up to the rooftop to take some time to think and sort through everything that had happened. He'd completely lost his mind, demanding Mae marry him the way he did. He didn't blame her for saying no; he'd acted exactly like the Neanderthal she'd accused him of being.

He was going to be a father. He'd already started selecting wood to build a crib. He'd been replaying memories with his parents since he found out. With each one, he became more and more excited about making some of those same memories with his own child. Teaching him or her to catch, learning to ride a bike, and reading a story at bedtime. Yes, he was scared, terrified if he let himself admit it, but also happy in a way he didn't know he could be.

He started to back away when Chloe noticed him and waved him over.

"Sorry, I didn't mean to interrupt."

"Not at all." Chloe smiled.

Jacob took a seat in one of the deck chairs arranged on the rooftop and took a sip of his coffee while Reid continued to tell Chloe about how he'd been traveling around to different farms with Mr. Wallace, selecting grain for the distillery.

"You're getting a full education, aren't you?" Jacob said.

Reid nodded. "I'm lucky. Primus is a master distiller. I… I hate to think what will happen when he passes on. I want to learn everything I can while I can."

"Sounds like a good plan," Jacob said.

Chloe nodded in agreement.

"Do you think Mr. Wallace would let you buy the Buckthorn someday?" Jacob asked.

Reid glanced at Chloe. "We were just talking about that. I'm not sure if it would be okay."

Chloe rolled her eyes with an exasperated sigh and looked at Jacob. "Maybe you can talk to him."

"About?"

"I thought when I came back to Colton, people wouldn't accept me for a lot of reasons, ever since I found out that Dax was my half-brother and that I wasn't who I thought I was," Reid said.

"I thought folks in a small town in the South would be even more prejudiced and discovered it's the opposite. People here care more about what church you go to than what color your mama or your daddy was," Chloe said.

Reid rubbed the back of his neck. "I'm still trying to sort things out. Who I am and what I want. The one thing I do know is I made the right decision to take the job at the prosecutor's office. I know I can make a difference there."

Jacob sat up straighter. There were several local officials who, thanks to Rhett's work, they now knew were part of the Klan. That included members of the prosecutor's office for three surrounding counties. Having Reid working as a prosecuting attorney would help them build their case.

Chloe's phone dinged with a text message. She looked down, and her eyes grew wide. "Shit, I'm late for a production meeting. It's nice to see you, Jacob. Reid, I'll catch up with you later."

Jacob glanced at Reid, his comment about working in the prosecutor's office playing over in his head. He watched his best friend's brother for a moment. Reid was a good guy. What he was about to ask him to do would mean Reid would be keeping a secret from his brother. Reid and Dax had just rekindled their relationship, and Jacob didn't want to do anything to jeopardize that. But Reid being offered a job at the county prosecutor's office was an opportunity that could help the investigation and help make sure Colton and Mae were safe.

"I want to talk to you about something, but I need to make a phone call first. Do you mind waiting for me for just a few minutes?"

"Sure." Reid nodded, looking at him with curiosity.

Jacob got up and walked over to the other side of the roof to make his call. Ten minutes later, he returned and sat back down.

"There's something I want to tell you, but if I do, I'll be asking you to keep a secret from Dax."

Reid sat forward, resting his forearms on his knees. He stared at Jacob for a minute before he nodded and said, "Okay."

"There's something I need you to know. It's a conflict of interest but, well, this is family. Maybe not the traditional kind, but...." Jacob exhaled. "I'm working with the FBI as a handler. We have someone embedded with a local Klan group. We've learned about certain people working in several county prosecutor's offices who are members of the group."

Reid sucked in his breath.

"I just spoke to the lead agent on this case, and he agrees that having you on the inside would be an incredible asset."

Reid gave him a solemn nod. "I'm in."

Jacob held up his hand. "Hold up, you need to think about this. No one else knows about this, including your brother. I want you to take time to think about if you're comfortable keeping a confidence from your friends and family."

"That's what you've been doing, isn't it? How long?"

"Since I came here."

Reid exhaled. "I can't believe Dax hasn't figured it out."

"Well"—Jacob's lips twitched—"in case you haven't noticed, your brother's been pretty distracted since he came back to Colton."

"Distracted? Try blinded by love."

"I'm happy for him. He's worked hard to make amends and turn his life around. It's good that he moved back here. But that's why I want you to think about this. I hate the idea of putting you in a position that might cause damage to your connection with your brother. You guys have come a long way in rebuilding your relationship."

Dax was damn lucky to have found the love of his life and to have a chance to rebuild his relationship with his brother. Dax, Callie, and Reid had come together in the aftermath of Dax's mother's lies to form a new family unit that was so much stronger than they were before.

Reid gave him an understanding nod. "I hear what you're saying, but I don't need time to think about this. I've handled a few cases with the Proud Boys in Chicago. I've seen the kind of hate and evil they perpetrate. Colton is my home. If I can do something to help my community and the people I care about, then I'll do it."

"Appreciate it."

They discussed their plan; Reid would contact the prosecutor's office and let them know he would accept their offer. He'd already transferred his law license to Mississippi so he could start right away. Since they lived in the same building, communication would be easy.

"I appreciate you trusting me with this," Reid said, "and I'm glad I can help."

"I'm happy to have you on the inside. I know you'd rather be making spirits with Mr. Wallace."

"Don't worry, I'll make the time to keep working with Primus, and I can leave the prosecutor's office anytime." Reid rubbed the back of his neck. "I've been feeling aimless lately. Wondering where I fit in. Knowing I can help, it feels right."

Jacob nodded. "Makes sense, and I'm grateful."

The door opened, and Dan walked onto the deck. Jacob stood up and shook his hand when he approached.

"Thanks for getting here so quickly. I just filled him in," he said, while Reid stared at them with surprise.

"Reid, you've already met Agent Nguyen."

Dan nodded to Reid with a sheepish smile. "Hey."

Reid looked at Jacob with a raised eyebrow. "Any other secrets you want to share?"

Jacob thought about Mae.

"Nope."

Reid leaned forward when Dan and Jacob sat back down. "What else do I need to know?"

They talked through more of the details, with Jacob letting Dan take the lead on how much to share with Reid.

"I'M SO sorry," Presley said for the hundredth time.

"You need to stop apologizing, I know you didn't tell Jacob I was pregnant on purpose."

Presley twisted her hands in front of her while chewing on her lip. "I just want you to know I'm not going to make any more mistakes, I swear."

Mae laughed. "I hate to break it to you, but that's not going to happen. We all make mistakes."

Every day since Jacob barged into her office, Presley had been apologizing to the point where Mae was starting to feel sorry for her.

"What can I do to help?" Presley asked.

"Nothing, just keep your mouth closed for now. Anybody else that finds out, I'd like it to come from Jacob or me."

"You haven't told your friends or family yet?"

"Not yet. We're still processing this news ourselves."

"Is everything okay with you and Jacob?"

Mae smiled. "We're good. Still in shock, but we're going to be okay."

"For what it's worth, I think you're gonna make a great mom."

"What makes you say that?"

"You're always so confident, and you always find a way to get things done. I've been watching you while I've been workin' here, and you're just so... pulled together."

"Thank you, Presley. I appreciate that, but I have to say I always figured I'd see you pushing a baby carriage around the park."

"I've always wanted a big family." Her face fell. "I'm afraid I may have lost my chance with anyone around here."

Mae got up from her desk and put her arm around Presley's shoulder. "You've made real progress, Presley, but change doesn't happen overnight. Give it time."

"I wanted you to know I went over and apologized to Callie for how hateful I've been, and Dax too."

Mae looked at Presley in surprise. "Good for you. I know that wasn't easy for you. I'm proud of you, Presley."

That night, as she and Jacob lay in bed, she shared her conversation with Presley.

"She's not perfect, but I give her credit for trying."

Jacob chuckled. "I expect she's still going to trip up now and then."

"Probably, but it makes me hopeful. If Presley can decide she wants to change, maybe other folks like Rhett and some other folks around here might change their way of thinking. I'm not naive, I know not everyone will, but Presley has me feeling more optimistic."

She still didn't know, and Jacob didn't like that he couldn't tell Mae the truth about Rhett, not until he was given permission by the agency.

"This is one of the things I love about you. You always have hope."

Mae raised herself up on her elbow. "Not all the time. I almost gave up on you."

Jacob pulled her on top of him, cupping her face with his hands. "Almost, but you didn't. I'll never be able to love you enough for that."

Mae's lips curled into a smile. "But you have the rest of your life to try and show me."

CHAPTER TWENTY-THREE

MAE SAT at the small table, looking at the men around her. "This is like one of those FBI shows on TV."

Jacob snorted. "Those shows are bullshit."

Dan nodded in agreement.

"Well, I guess I'm about to find out how it's done for real," she said.

Jacob frowned and pulled her chair closer. He put his arm around her shoulder and waggled his finger in her face. "You are going to stay safe and let me do my job."

Mae bumped his shoulder with hers. "We're all going to do what we need to do to keep our town safe."

Jacob grunted. As much as Mae wanted to be annoyed by the way he was acting all possessive, her heart filled with joy. The days since Jacob's disastrous attempt to make her marry him had been spent having long conversations ending in late nights. There were arguments and lots of making up. Most of their disagreements were minor, but the one point they couldn't come to agreement on was Jacob's insistence that they get married.

It wasn't that she didn't want to marry him, she just wanted to make sure they were doing it for the right reasons. Marriage wasn't a requirement for raising a family. The one thing Mae was confident in was that she and Jacob would be able to work together loving and raising their child. They'd even been able to laugh, talking about what it was going to be like to be parents.

But now wasn't the time to think about marriage and a family. May stopped musing on the state of her personal life and turned her attention back to the men at the table. She glanced at Jacob and saw the anxiety in his eyes and gave him a small smile.

"I'm not going to take any unnecessary risks, Jacob."

He paused, his eyes flickering to her stomach. "I know you won't," he said tenderly.

They were a team, partners in whatever the future would bring.

"Is there anything we've missed?" Dan asked.

"I'm worried about Emma," Mae said.

"What does Emma have to do with any of this?" Dan asked.

Mae glanced at Reid. "She mentioned a while ago that her father said he has friends who could make his charges go away and would make sure he was elected mayor."

Jacob swore under his breath.

"That might be what he's saying, but it's doubtful that could actually happen. Between the case the DA's building and the evidence we've been gathering, Clyde Walker isn't going to have a future that doesn't include time behind bars."

Reid nodded. "I'll check the files and look to see who's been involved in his case. I just want to make sure that no one at the DA's office is trying to help Clyde get his charges dropped or reduced."

"There's something else that I'd like you to look into if you can," Mae said. "Emma said her dad hasn't been paying her, just giving her a small allowance. That can't be legal. Is there anything that we can do to help her?"

Reid pressed his lips together into a thin line. Anger flashed in his eyes. "I'll look into it."

"Thanks, Reid, I'd appreciate it."

Dan leaned forward, looking down at the notepad in front of him. "In the meantime, let's review what we know. We have a credible threat against you, and now we have intel that whatever these guys are planning, they're targeting the Fourth of July."

"How patriotic." Mae's voice dripped with sarcasm. "So what's the plan?"

"You're going to a safe house," Jacob announced.

Mae reared back. "The hell I will. I can't just up and leave now. First, I have too much going on with the Fourth of July celebrations, and secondly, it would look awfully suspicious if I were to just up and disappear."

"She's right." Dan nodded.

"Okay then, how about this. It won't look suspicious if we're on our honeymoon."

Mae sighed and leaned over to whisper, "Stop it."

She turned to Dan and Reid and announced, "That's not an option."

Jacob glared at her for a moment. "Whatever we do, the most important thing is that we keep her safe."

Dan and Reid both nodded in agreement.

"I've been wondering, were you planning on including Isiah on this?" Reid asked. "It seems like now would be a good time."

"That's not my call to make," Jacob replied. "Dan, what do you want to do?"

"Bringing the sheriff in will help with security. With the station being in the same building as Mae's office, it will be easy to keep an eye on her office and anyone coming and going from there. And we know Isiah won't be a security risk with his background."

"It makes sense," Mae added.

"Do you want me to brief him?" Dan asked.

"No, I need to be the one to do it," Jacob replied.

Mae reached over and threaded her finders with Jacob's, feeling the tension radiating from him. Without realizing it, Jacob had created a new family, and as much as he tried to guard his heart, he loved Dax and Isiah.

"What about Dax?" she asked.

Jacob's mouth pressed into a thin line, and he shook his head.

"This doesn't go beyond the four of us and Isiah," Dan said. "Don't forget about Robert Ellis. He'll help anyway he can if we need it."

Dan looked at Reid. "I still can't believe your uncle is Robert Ellis."

"I'll take you out to meet him if you'd like," Reid offered.

Dan's eyes lit up. "I'd like that."

Mae gave Jacob's hand a squeeze and tipped her head in their direction.

He leaned over and whispered in her ear, "Don't meddle."

Dan turned to Jacob. "Have you had any contact with our informant?"

"No, he only reaches out if he has information to pass on or if there's something urgent."

"That's a good thing, right?" Mae asked.

"That's one way of looking at it. Or maybe things are too hot for him to make contact." Jacob sighed and shook his head. "I don't like this. We need more information."

The death grip he had on her hand showed just how worried he really was.

"There's nothing we can do, Jacob. We just have to be watchful and wait," Mae said.

"Hopefully, we'll get some kind of advanced warning, but we have to plan as if we won't," Dan said.

"I know you're not looking forward to telling Isiah," Mae said to Jacob. "Do you want me to be there?"

"No"—he exhaled—"I feel bad enough about Reid, but now I'll be putting Isiah into a position where he'll have to keep a secret from Dax too. I don't know if he'll forgive me for this when it's over."

Mae kissed his temple. "Of course he will. He might be mad for a while, but he'll forgive you. He loves you, Jacob. You're family."

He put his hand on her stomach. "You're my family."

Dan cleared his throat. "Y'all can canoodle later."

Reid choked on laugh and looked at Dan. "Canoodle?"

"You heard me."

Mae watched the two of them with growing amusement. It was clear there was some chemistry there.

Dan grew serious. "I'm going to have agents stationed throughout the town and the park on the Fourth. If anything happens, we'll be able to move in quickly."

"Let's hope that your person on the inside is wrong, and nothing will happen," Mae said.

Jacob reached for her hand, holding it in a tight grip, his face a mask of worry.

Once Dan and Reid left, Mae pulled him over to her sofa and pushed him down and settled into his lap.

"I know you're worried, but everyone is doing everything they can to make sure nothing will happen."

He nodded and pressed his forehead against hers. "I'm worried about what life will look like once we get beyond this."

"What do you mean?"

"All of the sudden, I have a future that I never thought I could have, with a family and friends, and it's still a little scary to me."

Mae's heart softened. "We are so alike. We both get scared when good things happen."

She pressed her lips to his. Jacob's large hand reached up to cup her face while his other arm wrapped around her, holding her gently. It started as a slow and gentle kiss that reassured them of their love for one another.

She shuddered when they finally broke apart.

"I love you so much, Mae. I don't know how I thought I could live without a lifetime of memories with you."

CHAPTER TWENTY-FOUR

SHADES OF pink and orange were just beginning to tinge the sky when Isiah came up to the roof. Jacob picked up the thermos sitting next to him and poured a cup of coffee, holding it out to his friend as he took his place next to him. He kept his flask in his pocket for now.

After discussing bringing Isiah into the loop with Dan, his superiors wanted to do it at the office in Jackson. Jacob refused—this conversation needed to happen with just the two of them. If he was going to lose a friend, he didn't want an audience.

They sipped their coffee in silence for a few minutes, watching the sky lighten and listening as the birds began their morning song.

He didn't beat around the bush. It wasn't his style, and Isiah wasn't going to put up with any bullshit. "I've been working as a handler for the FBI since I came to Colton. My assignment is embedded with a White supremacist organization. I've been cleared to share this information with you now because we've become aware of a direct threat to someone here in the community."

Isiah's jaw ticked. He looked down at the cup in his hands for a minute before setting it aside. He kept his eyes on the horizon when he spoke.

"I know you can't tell me who your contact is, but can I ask who the threat is against?"

"Mae Colton."

Isiah sucked in his breath and looked at Jacob. "Does she know?"

"She does."

"What intel can you share with me?"

"They are a threat to the whole community, but there is one person who they have threatened directly. There's been chatter about Mae. You've also been mentioned, but there's no specific threat right now. As soon as we have concrete proof of any plan, we'll move in."

"Why are you telling me now?"

Jacob exhaled. "I need as many assets as I can get to keep Mae safe."

Isaiah nodded. "That's understandable."

"There's something else I need you to know... Mae's pregnant."

Isiah looked at him with wide eyes.

"Yeah, I know"—he sighed—"it wasn't supposed to happen, but now that it has, I'm... happy."

"You always said you would never commit to someone, that you couldn't. Look, man, you're my friend, but I care about Mae, and I don't want to see her get hurt or abandoned."

Jacob fought back a flash of anger. "I would never abandon my child or Mae," he said between clenched teeth.

"I wasn't saying you would. We've been friends for a long time. I know what kind of man you are."

A small bit of tension eased out of Jacob's body.

"But I also know you," Isiah continued. "You won't be the father this baby needs or a good partner for Mae if you're always holding a part of yourself back. Did you think I didn't notice that's what you do? Come on, Jacob, we've been through a lot together. We're family, and I know you."

Jacob huffed a laugh. "Honestly? I'm scared shitless."

"Good, I'd be worried if you weren't."

"I hated keeping all this from you," he confessed.

"It couldn't have been easy for you. Can I ask, does Dax know?"

Isiah sighed when Jacob shook his head no.

"That's heavy."

"I just hope when all this comes out, he'll forgive me, that both of you will forgive me."

"You're family, and you're serving your country, There's nothing to forgive."

Jacob dropped his head and blew out a shaky breath. He didn't realize just how scared he was that he would lose Isiah's friendship. Mae was right, as much as he'd been trying to keep himself apart and protect his heart, he'd failed. Admitting he loved Mae opened a gateway that allowed him to admit that he loved his friends, and he couldn't imagine his life without them. He wanted the memories he'd made with Isiah and Dax. The good ones outweighed the bad.

"I feel better now that you know," he said quietly.

"Good. Now, what happens next?"

"The intel we have indicates the Fourth of July is the timeframe they're looking at."

"So we wait for another couple of weeks, set up surveillance, and hope these guys brag about their plans to somebody."

"Pretty much."

Isiah put his hand on Jacob's arm. "Hey, we've got this. We're going to do everything we can to keep Mae safe."

"Anything you can do to help persuade her to marry me?"

Isiah threw back his head and laughed. "I love you, man, but I'm not touching that with a ten-foot pole." He sobered. "I'll do some extra drive-bys at May's parents' place."

"I don't want to stretch you any thinner than you already are."

Isiah smiled. "Don't worry, I'm good."

Jacob squinted against the sudden burst of sunlight. He spied Mae making her way across the park, head held high, waving and calling out greetings to a group doing Tai Chi in the park. His heart squeezed until it was painful. The same truck Rhett had gotten into when he came to the hardware store came barreling down the street just as Mae was starting to cross to the town hall.

Both men jumped to their feet, watching from the rooftop. Mae jumped back onto the sidewalk just in time, yelling at the truck to slow down as it went past.

Isiah muttered an expletive under his breath.

Mae stood with her hands on her hips, watching the truck turn the corner and disappear before continuing on her way. Jacob rubbed his chest, trying to catch his breath.

"You okay?" Isiah asked.

Jacob forced himself to nod, not trusting his voice. He wasn't okay, not by a long shot. His heart still hammered in his chest, and every time he blinked, the scene he just witnessed replayed itself.

"I see everything as a threat. I've got to stay objective. Maybe that was just someone being reckless, but it could also be something more."

Isiah dropped his head and sighed. "Got it."

"I didn't want to burden you with this."

"I know," Isiah said quietly as he turned and walked away.

Jacob stayed on the roof as long as he could. He liked this view of his world; he could see the entire town square and assess any risks. He looked at his watch and muttered an expletive. He was going to be late opening the store if he didn't get a move on. Jacob made quick work of showering and changing before scooping Petunia up and heading to the hardware store. She was getting too big to fit in his pocket, but she seemed perfectly content to perch on his shoulder as he strode across the park. He scanned the area on high alert, watching for anything suspicious but only seeing familiar faces waving hello.

Dan was sitting on the bench outside waiting for Jacob when he arrived. It was nice to have someone to work with. When it was time for Dan to go back to Jackson, Jacob decided he'd place an ad at the trade school and hire another full-time employee to replace him. Petunia leaped from his shoulder and began her morning inspection of the store, batting at imaginary bugs and proceeding to engage in a battle with a display of feather dusters.

"Everything go okay with Isiah this morning?" Dan asked.

"Yeah, he's on board."

Jacob went on to tell Dan about the incident he'd witnessed with the truck earlier. "Maybe I'm being overly sensitive, looking for danger where there isn't any."

Managing to keep Mae safe without blowing his cover wasn't going to be easy. There were too many ways that this assignment could go wrong, and Jacob didn't see where he was going to be able to come away at the end without Mae being furious with him for keeping this secret, or him not being able to keep her safe. His heart and his conscious were twisted up in a tangle of knots that threatened to bind him until he couldn't do anything at all.

"Shit," Dan muttered. "I don't like this."

"I'd feel better if we could get an update from Rhett," Jacob said.

"Listen, I want to get these guys as much as you do. They're making threats about the Asian community too. More than one member of my family has said that they are really scared right now. It's not just being Asian; they feel vulnerable as immigrants." Dan shook his head. "I was born in this country, and people treat me like I don't belong here. My grandparents came here in the '70s and worked hard to build what they have. I hate the idea that they don't feel safe in their own homes because some jerk thinks the color of his skin gives him more rights than everybody else."

"Sometimes I feel like we're playing whack-a-mole with these guys. Just when you get rid of one group, another one springs up."

"I've gotta say, I appreciate having you working with us. For the first time since I started, I feel like we're starting to make some headway."

Jacob turned away and started straightening the already tidy countertop. Dan meant it as a compliment, but it made him uncomfortable. He was no hero. Heroes made sacrifices, and so far, Jacob had gained more than he'd given up coming to Colton.

The bell over the door opened, and Mae's father walked in.

"Morning, Jacob. I stopped by to—ouch! Son of a—"

"Sorry, Mr. Colton." Jacob rushed over to pluck Petunia off Joseph Colton's leg.

Joseph looked at Petunia and chuckled. "Well, what do we have here?" He reached out and scratched the kitten between her ears.

"This is Petunia."

Joseph chuckled at the name. "Well, it's nice to meet you, Petunia," he said, giving the little cat another pet. "Jacob, I came by to pick up the garden bench for Ella."

"Of course. Come on back to the workshop, and I'll grab it for you."

He'd been in some tense situations in the past, but he'd never had to face the father of the woman he'd gotten pregnant before. They were still trying to figure out when to tell Mae's parents about the baby. They were both nervous about their reaction. Jacob didn't want Joseph and Ella to think that he wasn't going to take responsibility. He wanted to be able to announce that they were engaged at the same time they told them about the baby, but Mae was still being stubborn.

"This is beautiful work, Jacob. Ella's going to love how you inlaid the magnolia in the top."

"Thank you, sir."

An awkward silence settled around them, only broken when Mae burst into the room.

"Jacob, I—" She shot Jacob a worried glance before coming over to give her dad a kiss on the cheek. "Hi, Dad."

"Well, this is a nice surprise. What brings you here?"

"Oh, I just wanted to make sure Jacob had ordered enough flags for the Fourth of July parade."

"Since you're here, can I buy you lunch at the Catfish?" her dad asked.

"Yeah, sure."

Joseph pulled out his wallet. "How much do I owe you?"

"Don't worry about it, Mr. Colton. You go ahead and take Mae to lunch. I'll bill you later."

Joseph slowly slid his wallet into his back pocket. "Make sure you do."

"Yes, sir."

"Come on, Dad, I'm starving." Mae led her dad away.

Jacob slumped against his workbench and exhaled, the solid wood of the bench the only thing keeping him up. Petunia sauntered in and sat at his feet, looking up at him.

"Don't look at me like that," he grumbled.

She sniffed and walked away with her tail twitching in the air.

THAT NIGHT, he sat snuggled on the couch with Mae tucked beside him. Mae had her computer on her lap, entering numbers in a spreadsheet, periodically muttering to herself and using some very unsavory language about the former town council. Finally, he couldn't stand it anymore. He put his book down and turned to Mae, gently pulling the laptop out of her hands and setting it aside.

"We need to talk."

Mae bit her lip. "You want to talk about telling my parents, don't you?"

"This isn't going to stay a secret for long, Pixie."

Mae pressed her hand to her stomach. "I know."

"I still think it would ease the blow if we also told them we were engaged."

Mae shook her head with a smile. "Nice try, but no. Can we just get through the Fourth of July celebrations first?"

He nuzzled her neck. "July fifth, we tell your folks."

"The fireworks are gonna start all over again, you know that, right?"

Jacob kissed along her jaw until his mouth captured hers. "I think the fireworks are starting right now," he growled, nipping at her lips.

MAE DREAMED she was sitting on her rock at Turtle Pond. The sun was shining, and she was lying on her back watching the clouds roll by. In the dream, her body had transformed; her belly was now round. When the baby kicked, she sighed, a small smile playing over her lips as she rubbed her stomach. The air became warm and heavy, filled with the minty, woody scent of eucalyptus.

"He's going to be a fine, strong boy."

Mae turned to see an old woman wearing a white dress, her black curly hair threaded with gray piled high on her head. She drifted toward Mae, standing over her with a smile filled with so much love she put her hand over her heart, afraid it couldn't contain the feeling that swept over her.

"You're Ada Mae," Mae said, gasping.

The smile faded from the woman's face, and her gaze became filled with sadness.

"I cannot stop what will happen, my child. You will not be alone. I will be with you even when you cannot see or hear me."

Mae struggled to stand, but the woman held out her hand to pull her up. The woman placed her hands on Mae's face, stroking her cheeks with her thumbs.

"I wish I could have come to you sooner, but I can only come when I am needed. You are the last of my daughters, my namesake. You have each honored my memory in your own way. Callie is forgiving, Josephine is protective, and you, my child, you are so strong." She pressed her forehead against Mae's. *"Your strength has not failed you before, and it will not fail you when the time comes."*

"What's going to happen, what am I going to be strong for?"

"That's my girl, always seeking, always questioning. I cannot tell you of things I am not able to see, but I see your strength and your love, and it will be enough."

Mae backed away, looking off into the distance, listening. Was that someone calling her name?

"Mae, Mae, wake up, sweetheart, you're dreaming."

Jacob was looking down at her, a concerned expression on his face when she opened her eyes.

"I was dreaming?" she murmured.

She could still smell Ada Mae, the scent of eucalyptus, the sunlight, the warmth of her hands when she held her face. Mae didn't realize she was crying until Jacob reached up to catch another tear before it fell.

"Was it a bad dream?"

"Yes"—Mae wrinkled her forehead—"no, it was… beautiful. She was beautiful."

He caressed her face and whispered, "No one is more beautiful than you are."

"She told me that no matter what happens, everything will be okay."

Jacob gathered her into his arms, holding her tightly. "Whoever you were dreaming about is right. I'm going to make sure of it."

JACOB HELD onto Mae long after she drifted back to sleep. She must have been dreaming about Ada Mae. If she told Mae she would be okay, did that mean he'd done enough to keep her safe? If he didn't, how could he live with the memories of his failure? He closed his eyes, conjuring up the image from his own dream. She appeared in his memory, hazy, her voice far off and distant. His heart thundered in his ears, drowning out what she was saying. All he could remember was the sadness in her eyes.

CHAPTER TWENTY-FIVE

PLANNING THE first big celebration the town had seen in years was a challenge. Doing it with an overprotective boyfriend was almost impossible. The closer they got to the Fourth of July celebrations, the more the whole town vibrated with excitement. Ms. June's weekly visits became daily visits as the holiday grew near, and Jacob started showing up at her office at five o'clock every day to take her home, where he insisted that she put her feet up while he made her dinner. Thankfully, now that her first trimester was almost over, Mae's appetite had returned with a vengeance.

Her days were filled with the mundane tasks of small-town politics, and that was fine with her because her nights were spent in Jacob's arms. He wasn't holding any part of himself back anymore, and she'd lay in bed with him, Petunia purring between them, while he told her stories about his parents and his childhood growing up on Staten Island.

They still argued, mainly about Jacob's overprotectiveness. Mae refused to hide, and he'd have her locked in the apartment all day if he had his way.

MAE WALKED through the park on the morning of the Fourth of July, admiring the results of the community working together to observe the nation's birthday.

She waved at her mom and the Jewels, who were hanging baskets overflowing with red geraniums, white petunias, and blue lobelia in every archway of the gazebo. Red, white, and blue mingled with the deep summer green of the trees and grass in every corner of the park. The whole town had been transformed, with every storefront, empty or occupied, displaying an American flag and the new Mississippi state flag. All except Walker's Pharmacy, which flew the old state flag that featured a Confederate flag as part of its design.

Mae sighed. She hadn't seen Emma lately, and she worried constantly about her friend.

Lawn chairs were already set up on the sidewalks for the parade later that afternoon. Nate and his new rookie firefighter were in front of the firehouse washing the firetruck, getting it ready to lead what would be the world's shortest parade route of one block. After a lot of debate, the planning committee decided that the parade would circle and make a second pass down the parade route. Her dad's convertible was already parked next to the firehouse. Mae was going to be part of the parade as well, sitting on the top of the backseat. She was going to feel silly sitting there waving to the crowd, but Presley was the one who pointed out that it was important for her to participate, and by being there, she was showing her support for the event. Presley even gave her a lesson in waving, teaching Mae the elbow, elbow, wrist, wrist, wrist technique. But Mae declined Presley's offer to borrow one of her tiaras. She did give in and agreed to wear a sash that said Mayor on it, mainly because Presley looked so crestfallen when she'd first dismissed the idea.

Jacob was furious that she was going to ride in the parade and be exposed the way she was, but Mae wasn't going to hide. She would be in the parade and at the park with the rest of the residents of Colton. Mae reminded Jacob that there was safety in numbers, and she would be surrounded by friends and family throughout the night.

She glanced to where Jacob balanced on a ladder, hanging a flag banner from one of the light poles in the park, with Dan helping him. He had closed the hardware store early that day to help. But Mae knew he really just wanted to keep an eye on her. She smiled and waved while they both looked at her, their faces clouded with tension and worry.

Presley came over with the bright pink glitter clipboard that had become a permanent appendage lately.

"I've got two buckets filled with little flags for the kids to wave during the parade. I'll hand those out when the kids are lined up and ready to go." Presley looked over her list again, chewing her lip. "I feel like I'm forgettin' something."

"You've done a great job, Presley. I'm sure everything is fine."

Mae was proud of how her new administrative assistant had dug into her job. Presley continued to work on changing for the better, going to the library and apologizing to Callie for the way Presley had treated her in the past and asking to join the planning committee for the Fourth of July celebrations. She ended up taking over most of the planning and did a wonderful job pulling together all of the small details.

Presley looked around the park. "It looks nice, doesn't it?"

"It really does."

"Are you gonna make your announcement tonight?" Presley asked in a hushed voice.

Mae nodded and smiled. "Yes, I'll be announcing that I'm going to run for mayor."

Presley had been bursting at the seams for Mae to make her announcement, and her brother Ashton was eager to make good on his offer to manage her campaign. Mae was just as excited as they were. No one else had thrown their hat in the ring yet, and that included Emma's dad. As far as Mae was concerned, Clyde Walker was all bluster and no bite.

Presley looked down at her clipboard again and gasped. "Oh no, I left the corsages for the veterans in the refrigerator at home."

Mae chuckled, watching Presley make a beeline across the park toward her car. A minute later, a yellow convertible sped past the park. Mae shook her head, hoping Isiah didn't catch Presley speeding again. Colton's sheriff was running out of patience with that girl.

Jacob appeared at her side. "You ready for lunch? You need to eat and rest. It's going to be a long night."

Mae opened her mouth to argue and closed it again. She was hungry, and she wouldn't mind a nap.

Back at her apartment, Jacob fed her and insisted she put her feet up for a while.

He perched next to her on the couch, tucking a blanket over her. He looked down at the baby blanket she'd almost finished knitting in a delicate lace pattern, fingering the blue yarn that started out being a sweater for him.

"What if it's a girl?" he asked.

Mae frowned. "Jacob Winters, are you going to be old-fashioned and insist on blue for boys and pink for girls?"

He kissed her temple. "Of course not, but I'm probably going to be one of those old-fashioned dads who's overprotective of his daughter."

"My dad can give you notes."

Jacob's expression grew pensive. "Are you nervous about telling them?"

"I am. Part of me thinks there's no reason to worry and they'll be fine, but there's just a little niggle of worry that they might let me down."

"Your parents love you unconditionally. They remind me of my parents. They'll be surprised, but they would never turn their back on you."

Mae yawned. "We'll tell them tomorrow at Sunday dinner."

Jacob gave her a gentle kiss. "Get some rest. We've got a long night ahead."

JACOB WAS reluctant to leave Mae. He would have been happier staying close by, but Isiah and Dan were waiting to do one more security check around the park before the festivities started. They were waiting outside on the sidewalk, and the three of them walked around the perimeter of the park looking for anything that might seem suspicious.

"I don't like that we haven't had any contact with our informant," Dan said.

They hadn't heard from Rhett since his last message, and Jacob was ready to crawl out of his skin with worry.

Dan looked around the park with a frown. "I asked for a dozen extra agents to be in the crowd, but I was only given four. They'll be arriving in the next hour or so, and I'll have them cover the perimeter of the park. They'll mingle with the rest of the townsfolk."

Jacob's phone pinged. He looked down and frowned.

"Is there a problem?" Isiah asked.

Jacob looked at Dan. "It's from our contact. It looks like coordinates."

"Can you send them to me?" Dan asked.

Jacob forwarded the message.

Reid walked over to where they were gathered. "Is there anything I can help with?"

"Can I use your computer?" Dan asked. "I want to look up maps of these coordinates."

"Sure." Reid jerked his head toward the Barton Building.

Isiah took his hat off and wiped the sweat from his brow. "I'll be glad when this day is over."

"If we make it through the day without an incident, it doesn't mean the threat is gone," Jacob said. "I won't rest easy until all these White supremacist groups are put out of business."

"Colton or Chicago, or anywhere else in this country, there's always going to be folks who think their rights are more important than others, that somehow, they are inherently superior for some reason or another. You can't fight them all, Jacob. But we can take care of our community."

Jacob folded his arms in front of him. "I hate it when you're calm and rational."

Isiah chuckled. "We always took turns. Remember that time we were on a mission in that desert hellhole that was supposed to pass for a town, and I went after that newbie for disrespecting the locals? You pulled me back and took him aside to talk to him about diplomacy."

Jacob nodded with a grim smile.

"I know you're worried, but we're going to do everything we can to make sure Mae is protected tonight."

"I appreciate it, and it's good to know you've got my six again."

Isiah said goodbye and headed toward his office in Town Hall. Jacob made one more circuit of the park before heading back toward the Barton Building. Dan and Reid met him halfway.

Dan pointed to a printout of a map. "The coordinates the informant sent are for a cabin about thirty miles out of town."

"It's in the middle of nowhere, so my guess is it's a hunting cabin," Reid added.

"I'm redirecting two of the agents that were supposed to come here to head out that way and check it out," Dan said.

Despite the late afternoon heat, Jacob felt chilled. Why was Rhett sending coordinates to a cabin in the middle of nowhere?

CHAPTER TWENTY-SIX

JACOB HAD Mae's hand clasped tightly in his as they made their way across the park. The parade had been a big success, and the children riding their trikes and bikes decorated with red, white, and blue streamers were adorable. The littlest ones were pulled in wagons while everyone cheered and waved as they went by. She did feel silly wearing a sash and riding in her dad's car, but the smiling faces and cheers from her family and friends warmed her heart.

Banners hung from the lampposts around the park with the American flag on one side and the new state flag on the other. Presley, Callie, Ashton, and the rest of the planning committee had done an amazing job pulling together the festivities. Nate and Mason waved from over at the firehouse, where they were huddled together going over their safety protocol with a few volunteers, who would be on standby while they set off the fireworks from the parking lot.

Jacob was waiting for her at the end of the parade route, his face pinched and drawn. Mae could tell he hated every minute she was so exposed. Her own concerns were swept away by her friends and neighbors waving and cheering for her as she passed.

Her mom came over and pulled her into a hug. "I am so proud of you, sweetheart." She turned to Jacob. "You did a wonderful job putting up all the bunting around the gazebo, thank you."

Jacob nodded. "It's my pleasure, ma'am."

The parade took place late in the day, and now the children were running around the park with sparklers, and everyone was getting ready for fireworks.

The Jewels waved from where they were setting up their lawn chairs. Mae watched with amusement as Uncle Robert tried to set up his chair a little closer to Ruby's, and Opal and Pearl shooed him away. Reid was talking to Dan over by one of the large oak trees. Mae smiled when Dan reached out and took Reid's hand in his for just a moment. She'd noticed the looks they'd shared more than once and hoped the spark between them would grow into something more. She laughed at herself;

pregnancy hormones had turned her into a mushy romantic. She wanted everyone to be as happy as she was.

"I better go find your father and make sure he's found us a good spot for the show," her mom said.

Jacob's hand briefly brushed against hers before he stepped back to stand in front of her. His eyes were filled with worry. "Are you feeling okay?"

"I'm fine, Jacob, really."

Mae's heart swelled, looking at the man in front of her. Jacob was going to be a wonderful dad, maybe a little too overprotective, but their child would never question they were unconditionally loved. As scared as she had been when she first found out she was pregnant, now that she had some time to come to terms with the expected turn her life had taken, she was excited for the future. Their future, as a family.

Dax waved over at them from the other side of the park, and they started to head in their direction when she tugged her hand out of Jacob's. "I'm just going to make a quick circuit around the park and make sure I've said hello to everyone and do a little campaigning."

Jacob frowned. "I need to be able to keep an eye on you."

"I'll stay in the park, I promise. You'll be able to see me the whole time. Go talk to Dax, and I'll meet you there in a minute."

Jacob exhaled and bowed his head. "Okay."

Mae gave him a quick kiss on the cheek and went over to say hello to a family sitting on a picnic blanket nearby.

Ms. June rushed over. "Oh, Mayor Colton, I'm so glad I found you. I need to talk to you for just a minute. I have some exciting news."

Turning to Ms. June with a forced smile, she asked, "What can I do for you?"

"There are two gentlemen here from *Southern Living* magazine, and they want to meet you. I met them last week at the farmers' market, and they were asking about you. They seemed very impressed with everything you've done as mayor."

Mae looked over at the two men wearing jeans with button-down shirts and blazers, standing next to a black SUV in front of Town Hall. They waved with friendly smiles.

She glanced back to where Jacob was talking to Callie and Dax. She and Jacob agreed that they wanted to share their news with them tonight. Some secrets didn't stay secret for long in a small town, and as she felt the little butterfly flutter in her belly, she knew that Callie and Dax might be surprised, but they would be happy for them. Her parents were another matter altogether, but she'd face that tomorrow. She was anxious to go to her friends, but Ms. June's eyes were filled with excitement, and Mae felt a tinge of guilt for not giving her as much attention as she had been. Plus, a feature on Colton in a national magazine would be good for the town.

"They said they're interested in doing a story about our town." The older woman was vibrating with eagerness.

"The Fourth of July isn't the best time for this, but okay. The fireworks are just about to start, so I'll only have time to introduce myself, and we can set up a time to meet in my office next week."

"Yes, yes, of course," Ms. June agreed as she practically dragged her to where the two men were waiting.

JACOB WAS listening to his friends while he watched Mae out of the corner of his eye.

"The thing is, it's the person you're least likely to suspect."

Jacob jerked, looking at Dax. "What did you just say?"

"I was just talking about Presley and saying sometimes you can be surprised at how they can change."

Jacob's heart started thundering in his chest. He looked over to where Ms. June was leading Mae away from the park. Fireworks from some of the surrounding farms lit the night sky. The air around him crackled and popped as his protective instincts went into overdrive.

"Jacob, what's wrong?"

Dax's voice faded away as he started making his way across the park. Dan was on the opposite corner talking to Reid. He caught Dan's eye and jerked his head in the direction he was headed. Dan nodded, circling from the other side. Tension coursed through his body as he calculated the distance to Mae.

MAE APPROACHED the two men with her hand outstretched. "Hi, I'm Mae Colton."

"Mayor Colton, it's a pleasure to meet you."

He was smiling, but it didn't reach his eyes. He grasped her hand and pulled her to his side, where she felt something pushed into her ribs.

"What are you doing? Why do you have a gun?" Ms. June asked, looking at the men wide-eyed.

"We don't need you anymore, old lady," the other man said, pushing Ms. June roughly to the ground and then kicking her in the ribs.

Mae watched in horror, her heart thundering in her chest as she was shoved into the car and a piece of duct tape was slapped over her mouth.

MIDWAY ACROSS the park, Dan caught up with Jacob. The sky was quickly growing dark around them. There were already some fireworks going off in the distance from other towns, filling the sky with flashes of color.

When he saw the top of Mae's head disappear behind the car, his heart seized.

"Run," he shouted at Dan.

He didn't question his instincts. He just knew that whatever was going on, they weren't going to make it in time. They came out of the park just in time to see the flash of taillights as a black SUV pulled away from the curb, revealing a figure lying motionless on the sidewalk.

Ms. June was clutching her side, trying to sit up.

"Those men told me they wanted to interview the mayor," she said, looking around in confusion. "I don't understand." She let out a low moan and coughed. "They said they were from *Southern Living*. They were going to do an article about the town."

Reid came running over and knelt by the older woman. "Take it easy, Ms. June. You've probably got a couple of broken ribs."

"It's okay, ma'am, we're going to get you some help. Just stay still," Dan added.

"They had a gun," she said, looking at Jacob, her eyes wide with fear.

An eerie silence punctuated with hushed whispers settled over the park as it became clear that something was wrong, and the crowd from the square began to surge forward.

Isiah pulled up in his cruiser and rolled down the window, shouting, "Get in, I've got gear in the back."

Jacob jumped in, and Isiah gunned the engine.

CHAPTER TWENTY-SEVEN

MAE'S EYES grew wide when she saw the man next to her in the back of the SUV. Rhett Colton looked at her with a frown. He turned her so her back was to him and grabbed her wrists, taping them before turning her back around and shoving her back in her seat. He reached down and tugged at the sleeve of his shirt, tapping the smartwatch on his wrist. He tilted his arm so that she could see its face.

Friend, not foe.

She gasped behind the tape on her mouth. Rhett Colton was the contact they had on the inside.

Her eyes flicked to the men sitting in the front of the car, and then back to Rhett. He looked straight ahead but tapped his watch again.

Stay calm. Do what I say, no matter what.

"She's gonna make a mighty fine ornament hangin' from a tree," one of the men in front sneered.

Mae began to shake, not from fear but anger. Her body tensed, ready to fight. Rhett's jaw ticked, but he remained silent while the two in the front discussed how great the party they were going to have that night would be. A party where they planned on killing her.

THE AIR was warm and tinged with the smell of wood burning from the bonfire that had been lit. Jacob wiped the sweat from his forehead and kept his weapon trained on the man who held Mae. Clyde Walker.

"Jacob, I know what you're thinking. I want to kill them too, but you have to stay focused on the mission," Isiah said quietly.

A few minutes ago, someone had slung a noose over a tree.

They were waiting in the woods just beyond the cabin Rhett had sent them the coordinates to, with the two agents Dan had sent ahead to check the place out.

When he took off after Mae and her kidnappers with Isiah, he looked at maps Dan had printed of the coordinates and found a shortcut. He gave Isiah directions while he updated Dan.

The shortcut would give them time, but not much.

They pulled off the road and into a cornfield where the car would be hidden. They worked quickly, putting on the tactical vests Isiah had stashed in his trunk. Jacob knew he could count on his friend to be prepared. As soon as they were geared up, they headed across the field and into the woods.

The SUV with Mae had pulled up just ten minutes after they arrived. But there were over twenty men at the cabin and only the four of them; they had to wait for backup.

If they had time.

Jacob's finger flexed on the trigger.

MAE FOUGHT to keep down the bile rising in her throat. She glanced down at Emma. Her lip was bleeding, and she had an ugly gash on her cheek. There was a man standing next to her holding a bullwhip.

"First, I'm gonna give your friend the whippin' she deserves, and then I'm gonna give you your lick for being a traitor to your race, little girl." Spittle flew from Clyde Walker's mouth as he sneered at his daughter. Her eyes darted toward Rhett, but he was looking dead ahead, his face a mask of grim determination.

Someone lit a string of firecrackers and threw them at Mae's feet.

JACOB GROWLED low in his throat, fighting to breathe when Mae jumped and almost lost her balance.

"Stay on mission," Isiah said quietly.

His jaw ticked. Isiah had seen him in battle enough times to know where his head was at in that moment. Isiah was right; Jacob wanted to kill every single man who pulled up to the cabin. His muscles burned from waiting, tense, ready to strike. He welcomed the pain. It gave him something to feed off of besides his anger.

They were having a goddamn tailgate party, laughing, drinking, and joking around. He clenched his hands at his side. He couldn't allow himself to touch his gun until it was time. The ability to wait patiently for his target to come into view had made him one of the best sharpshooters in his company. He'd spend hours, even days, patiently waiting for the right time to strike.

Not this time.

He wanted to pick off each and every man standing in the clearing outside of the cabin.

"They'll be pulling in any minute now," Dan said, looking down at the geo tracking software on his smartwatch. "Remember, we have to give the agents enough time to encircle the area before we move in."

Jacob nodded, his gaze never straying from the group at the cabin. He'd been analyzing every element of the place since they took up their position, studying every angle, the strengths and weaknesses.

"Take up position," Dan said quietly into the mic on the shoulder of the tactical vest he wore.

It felt strange to slip back into the gear he hadn't worn for two years now, like welcoming an old unwelcome friend.

They would go radio silent from there on out, communicating with hand signals and text. They weren't taking any chances.

A second later, Dan gave the signal. Jacob lowered his gun and started moving through the woods toward the group, his eyes locked on Mae.

He moved silently through the trees and bushes, the crackling from the bonfire disguising any twigs that snapped under his feet.

Dan put up his hand, signaling them to stop. He tapped into his smartwatch and then counted down three, two, one on his fingers.

"FBI, everybody freeze!" Agents charged from all sides of the clearing.

Jacob ran forward, his eyes on Mae, pushing past anyone in his path and ignoring the shouts and gunfire around him.

Rhett was trying to pull her out of the fray when Clyde Walker wrenched her out of his grasp. He had his arm around her neck and pointed his gun at the agents charging toward him.

"Everybody get back," he shouted, tightening his hold on Mae's neck.

Rhett had his gun drawn, trained on Clyde. He glanced at Jacob and lowered it just a fraction before stepping back.

"I'll kill her. Ain't nobody going to miss another uppity bitch," Clyde shouted.

Jacob pulled his gun away from his eye for a moment. Mae was looking straight at him. He would remember every second of this moment, but what would stay with him was the trust and love he saw in her eyes.

He lifted the gun back up, looking through the scope.

Jacob took a deep breath, allowing his body to relax and sink into that special place where everything was still for just a fraction of a second. A trickle of sweat started falling from his temple. The bullet hit Clyde square between the eyes. He was dead before he'd even realized he'd been shot. Emma screamed, burying her face in her hands. Clyde's knees buckled, and Mae wrenched herself out of his grasp before he could pull her down with him.

Jacob whirled around, his gun butted against his shoulder as he looked through the scope. A man lunged at Isiah from behind, and Jacob fired again. More agents burst into the clearing in front of the cabin with their guns drawn. A few of the men ran off into the woods. There was no need to chase them; they could run as far as they wanted, but they'd be caught eventually. The smell of gunfire mingled with the smoke from the bonfire. The men who had been celebrating just a minute earlier were quickly outnumbered. Some fell to their knees and surrendered. The few that were belligerent enough to keep fighting either lost their lives or were wounded enough to lose their ability to fight.

Jacob turned back toward the cabin and ran to Mae. Rhett was cutting the duct tape that bound her wrists, and as soon as her arms were free, she grabbed at the tape on her mouth, wincing as she peeled it away.

"Go slow, baby, it's gonna hurt," Jacob said.

As soon as the tape came off, she let out a sob and grabbed at his vest, burying her face in his chest. Jacob wrapped his arms around her, hugging her so tight he could feel her heartbeat in his chest, and that was the only thing that reassured him.

He grasped her face in his hands, scanning for any sign of injury. There was a little bit of blood splatter on her face, but nothing else he could see.

Someone shouted "Cut that goddamn noose down" in the background, and Jacob squeezed his eyes closed, pressing his forehead to hers.

"It's okay, you're okay," he said, trying to reassure himself as much as he was comforting her.

Rhett stood by, watching them anxiously. "I'm sorry I couldn't give you any more warning. I didn't know what was going to happen until they walked over to the car with Mae and Ms. June."

"You did fine. I knew you were prepared to do anything you could to keep her safe."

"Where's Emma?" Mae cried, frantically looking around the clearing.

"It's okay." Rhett pointed to where Emma was being wrapped in a blanket by one of the agents. "I'm sorry you had to go through this." Rhett shook his head. "I should have done more."

"Don't you dare. You've sacrificed two years of your life. Look around you, Rhett." Jacob pointed to where agents had rounded up everyone who was at the cabin and had them on their knees in zip-tie handcuffs. Some still looked belligerent, a few had their heads hung in defeat, and just a few were crying like babies. "You did this, Rhett. You should be proud."

Rhett swallowed and turned away. "Thanks," he muttered.

There were low grumbles of *traitor* and *Judas* as he walked through the men toward the mobile command vehicle that had arrived. A couple of the men cried out that it was all just a joke, and they weren't really planning on doing anything wrong.

Rhett stopped by one of them and leaned over him. "I've got enough evidence against you to make sure everyone knows you're no comedian."

The man shirked away, muttering about how Rhett was going to pay for betraying them.

"Poor Rhett, we all thought he was such a terrible person," Mae said.

Jacob wrapped his arm around Mae, pulling her close to his side. "He'll be all right."

Jacob wasn't sure if that was really true. He'd seen other men with that same haunted look in their eye, and they hadn't fared all that well.

He put his hand on Mae's stomach. "Come on, let's get you checked out and make sure you're okay."

Her eyes darted toward the dead man lying next to them.

Jacob stepped between Mae and the body. "Don't look. He's gone."

She nodded and let him guide her to the ambulance waiting nearby.

Mae rushed over and hugged Emma, who was being led to another ambulance.

"We'll make sure she's taken care of," Dan said, heading their way with another agent.

"I'm fine, Mae, honestly. Don't worry about me," Emma said. "Let them make sure you're okay."

"Oh, Em, I'm so sorry. Your dad—" Mae glanced over her shoulder and saw a sheet being draped over Clyde's body.

Emma's cornflower-blue eyes filled with tears. "I'm glad he's dead." She buried her face in her hands. "Maybe that makes me a terrible person, but I don't care."

Mae held Emma while she cried. "You aren't a terrible person, Em. You are one of the bravest people I know."

A paramedic came over. "Ma'am, I'm sorry, but we need to get you both checked out."

Mae gave her friend one more hug as she looked at her black-and-blue face with worry before she let Jacob guide her to another ambulance.

Jacob watched anxiously while Mae was getting her vitals checked. Mae looked okay, but he wasn't reassured that she or the baby hadn't been hurt.

"Jacob, we're going to need to get a statement from you," Dan said, walking up to the ambulance.

"Understood." He hesitated, unwilling to leave Mae's side.

Dan gave him a sympathetic look. "I can come by the apartment later, unless you're going to the hospital."

"No." Mae shook her head.

"Yes." Jacob gave her a stern look.

"Jacob, I'm fine. The baby is fine."

Dan did a double-take when she mentioned the baby. The blood drained from his face. "You are absolutely going to the hospital."

"Don't argue with us, Pixie. I need to make sure you're both okay."

Mae nodded, and he climbed into the ambulance with her. He held her hand, bringing it to his lips as the ambulance sped away.

Chapter Twenty-Eight

THE LAST thing Mae wanted to do was go to the hospital. She wanted to go home and wash away the sweat and stench and have Jacob hold her in his arms. But this was a small thing she could do to help take away the worry that clouded his face. Not that either of them would be able to wipe away the memory of what happened for a very long time. Mae reached up and grasped Jacob's hand. For him, the memory might fade, but it would never go away.

She looked at him with a new understanding. What just happened was exactly the kind of memory Jacob didn't want to have to live with, the ones he'd been avoiding trying to make by pushing her away.

"Jacob, look at me. We're going to be okay."

Jacob jerked his head in a nod. He remained silent and stern on the ride to the hospital. Now he'd taken up a position in the corner of the exam room with his arms folded, looking intimidating in his tactical gear.

"Jacob, stop looking so angry. You're scaring people," Mae said when the nurse gave him another nervous glance. It was bad enough that Dan had insisted on having an FBI agent with them, who was currently standing guard outside the door.

The adrenaline she'd been feeling began to fade away, and she shivered from the chill that swept through her body.

The nurse finished and let them know the doctor would be in shortly.

As soon they were alone, Mae held out her hand. "Come hold me, Jacob."

JACOB PEELED off his tactical vest and came over to sit on the edge of the bed, clasping Mae's hand in his. As scared as he had been for her safety, he was paralyzed with worry that the kidnapping had hurt her or the baby. Now that he'd embraced the idea of having a family, it was hard to breathe, worrying about everything that could go wrong.

"Jacob, look at me"—Mae reached up and cupped his cheek—"I'm fine, we're fine. Breathe before you pass out."

Jacob exhaled and kissed the top of her head. Just then the doctor came in, an older Black man with a salt-and-pepper beard and a wide smile.

"Well, let's see what we have here," he said, looking over Mae's chart.

Jacob got off the bed, but Mae clenched his hand tighter, keeping him at her side.

"Your vitals look good. Any cramping?"

"No, I feel fine," Mae said.

He listened to Mae's heart and shined a light into her eyes. All the stuff doctors usually do, that didn't seem like nearly enough to Jacob. The doctor went over to one of the built-in cabinets along one side of the room and pulled out something that looked like a tape recorder.

"Let's have a listen. Can you just pull your shirt up a bit, please?"

Mae pulled up her shirt, and the doctor pressed a little wand thingy against her stomach. He pressed a few buttons, and a second later Jacob heard his baby's heartbeat.

Mae looked up at him with a smile, her eyes filled with light and love. Her face blurred from behind a sheen of tears. He'd heard it at their last OB/GYN visit, but he didn't realize just how much he needed to hear it at that moment.

The doctor finished up and patted Mae's arm. "Everything looks just fine. I want you to follow up with your obstetrician in the morning, but I'll go ahead and release you tonight. I expect you two would like a little privacy." He turned to Jacob. "Mr. Winters, I'd like to thank you and the rest of the agents. I heard what you all did tonight. Thank you for your service."

Jacob could only nod, still unable to speak past the lump in his throat.

There was a commotion outside the doorway, and Mae's parents burst in.

"Oh, my baby," her mother cried, rushing to the side of the bed.

The doctor turned to Mae's father. "Mother and child are just fine. You have nothing to worry about."

Jacob's stomach sank when he saw the twin expressions of shock on Joseph's and Ella's faces.

SHIT.

Mae swallowed and gripped Jacob's hand.

"Child, what child?" her mom exclaimed, looking at Mae wide-eyed.

Mae gulped, seeing her dad looking at Jacob with narrowed eyes.

The doctor started to back out of the room. "I'll just let you all talk." He mouthed with a grimace, *Sorry* to her before he left.

Mae took a deep breath, but it didn't work. There was nothing she could do to brace herself for the next few minutes.

"I guess there's no need for me to make an announcement," she said with a weak laugh.

"No, there isn't," her dad said in a clipped voice, his eyes still on Jacob.

Her mom looked between her and Jacob. "Are you getting married?"

"Yes."

"No"—Mae shook her head—"we're still working things out."

Jacob cleared his throat. "I don't want to be rude or disrespectful, but maybe we could continue this conversation later. It's been a long night, and I'd really like to take Mae home so she can get some rest."

"She'll come home with us," her dad said.

Oh Lord, her dad and her boyfriend were about to get into a macho pissing match. She needed to nip this in the bud.

"I'm going home with Jacob. I want to sleep in my own bed tonight."

"Doesn't seem like you've been sleeping in your own bed for a while now," her dad muttered.

"Joseph," her mother exclaimed, "now is not the time."

Jacob sucked in a breath and moved even closer to her side.

"I'm going home with Jacob." Mae did her best to sound calm. "I know this news is a surprise. Believe me, no one was more surprised than the two of us." She drew in a breath. "When you can have a civil conversation, we'll talk, but right now…."

Her voice broke, and her mom went over to her dad and started pulling him out of the room. "Come on, Joseph. Mae went through a horrible ordeal, and the important thing is she's all right. Let's let her get some rest, and we can talk about this later."

Her dad sighed and came over to the bed and kissed the top of her head. "I didn't mean to be harsh with you, sweetheart. We were frantic when we heard what happened, and then… well"—his eyes darted toward Jacob—"we can talk about this later."

Mae buried her face in her hands as soon as her parents left the room. She hadn't known what to expect when she told her parents about the baby, but it wasn't this. Her dad's comment about where she'd been sleeping hurt.

"Maybe you should go with them," Jacob said quietly.

"No, I want to be with you… I need to be with you."

Jacob sat on the edge of the bed with an arm around her. "I'm so sorry, Pixie."

"It's not your fault." She sniffed and wiped her eyes. "Well, it's kind of your fault."

"Don't joke about this. I hate that your parents are upset with you because of me."

"They aren't. My parents love me no matter what."

Even though she said it with confidence, there was a small kernel of worry in the back of Mae's mind. But she was confident in one thing. She loved Jacob. Their lives were connected now, and the only thing that mattered was that they worked together to raise their child.

Dan was in the waiting room with Reid when they finally released her. The two were sitting in a corner holding hands and talking quietly. They jumped up and came forward when she walked out with Jacob, the agent who had been guarding their room following behind.

"Thanks, Steve." Dan nodded to the agent. He turned to Jacob. "There'll be another agent at your apartment. You'll have security for the next few days, just as a precaution. I'm sorry for what you had to go through, Mae, but tonight was a success. We made some significant arrests, and with Rhett's help, we have enough evidence to put down at least three groups that have been operating in the area, and possibly more."

"What about Emma. Is she okay?" Mae asked.

Reid nodded. "Callie and Dax took her home with them."

"We're going to provide her with security as well. She's been incredibly helpful in our investigation. It won't be easy for Emma to testify about what happened. You're going to have to testify as well, both of you," Dan added.

Jacob looked at Reid. "How upset was Dax?"

"He's pretty pissed at both of us, but he understands."

"He loves you both. He's going to forgive you for keeping this from him," Mae said.

"Are you heading back to Jackson?" Jacob asked Dan.

Dan and Reid exchanged a look. "Actually, I'm going to stay in Colton. Jackson is just a couple of hours away, and I can work remote."

Mae grinned. "That's great news."

"And I'm going to stay on at the county prosecutor's office for a while longer while they rebuild their staff," Reid said.

"Thank you, both of you. Tonight could have ended very differently without both of you," Jacob said in a gruff voice.

"Take your family home. We can finish up any paperwork and interviews tomorrow," Dan said to Jacob when Mae stifled a yawn.

JACOB MANAGED to keep it together while Mae was checked out, they talked to Dan and Reid, and he drove them home. But as soon as they walked into his apartment, he sank to his knees and pressed his head to Mae's stomach and wept.

"Sweetheart, it's okay," Mae said, stroking his hair.

Eventually he found the strength to stand up and wrap her in his arms. "I was so scared," he confessed.

"So was I," she admitted.

He cupped her face with his hands, kissing her tenderly. "You're going to have to bear with me. It's going to take me a while to reassure myself that you're really all right."

"Take all the time you need. I'm not going anywhere."

He nodded and pressed his forehead against hers. Their moment ended when there was a loud *meow*, and they both looked down to see a very angry-looking Petunia sitting at their feet.

"Sorry, kiddo, you must be hungry."

He'd left some extra food out for her when he'd left that day, but now it was almost morning and well past her feeding time.

"What about you? You must be starving by now. You didn't eat anything other than a granola bar at the hospital," he said to Mae.

She nodded and yawned.

Jacob scooped up Petunia and put his arm around Mae's shoulder. "Let's get my family fed."

He fed Petunia and made breakfast while Mae showered and changed. As soon as she finished eating, Jacob scooped Mae up and tucked her into bed. She was asleep before her head hit the pillow.

The hot spray from the shower washed over him. The water was on the hottest setting, and it still wasn't warm enough. He braced himself against the wall and let the fear and tension flow out of him. He stayed in the shower until the water began to cool and then dragged himself into bed as streaks of purple began to appear in the sky.

Mae sighed and snuggled up next to him. He took a deep breath, inhaling the scent of his shampoo against her skin. The aroma of eucalyptus surrounded him as his eyes drifted closed.

"*I wanted to come one last time.*" Ada Mae smiled down at him from the foot of his bed. "*Your memory is long, and you have such a full life of them ahead.*" She moved over to the side of the bed and reached out to briefly cup Mae's cheek. "*Take care of my namesake. Be happy*"— she looked at Jacob—"*and remember everything.*"

Chapter Twenty-Nine

THE DAYS following the kidnapping attempt were chaotic and stressful. The evidence Rhett had been collecting for the past two years would make sure the men apprehended the night Mae was kidnapped would stay behind bars for a very long time.

Mae's parents were slowly coming around to the idea of becoming grandparents. Her mom was a little more enthusiastic about the idea than her dad, but they were both supportive of Mae, and that's all that mattered to Jacob. The only wrinkle in their lives was Mae's continued refusal to marry him.

They'd been arguing for months when Mae finally decided she was ready. It wasn't one particular thing that Jacob said or did. It was a perfectly still and calm morning, when they were sitting on the roof deck, watching the town slowly come to life. Maybe that's why she proposed... because life seemed settled in that moment.

She set down her cup of tea and stood up. Or at least tried to. Jacob jumped up to help her. She stood there for a minute, her hands in his, looking into those blue eyes that could be as stormy as the seas and then as calm as the waters in the pond, in each case fathomless in the love she saw in them.

His eyes bulged when she went down on one knee. "Are you having a contraction?"

"No, I'm fixin' to propose," Mae said between clenched teeth.

"You're not supposed to propose. I am."

"Says who? I can propose if I want to, and I've decided I want to." She took his hand in hers. "Jacob Winters, will you do me the honor—"

"Absolutely not," he said loud enough to startle a group of starlings into flight. They argued about it until Jacob ended up on a knee with her. They argued some more about who was going to propose to whom until they finally ended up kissing just to shut each other up. They were on their knees facing each other when Mae put her hands in his.

Mae took a deep breath and smiled. "Jacob, I'd like to marry you and spend every day making a new memory with you. Will you please marry me?"

Jacob shook his head, his eyes shining with love and mirth. "Mae, will you do me the honor of marrying me? I know a grumpy lumberjack isn't what you had in mind for a life partner, but I promise I'll give you at least one happy memory every day."

Mae threw her arms around Jacob's neck. "A grumpy lumberjack is exactly what I need to make me happy," she whispered against his lips. "I don't have a ring." She sat on Jacob's lap after another toe-curling kiss.

"Well, I do. I just don't have it with me."

"I don't want a fancy wedding, but I do want to get married before the baby is born."

"That doesn't give us much time."

"As long as you're standing in the gazebo with me, and we have Judge Beaumont and Rabbi Singer to officiate, that's all I need."

Jacob drew back. "Rabbi Singer?"

"He's the rabbi at the reform synagogue in Greenwood. I've kind of been meeting with him." She linked her hands with his. "I know you're not religious, but your Judaism is a part of who you are. I want our children to have that connection too."

"I... I don't know what to say," Jacob said, tears hovering at the corners of his eyes.

"Say yes, you'll marry me, and if we plan it right, we might just have a Hanukkah wedding."

"Yes, Pixie, I'll marry you. But there's just one thing. I've got to get your parents' blessing first."

"You know I'm a grown independent woman, and I think those old traditions are unnecessary."

"I do too, but I respect your parents, and if we aren't going to do anything else by the book, I want to do this one thing. My dad"—his voice broke—"I remember my dad telling me it was a tradition I should always respect."

"I CAN'T give you my blessing. I'm sorry, but I just can't. He's not right for you."

Mae sat on the stool in her parents' garage, watching her dad clean off his wrench in shock. When she had asked how it went when Jacob came back from her parents' house that morning, she was met with grim silence and Jacob looking visibly shaken. His voice was gruff when he broke the news to her that her dad had said no. After reassuring Jacob that she was going to marry him no matter what, Mae jumped in her car and drove straight over to her parents' house.

Her mom locked eyes with her when Mae burst through the back door. She tried to reach out for Mae as she continued on her path to the garage.

"I'm sorry, baby," she called out, her voice low and shaky.

Mae held her hand up and walked past her and out to her father's workshop. She'd deal with her mom later. Right now, she needed her dad to look her in the eye and explain why he wasn't giving his blessing.

Now her dad stood in front of her, his eyes on the polishing cloth in his hand, not on her.

"In what way? How is he not right for me?" Mae yelled, her voice shaking.

"Jacob's a good man, and I'll always be thankful to him for protecting you and our community, but you can do better, sweetheart."

"Who would be better?"

"A man with a college degree, someone who's a professional, and I have to say it, but I'd be happier if you married a Black man."

Mae sucked in a breath.

"Because that's worked out so well for my sister, hasn't it?" she spat out.

Her dad pressed his lips together.

"It's—"

Mae held her hand up. "Don't you dare say it's different. I can't believe you're being so biased."

Her dad shook his head. "I am not."

"Why because you're Black and Jacob's White? You're being just as biased against Jacob as people have been against you. You say you want what's best for me, and that's Jacob. He loves me and respects me. Everybody around here assumes they know what my hopes and dreams are, but you know what? Jacob's the only one who ever asked. And when I told him, he listened."

"I appreciate that, but he's White and Jewish, and—"

"Don't you dare." Mae jumped off the stool and poked her dad in the chest. "Don't you dare bring up Jacob's religion."

Joseph sighed. "I'm just trying to say the two of you are too different. You come from different cultures and traditions. He won't be able to understand and support you the way someone who comes from the same background as you would."

"That is the biggest load of horseshit I have ever heard," Mae sputtered.

"I'm sorry, sweetheart, but this is how I feel."

"So it's okay for Callie to marry Dax, but I can't marry Jacob?"

"It's different. Callie's mixed."

"And I'm what… pure? Come on, Dad, you're better than this."

She stared at her dad. He'd let her down. It hurt. A lot.

"I'm going to marry Jacob, Dad, we're going to have a baby, and that baby will be a part of both of us. Are you only going to love the part from me?"

Her father's mouth opened and closed. "Of course not. We're gonna love and spoil that child to death."

Mae shook her head sadly. "Not if you can't respect his father. I would never keep you from your grandchild, but…." She drew in a deep breath. "There will be boundaries if you can't love all the parts that make our child a whole."

She put a trembling hand on her stomach. "I'm gonna be a Colton bride, Dad. It would be nice if you and Mom were there to see us take our vows, to—" She choked back a sob. "—to walk me down the aisle. I'll be sad if you aren't there, but I'll be okay, because I'll have the man that I love with my whole heart at my side."

"Mae, honey, wait," her father called out as she walked as quickly as she could out of his workshop.

She got into her Jeep, wiping tears from her eyes as she pulled out of the driveway. Instead of going home, she went to Callie and Dax's house.

"Mae, what's wrong?" Callie asked when she opened the door.

"Can we talk?"

"Of course. You want to sit out here?" Callie gestured to the porch swing.

Mae nodded.

"You take a seat. I'll be right back."

She sat down and pushed against the floorboards with her toe, setting the swing into motion.

Callie returned a minute later with a box of tissues and a glass of water, setting them down on the porch railing behind them.

"I thought we might need these."

Callie's understanding of what she was going to need burst the dam, and Mae started to cry.

"Oh, honey, what happened?"

"My d-dad." Through her tears, Mae told Callie about her conversation with her father.

"I am so sorry, Mae. I wish you didn't have to go through this," Callie said when Mae finished.

"You don't seem so upset."

Callie sighed. "I've learned from my experience growing up as a biracial child. People are surprising. Sometimes the ones you think won't have a problem with you or your parents do. I'm disappointed in your dad, but I also understand."

"What do you mean?"

"Some people think that if you're in a relationship with a White person, or biracial, that somehow you're giving up your Blackness."

Mae drew back. "That's ridiculous."

"No"—Callie shook her head—"it's just a different way of thinking. You may not like it. I certainly don't like what he said, but you can't dismiss your dad's feelings."

Mae rubbed her belly. "I always thought he'd walk me down the aisle."

Callie gave her a sympathetic smile. "I know, and I think he will. You just have to give him some time. Give him some space to work through his feelings. He loves you, Mae. He'll come around."

"You're right, I know that. I'm just so… angry, and I feel… betrayed, I guess."

"It's a hard thing when your parents let you down."

"What if he doesn't change his mind?"

"Then I'll be right there by your side. Or Uncle Robert, or Nate. People will fight over the honor, Mae. You should know by now how many people are fighting for you, rooting for you."

Mae nodded. "Would you walk with me if my dad doesn't and stand up with me as my maid of honor?"

Callie gave her arm a squeeze. "Of course, I will."

"We're getting married, and I'm having a baby. Everything is changing." She blinked back another round of tears. "It's all good. Good, but scary at the same time. And I'm feeling just a bit overwhelmed."

"I'd be worried if you didn't feel that way."

"This roller-coaster ride isn't going to end, is it?"

Callie laughed softly. "No, I don't think so. I think this is what living a full life is supposed to look like."

"Callie, I'm going to have a baby, and I'm getting married, two things I never thought I wanted. But if it's with Jacob, I want it all."

Mae heard a sniff and looked over to see Callie pulling a tissue out of the box and dabbing at her eyes.

"Why are you crying?" she asked.

"Because I'm happy, I'm happy for you, for us. Our kids are going to grow up together, and we'll get to live here and be neighbors, friends and family, all here in this place we both love, that we fought so hard to make better. I think my grandpa and grandma would be so proud of us right now."

Mae's eyes grew wide. "Are you...?" She pointed at Callie's stomach.

"No, not yet," she answered with just a tinge of sadness in her voice. "But we just started trying, so there's time."

Mae grasped her best friend's hand.

"Do... do you think Ada Mae is proud of us?" Mae asked.

Callie gasped. "Did you dream about her?"

Mae smiled and nodded. "Eucalyptus."

"I think she's happy now and can finally rest."

"She said you, Jo, and I were the daughters of her hopes and dreams. I like that."

"That's beautiful," Callie said in a teary voice.

They sat with their arms around each other, letting go of the past to embrace their futures. They weren't the same little girls who made fairy mud pies and fought off imaginary foes and real bullies.

Eventually, the shadows grew long, and the air cooled.

"I should head home. Jacob's going to be worried."

"I don't think he's too worried." Callie smiled and pointed to where Jacob was sitting against a large oak tree down the road reading a book.

"He called to see if you were here and walked over. He's been waiting for you."

Mae turned and gave Callie a hug. "Thank you, and I love you."

"I love you too."

Jacob didn't look up until she was standing in front of him. He closed the copy of *What to Expect When You're Expecting* he had been reading and stood up.

"You ready to go home?"

Mae nodded. Standing on tiptoes, she wound her arms around his neck and gave him a kiss. They walked arm in arm to her car and waved goodbye to Callie and Dax, who had come out to join his wife on the porch swing.

Jacob kept one hand on the steering wheel and grasped her hand with the other on the drive back. "You okay?"

"Yes, and no." She sighed. "I'm so disappointed in my dad."

"He's human and entitled to his feelings."

"Can we just go to Vegas?" Mae asked.

They pulled up in front of the Barton Building. When they got out, Jacob took her hand and guided her into the park and to the gazebo. He sat down on the top step and pulled her into his lap.

"We're not going to Vegas," he said, kissing her temple. "Your dad will come around, and if you want to postpone the wedding, I'll wait as long as you want."

Mae took Jacob's hand and placed it on her belly, covering it with hers. "No, I don't want to wait. Not just because of the baby. I'm ready to start my life with you. For the first time in a long time, I'm not stressed out about the future, about what people expect me to do. I don't know if I'll get re-elected or what will happen with my dad, but I know that if I have you by my side as my partner, I can face whatever comes next."

"I love you," Jacob said, nuzzling her ear.

"I love you too."

They sat watching the stars together for a while until Jacob sighed and asked, "Did you talk to your mom?"

"Honestly, I was so mad at my dad I didn't stop to talk to her."

"Maybe you should?"

"You're right, I should. I'm afraid she's going to object too."

"Do you want me to come with you?"

"Let me think about it. I know I need to do it; I just need some time."

IT TURNED out the decision was made for her when her mom walked into her office the next morning.

"Sweetheart, can we talk?"

"Um, sure. I was going to come talk to you, I just… I wasn't ready yet," she admitted.

Her mom closed the door and sat down across from her, folding her hands in her lap. Mae watched her mother, looking for any sign that might tell her how this conversation was going to go.

Ella sighed. "Yesterday was… well, it wasn't how I hoped things would go. I have to admit, Jacob Winters isn't the kind of man I dreamed of for you"—she held up her hand when Mae objected—"but it's not about what I want, it's about your dreams, and it's clear that Jacob loves you, and you love him.

"You've always been so self-assured and confident, but I've been watching you with Jacob. If you said you wanted to be an astronaut, he'd have you enrolled in space camp by the end of the day." She shook her head and smiled. "You're both stubborn and passionate, but the two of you support each other in a way that's… well it's something special. It's the kind of love that if you're lucky enough to find it, you should hold on to it, cherish it."

Tears were streaming down Mae's face by the time her mom finished speaking. She got up and threw her arms around her. "Thank you. I wish Dad understood the way you do."

"Oh, honey, he does. He's just having a hard time letting go of what he thought your life was going to be. He's scared."

"That's what Callie said." Mae sniffed.

"She's right."

"So what do I do?"

Her mom patted her cheek. "You let me deal with your dad."

Mae frowned. "I don't want you to force him to do something he doesn't want to."

"I won't do anything like that. Joseph just needs a little time and some perspective to come around. He's stubborn like his youngest daughter. You keep planning your wedding and"—her voice broke—

"and if you'd like some help, I promise not to try to force my own vision on you."

Mae hugged her mom again. "Oh, Mom, I love you."

"I love you too, I love both of you, I mean, all three of you." She laughed, putting her hand on Mae's belly.

CHAPTER THIRTY

JOSEPH COLTON could be a stubborn man. It was a trait he shared with his daughter. She was surprised that it was less than a week before her dad showed up on her doorstep.

"May I come in?" he asked when Mae opened the door.

"Of course."

Jacob got up from the couch and extended his hand. "It's nice to see you, sir. Please, sit down."

Of course, the minute he sat down in the chair on the other side of the sofa, Petunia came over to investigate their visitor, sniffing around his feet for a minute before she jumped into his lap and started kneading on his thigh. Mae bit back a smile, watching her dad bite his lip, enduring the discomfort the little cat caused.

"Would you like me to leave?" Jacob asked.

"No," Mae's father said, "please sit down. I'd like to talk to both of you."

They sat together on the sofa. Mae took Jacob's hand in hers and held her breath, her body split between hope and worry about what her father was going to say.

"Jacob, I owe you an apology. You too, sweet pea. I just"—he shook his head—"it's a hard day when a father realizes that his little girl has grown beyond childhood. Mae's sister married and moved out before we ever had a chance to know her as a woman, but with Mae, we've been blessed to see her mature and grow. I was selfish in not wanting to give that up, to let another man stand by her side. The things I said…. I don't care that you're White or what your religion is, son. I know Mae won't lose any of her identity and her history marrying you. I… I was looking for any excuse not to give her up."

"You aren't losing me, Dad," Mae said.

Joseph patted her arm. "I know that, but it feels like I am."

"I don't know if this helps, but Mae and I have been talking," Jacob began. "Your connection and history in this town is important. Mae's going to take my name when we get married, and I'm going to take hers. Winters-Colton seemed like the right thing to do."

Her dad smiled. "Thank you, son."

"Dad, promise me you aren't doing this because Mom made you."

"Well, your mother did threaten to make me move into the garden shed," Joseph said with a wry smile, "but no, it was Robert Ellis, Nate, Sam, and the rest of the guys at the barbershop who talked some sense into me. You have a lot of friends around here, Jacob."

Mae leaned over and whispered to Jacob, "Remind me to give the barbershop some kind of mayoral award."

He chuckled, kissed her cheek, and whispered back, "I'll carve the plaque."

Joseph carefully set Petunia down and got up. "Look, I'm not going to lie and say this is easy for me, but I'm going to try, and I hope you will give me a chance to keep talking with you and work through my feelings." He chuckled. "I mean, if you're willing to give Presley Beaumont a second chance, I hope you can give me one too. You two are going to have your hands full. I hope when the baby comes, you'll let your mom and me help out." He hesitated for a moment before adding, "It would mean a lot to us if you'd keep coming for Sunday dinners."

Mae got up and threw her arms around her dad's neck. "Of course we will." She sniffed and buried her face in her dad's chest. "I love you, Dad."

He patted her back. "I love you too, baby girl."

Jacob offered his outstretched hand. A lump formed in Mae's throat when her dad took Jacob's hand and pulled him into a hug, slapping him on the back.

MAE LIKED to think Ada Mae planned a perfect early spring day for their wedding. Unfortunately, she hadn't planned on being in her final month of pregnancy and as big as a house on her wedding day. She sighed and ran her hands over the cream chiffon covering her belly.

"You look so beautiful," Callie said, handing her bouquet of lily of the valley, pale pink peonies, and eucalyptus.

She leaned over, ignoring the slight cramp in her side, and gave her friend a peck on the cheek. "Thank you."

Callie's baby bump was still small enough that the pale pink chiffon Grecian-style dress hid it.

Turning to the mirror for one last look, Mae was surprised by what she saw. She'd been worried about finding a dress, but Chloe reached out to one of her friends in LA who worked as a costumer for a historical TV drama, and she came through with an absolutely beautiful empire-waist gown in layers of fabric that draped over her body. The deep vee neckline showed off the swell of her breasts, and the sheer sleeves reached just above her elbows. It was simple, without any adornment other than the tiny buttons on the back of the bodice, but that's what made it beautiful. Her mom gave her a pair of pearl earrings with a tiny diamond stud at the top that had belonged to her grandmother to complete her outfit.

Her father came into her childhood bedroom, his gaze softening and his eyes becoming bright. "Your mother's on her way. Are you ready, baby girl?" he asked in a gruff voice.

She turned to him with a smile. "I'm as ready as I'll ever be. I'm not sure there's anything else we can do to make this"—she waved at her stomach—"look bridal."

He came forward and took her hands in his. "You look beautiful. No father could be prouder of a daughter than I am of you."

"Please don't," she choked out. "Presley will absolutely have my hide if I ruin my makeup."

Her father chuckled and tucked her arm around his. "Let's get you married. I don't know who's more anxious, the groom or your mother, but one of them is going to bust a gut if we don't get this show on the road."

Mae laughed as they made their way out to her father's Mustang that had been decorated with a white bow and flowers tied to the antenna. Her father had wrangled one of the high school kids to play chauffeur, and he stood by the car beaming at them as they came out of the house.

"It's a fine day for a wedding, Mayor Colton," he said, opening the door with a flourish.

Callie sat in the front while Mae rode with her father in the back seat on the short ride from her parents' house to the park. She clutched her dad's hand, nervousness sending another twinge of pain across her back. She'd woken up that morning with a low ache in her back from sleeping on her old mattress at her parents' house. Mae would have been much happier in the bed she shared with Jacob, but spending the night back home and not seeing the groom the night before the wedding was the one nod to tradition her mother requested.

When they arrived at the park, Mae wasn't quite able to exit the car as gracefully as she'd gotten into it, but with her dad's powerful hands to lift her up, she managed while looking somewhat dignified.

"Thank you, Daddy," she said, blowing out a shaky breath.

"Ready?" Callie asked, handing Mae her bouquet.

The funny thing was, she was ready —for the wedding, the baby, all of it. She looked toward the gazebo and saw Jacob standing with Dax, Isiah, Dan, his friend Marcus, and Uncle Robert. Jo, Emma, Chloe, and Presley stood on her side. Not once in all the wedding planning did her parents suggest that she ask her sister to stand up with her. Of course, Mae invited her sister, but predictably, she had an excuse for why she couldn't come. But Jacob's high school football coach and his wife made the trip, and it made her so happy to have the people he considered family there.

The ladies of the Colton garden club had outdone themselves, decorating the gazebo with tall pillars that Jacob made with large baskets on top that overflowed with pink peonies, white roses, and hydrangea. Every garden in town had been plucked clean. Eucalyptus was tucked in among the flowers, and ivy cascaded over the sides.

Her smile widened, seeing Jacob in his dark blue suit, the same color as his eyes. The men were all wearing dark pink ties, a slightly darker shade of pink than her bridesmaids wore.

Mae's eyes locked with Jacob's, and the rest of the world faded away; it was just the two of them.

The youngest of the Jewels, Ruby, stepped up and sang "Lovely Day" by Bill Withers.

Callie started down the path to the gazebo.

Her father patted her hand. "Let's go."

Walking up the brick path was the easy part. The gazebo stairs were a bit trickier, with her belly that seemed to decide at that moment to get even bigger.

But Jacob was waiting for her at the top. One look at the smile on his face and the love in his eyes, and she would have waddled up all the stairs of the capitol in Washington to get to the man she loved.

Unfortunately, at that moment their baby had a different opinion about the stairs. Her dad put her hand in Jacob's, and his mouth fell open when it sounded like someone had just thrown a pot of water to the floor. He looked down at the puddle of water at Mae's feet and then to her face with wide eyes. She didn't have time to be surprised, because a second later she was hit with a contraction that buckled her knees.

"This is not happening," she moaned as her body tensed with another wave of pain.

The town's new doctor, Dylan Colton, rushed to her side. "Let's get you to the clinic."

"Nope"—she grunted—"I'm afraid I'm not going to make it that far."

"Okay, then let's get you comfortable." Dylan called over his shoulder, "Ruby, I need my bag, clean sheets, and towels now."

Ruby and her sisters set off toward the clinic. Mae had no idea they were capable of running that fast.

"Someone... do... we need..." Jacob was spinning in a circle, running his hands through his hair, gaping like a fish.

Someone came up and spread out a blanket. "Here, I had this in my car."

Mae sank down as another contraction hit. "They're coming so quickly." She panted as wave after wave of pain crashed over her. A contraction would stop, and before she could catch her breath, another one would start.

"Everybody get back!" Jacob roared, running back and forth and waving his arms wildly in front of their guests.

"Jacob. Isaac. Winters," Mae said, blowing out a breath between each name. "Get your ass over here right now."

Jacob immediately stood at attention and came to her side, dropping to one knee.

"You would have made one hell of a drill sergeant." Uncle Robert chuckled.

Mae shot him a look that had him snapping his mouth shut and backing away.

"I'm just going to see how far along you are," Dylan said, gently lifting her dress. His eyes grew wide. "Good Lord, you're fully dilated."

She held her hand out to Jacob, and he grasped it to his chest, holding on for dear life.

"Judge Beaumont, Rabbi Singer, you have exactly one minute each to do what you need to do to get us married," Mae called out.

The two men knelt down on the either side of her while her parents hovered behind them.

"Dearly beloved… aww hell," Judge Beaumont snapped the Bible shut. "Do you take her?" He pointed at Jacob.

"Yes."

"And do you take him?"

"Yes," Mae half yelled, half screamed.

"Then as far as I'm concerned, y'all are married." He turned to Rabbi Singer. "You're up."

The rabbi took everyone by surprise when he began to recite the Sheva Brachot instead of singing the seven wedding blessings; he recited them as if he were auctioning off a prize bull at the weekly livestock auction in Greenwood. He got through all seven blessings in under a minute. As soon as the rabbi finished, both men moved out of the way.

Nate had taken off for the firehouse and returned with his new rookie in the brand-new ambulance the town had just received. Dylan called out to them, "We're not going to be able to transport until after the baby's born."

"Break the glass, Jacob," she said, blowing out short puffs of air.

"It doesn't matter. We'll do it later."

Mae shook her head, panting. "We didn't get to jump the broom. At least you can break the glass. It's tradition, Jacob."

He gave her a gentle kiss on the shoulder as Dax came forward and placed a glass wrapped in a handkerchief Callie had embroidered for the occasion.

Jacob stood up just long enough to stomp on the glass and then dropped back down to her side. Just in time for another contraction. Just like his mama, this baby was in a hurry to get where it was going. The Jewels returned, and Ruby was in full nurse mode, getting blankets and towels under her and helping hand Dylan the supplies he needed. Mae squeezed her eyes shut, partly from the pain and partly from seeing the bloody mess her wedding dress had become.

Jacob winced and wiped the sweat from her forehead when she let out another scream.

"It's going to be okay, sweetheart," he said with a grimace when she squeezed his hand.

"With the next contraction, I want you to push," Dylan ordered. "Jacob, get behind her and support her shoulders."

Mae nodded, looking up at Jacob to ask, "Ready?"

With the next wave of pain, she squeezed her eyes shut and sucked in her breath before bearing down with a groan while Dylan counted.

"The head's out, you're almost there," Dylan said.

"You're doing great, honey, just a couple more," Ruby said.

Mae grunted and then bore down with the next contraction, letting out a muffled scream between clenched teeth.

The next contraction started, and she pushed again. All of a sudden, the pressure was gone, leaving a stinging pain in place of the intense squeezing she felt before. There was just a second of silence and then a small cry.

"It's a boy," Dylan announced. "Jacob, do you want to come cut the umbilical cord?"

Mae smiled at him through her tears. "Go make a memory."

Jacob moved down to where Dylan was holding their son.

"Mama," Mae said, "help hold me up so I can see."

Her parents knelt down on either side of her and helped prop her up. Dylan handed the baby to Ruby and quietly instructed Jacob on what to do. As soon as the cord was cut, the rabbi began to sing the shehecheyanu, the blessing for celebrating new occasions while Ruby wiped off the blood and goo before swaddling the baby and handing him to Jacob. Mae's heart swelled so big she thought it would burst, seeing Jacob hold his son for the first time. Her giant lumberjack carefully held his son, so tiny and fragile, with a look of awe on his face.

He slowly knelt down and placed the baby in her arms. "Thank you," he said in a hoarse whisper, placing a kiss on her forehead. "I love you."

May looked into her son's eyes for the first time, unable to find the words to express how she felt in that moment. What an incredibly powerful thing it was to have the ability to bring a life into this world. She had no idea her heart was capable of so much love.

"Mom, Daddy, look, this is your grandson," she said.

Nate came forward. "You'll get to hold him when we get to the hospital. Right now, we've got to get you two checked out."

Mae was carefully loaded onto the stretcher. She let out a low moan. Now that the contractions had subsided, she was sore but felt a lot better than she had while she was in labor.

Nate grimaced. "I'm sorry, we're going to try to go as easy as we can."

Dax and her dad jumped in to help get the stretcher down the ADA ramp they had just added to the gazebo a few months ago.

As soon as she was loaded into the back of the ambulance, Jacob climbed in after her and put the baby back in her arms. Nate was taking her vitals and calling in her stats to the hospital on the mic on his shoulder.

"We'll be right behind you, honey," her mom said.

"Don't worry about the weddin' stuff," Presley said. "I'll take care of everything."

Dax came forward. "Here, we figured you'd want these." He placed something in Jacob's palm.

He held out his hand to Mae, showing her the two plain platinum bands they had chosen to exchange.

"With this ring, I thee wed," he said, slipping the band on Mae's finger.

"With this ring, I thee wed," she said, placing the ring on his finger.

He leaned over and gently kissed her. "My wife."

"My husband."

Jacob kissed the top of the baby's head. "Our family."

"Are y'all gonna tell us what you're naming him?" Tillie called out from the crowd assembled at the back of the ambulance.

She exchanged a smile with Jacob. The name had been the one thing they didn't argue about.

"Ladies and gentlemen, I'd like to introduce you to Dante Joseph Winters-Colton"—Jacob's voice broke—"Dante is for my dad and Joseph for Mae's father. He's named after both of his grandfathers, one man whose memory I'll always treasure and the other I look forward to making new memories with, watching him with his grandchild in the years to come."

Mae's dad wiped at his eyes while her mom blew them a kiss. Their friends and family broke out into applause as the ambulance pulled away.

JACOB WAS able to take his family home the next day. Quick first-time births were rare but not unheard of, and the doctor warned Mae that if she got pregnant again, she'd have to be monitored closely, but other than that, she was just fine from her ordeal.

Dante was a healthy seven-pound-fourteen-ounces baby, a perfect blend of his parents, with his father's eyes and his mother's curls.

Jacob climbed into bed next to Mae, their son lying between them. Petunia jumped up on the bed and carefully walked toward the baby. She sniffed at his head and then curled up next to him, resting her paw on his swaddled body.

"I think they're going to have lots of adventures together," Mae said with a smile.

"Just like we are."

He locked eyes with his wife and smiled. He lifted her hand, rubbing his thumb over the shiny platinum band on her finger.

"Good memories, beyond anything I ever could have hoped for," he said.

"I love you," she whispered.

He leaned over and kissed her. "I love you."

Together, they looked down at their son, and Jacob saw a lifetime of memories in his eyes.

Keep reading for an excerpt from
A Hidden Heart
Mockingbird Bridge Book Four
by Eliana West

A
HIDDEN
Heart

MOCKINGBIRD BRIDGE

BOOK FOUR

ELIANA WEST

Mockingbird Bridge Book Four

Rhett Colton has spent the last two years working deep undercover for the FBI. He's forsaken his friends and family to keep his community safe, but now that his mission is over, he's haunted by what he's done and is having a hard time returning to his previous life. Only two things are keeping him from becoming totally lost—his dog, Rebel, and the beautiful new town veterinarian.

Jasmine Owens is ready to start over in the charming town of Colton, Mississippi, by opening her own veterinary practice. Jasmine knows what it's like to constantly have her abilities questioned, but she's strong enough to persevere. When she agrees to board Rhett's dog while he's away in DC, they begin talking every night over the phone and she realizes Rhett isn't the man she thought he was. He's so much more and sparks quickly fly on both ends.

But when new threats surface, Jasmine and everyone in Colton's safety are threatened. Rhett will need to make a decision. He's always sacrificed everything for his job, but is he willing to risk their relationship too?

Scan the QR code below to order

CHAPTER ONE

RHETT COLTON reached for the worn handle with every intention of opening the door. He gripped the black iron knob tightly, took one deep breath, and then another before letting go. The cabin that brought happy memories hadn't changed over the years. Large, peeled logs, turned dark golden brown with age, were still solid, holding the little cabin together precisely the way his grandfather had built it. The green metal roof had faded over time, along with the screen door painted to match. Rhett imagined restoring both to their original deep hunter green. The floorboards under his feet were solid, and the willow rocking chairs his grandpa built were still lined up on the porch in front of the large living room window.

Ten pristine acres surrounded the cabin. The centerpiece of the property was a large pond, ringed with cattails and a small cluster of indigo bush at one end. In the evening, the pond's occupants put on a show, leaping out of the water to catch the skeeter bugs and mosquitos that also called the body of water home. A bright blue kingfisher with a brown band across his belly usually joined the fray, swooping in, competing with the fish to fill its belly with insects for dinner. The evening activity assured Rhett that the pond was still fully stocked, and its occupants had been left to their own devices for far too long. He looked at the empty fishing pole rack and wondered if the vintage fishing reels his grandpa had prized were stored somewhere inside. Everything, the pond, the cabin, and its contents, were all his now. It would be up to Rhett to make sure the rods were put back in their proper place.

He bowed his head. This wasn't the reward he'd expected or wanted for what he did.

"You shouldn't have done it," Rhett muttered, backing away from the front door, fingering the hair tie he kept on his wrist, snapping it. The slight sting wasn't enough to distract him from the more significant pain he felt at the loss of his grandfather.

The agency had wanted him to cut his hair before he went on his assignment, but he'd refused. It was one piece of himself he wasn't willing to give up.

His best friend, the only loyal friend he'd had for the last couple of years, whined and pressed himself against Rhett's leg, bringing him out of his musings and back to the present.

He glanced down at his watch. Somehow he'd lost over an hour standing in front of his grandpa's cabin.

"Not today, Rebel," Rhett said.

He'd been saying that just about every day for months now. An invisible wall of regret and guilt kept Rhett from opening the door and claiming what was rightfully his. Rhett's grandpa left him everything he owned. He knew what his grandpa was trying to do with his gift. It was his way of saying he was sorry.

Pictures flashed through his mind like flipping through pages of a photo album while Rhett walked down to the pond. He sat down on the large cypress log at the water's edge. How many hours had he spent here sitting next to his grandpa with a pole in the water?

Rhett's father would comment on how he and his grandpa were like peas in a pod. Rhett had shared a bond with him that was unbreakable. They understood each other. Of all his cousins, he was the one his grandpa spent the most time with. He hadn't always led a good life, but when George Colton took his last breath, he left this earth having done everything he could to make amends and be worthy of his family and friends.

Rhett wanted to make sure his grandpa's legacy would be one of honor. But that meant destroying his reputation. His parents no longer looked at him with parental pride. Now his father looked at him with pity and sorrow in his eyes. It was almost worse than the anger and disappointment.

"I've got to go away for a while," Rhett said, digging his fingers into Rebel's soft fur. I've got a little more business to do, and then we can get back to normal, whatever that is." Now that his assignment with the FBI was over, all Rhett wanted was to rebuild the life he had before. Only that wasn't turning out to be as easy as he thought it would be. Rebel nudged his hand in a not-so-subtle reminder for Rhett to keep petting him. He knelt down and gently stroked the fur around the dog's muzzle. "You're going to stay with Jasmine Owens. Jacob says Dr. Owens is a good person, and she's a vet, so I know she'll take good care of you. We have to trust people again at some point, don't we? She's doing us a big favor, so be on your best behavior, okay?" Rebel gave him a wet kiss. "It's just a couple of weeks while I go to DC. We can do this."

Rebel rested his paw on Rhett's knee. He needed Rebel's reassurance more than the dog needed him. Rebel was the one thing that kept him from losing his humanity, his hope. He'd saved Rebel, but it turned out that Rebel had saved him too.

Remembering the first time he saw the scared German shepherd mix still made his stomach clench and his heart race. Rebel was just a puppy and about to be thrown into a dogfighting ring as bait. Rhett almost blew his cover before his assignment had gotten off the ground. He had to think quickly when he snatched the small ball of fur from his cousin's arms and yelled for him to stop. Thinking quickly, he came up with a story about how he needed a guard dog and threw in a hundred dollars. Money, he said. He was going to bet on the fight to keep him. He clutched the shivering body covered in tan and black fur close to his chest. The puppy looked up at him with enormous amber eyes and then peed all over him. Everyone in the room wanted to know what he was going to name him. He had to pick something suitable for the person he was pretending to be, so he chose Rebel.

"It's almost over. Two more weeks. We can do that, can't we, boy?" he asked, stroking Rebel's back.

He received a wet kiss for his reassurance.

Fourteen days would be easy compared to the two years he'd spent undercover with a White supremacist group. He'd be on leave when he came back from Washington. Three months, time to decide if he wanted to continue with the FBI or forge an alternative path. The only problem was, he couldn't figure out what that would be.

A flash of dark gray caught his eye, and he looked over at the pickup truck pulling up to the cabin with dread. He took in the scenery around him one more time before he slowly got up. His future looked like the murky blue waters of the pond when he turned and walked away.

Jacob Winters, the man who had been his handler while he was undercover, leaned against the hood of his truck, emblazoned with Winters Hardware on the driver's side door in cream against the gray paint.

Jacob had come to Colton for the assignment and stayed for love and the community that embraced him.

"Thanks for doing this," Rhett said, shaking Jacob's hand.

"It's the least I can do."

"Let me just grab my pack and Rebel's stuff from the porch, and we can go."

He held his hand up, and Rebel sat while he jogged back to the cabin and grabbed his stuff.

Jacob looked down at Rebel. "He could have served as an MPC with my unit with the Schutzhund training you've given him."

Rhett had used the training method for police dogs, emphasizing tracking, obedience, and protection skills. He'd done it in part to keep up the story that he wanted a guard dog and in part to protect both of them. Rebel would defend Rhett with his life, and Rhett would do the same for him. They were a team, and he wasn't sure if he could function without his best friend at his side.

"Thanks." He reached down and scratched Rebel between the ears. "I thought about going overseas when this was all over, but they wouldn't take Rebel as a multi-purpose canine since I'm not a certified trainer. He'd be fine if he was with me, but—" Rhett pressed his lips together, shaking his head.

"The Army won't guarantee that," Jacob finished.

Rebel had already given him so much comfort. He couldn't ask his best friend to risk his life as well.

With the truck loaded, Rhett took one last look at the cabin as they drove away. The closer he got to town, the more uncomfortable Rhett became. He was thankful Jacob didn't attempt too much small talk on the drive. Jacob Winters had served him well as his handler, and Rhett was grateful that he let him do his job without a lot of interference. They were alike in a lot of ways. They observed before they acted and didn't waste words. But Jacob had softened in the last year. He had a lightness... happiness around him that Rhett envied. His marriage and his son's birth transformed him. Rhett wondered what it would take for him to find the happiness Jacob had.

It had become a habit to hunch his shoulders and duck his head when he was in town. He bowed his head, letting his hair fall forward to hide his face. Even then, people stopped and some pointed when they drove by.

Rhett felt split in two. Half the folks in Colton saw him as a hero who helped save the mayor when the group he was embedded with hatched a plan to kidnap her. The other half had a hard time believing he wasn't really what he'd been pretending to be. It had been easier to avoid both groups and keep to himself since his real identity was revealed. In a strange way, it was fitting. Colton was a town of halves. Half White, half Black, the citizens that lived in the Mississippi Delta town reflected two sides of history, descendants of the enslaved and descendants of their owners. Rhett looked at the gazebo, the centerpiece of Colton's town square, a witness to history for over six generations, and wondered if he would ever find the peace and happiness that folklore promised would come to any couple that married under its canopy.

It had worked for Jacob. His former handler was happier than he'd ever known him to be.

Jacob pulled up to the new vet clinic that had just opened a few weeks ago. Originally built as a cigar factory in the early 1900s, the brick two-story building became a dental office and then was abandoned for many years. Now the building sat newly restored, with Colton Animal Clinic written on the window with vintage script in a bright emerald green outlined in white and silver.

He glanced at Rebel sitting next to him. "What do you think, boy, can you hang out here for a little while?"

"I've known Jasmine Owens since she was in high school," Jacob said. "The Owens family are good people. I promise Jasmine will take good care of Rebel."

Rhett dipped his head in agreement. Everyone in town was happy to welcome sheriff Isiah Owens's sister and another new business to the town's restoration efforts.

The new sheriff made a good impression, and Rhett liked and respected him. Sheriff Owens was doing a good job bringing order back to the area after years of the town being run by a corrupt sheriff and town council. Colton, Mississippi, had a brighter future now with new leadership, including the mayor, Jacob's wife, Mae. Rhett closed his eyes and tried to breathe in air that was suddenly difficult to find. His undercover work had ended the night the group he was with kidnapped Mae. Rhett had kept any harm from coming to her, but for those horrible hours on the Fourth of July, while everyone else was celebrating the nation's birthday, he was in the middle of a fight, trying to keep Colton's mayor from being killed.

"Rhett!" Jacob gave him a gentle shake. "You okay?"

He opened his eyes. How long had he had them closed?

"Yeah, I'm fine I was just—"

"Remembering?"

Rhett exhaled.

"That night haunts us all," Jacob said quietly.

"How is Mae doing? Is she still having nightmares?"

"She's doing well. She hasn't had a nightmare in a few weeks now."

Rhett shook his head. "She shouldn't have had them in the first place."

"It's not your fault, Rhett. You've got to lay that burden down."

"I could have stopped the kidnapping before it happened."

"You were trying to make sure you had a bulletproof case against those assholes. You wanted to have as much evidence as possible. I signed off on it too. This isn't all on you, Rhett."

It was easier to nod in agreement than keep arguing, even though Jacob was wrong. Rhett was the one undercover. It was his assignment and his fault things went too far. Rhett opened the door, and Rebel jumped out behind him.

"Come on, let me introduce you to Jasmine," Jacob said.

Rhett crouched down and held Rebel's face. "You be a good boy for Ms. Owens, ya hear? You show her you know how to mind your manners."

Rebel flicked his ears forward and cocked his head.

Rhett swallowed, trying to get past the lump that formed in his throat. Rebel was his best friend and confidant, and they hadn't spent time apart since the day he first held him.

He took a deep breath and walked into the clinic. Rhett almost tripped over his own feet when he laid eyes on Dr. Owens for the first time. Her dark, tightly curled hair was pulled up on top of her head in a twisty knot. She looked up at him with a wide-open smile that was reflected in her dark eyes. The oversized scrubs she wore must have been at least two sizes too big for her. They disguised her body, but he could see her well-toned warm brown arms under the short sleeves of her top. She had to be strong, working with animals all day.

She came toward him with her hand outstretched, and when it slid into his, it was a key that slid into a lock, opening his heart for the first time in a very long time. She must have felt the spark that arced between them too, because her eyes widened for a fraction of a second before he let her hand go.

He could see her lips moving, but he didn't register what she was saying right away. His breath caught. His first instinct was to turn around and leave, to get as far away from Dr. Owens's kind eyes and inviting smile as possible. She was the first person who didn't look at him with pity in their eyes since his assignment ended.

"Can you repeat that?" he murmured when he realized she was looking at him expectantly.

"I was asking how long you've had Rebel?"

"Two years, ma'am. I mean, Doctor."

She smiled. "Just call me Jasmine."

"I appreciate you doing this for me. I hope having Rebel won't be an added burden with your work."

Jasmine reached down and scratched Rebel between the ears. "Not at all. It will be nice to have a roommate for a while. I have an apartment above the clinic, so it will be easy to check on him throughout the day."

"I promise he won't chew up the furniture or anything like that."

"I'm sure he won't. We're going to get along just fine."

Rebel looked up at Jasmine, already smitten with his new friend. Rhett couldn't blame him. Jasmine Owens was someone he already knew he wanted to get to know better. Romance and a life undercover didn't mesh. The sudden desire to get to know this woman standing before him took him by surprise. If life were different, if he was any other man, he would have asked her out, but that wasn't possible. Rhett couldn't ask that from anyone, and especially not this woman. What woman would want him with his scars, especially a Black woman?

She was smiling at him. The light had shifted, and he noticed the flecks of green and gold in her brown eyes. They were kind eyes, but there was just a tinge of something in them that let him know that she'd experienced sorrow on some level. It made him want to miss his flight, stay, and talk to her. It had been a long time since he wanted to talk to anyone. He was wrong for her, but that didn't stop him from returning her smile and wondering, *What if?*

ELIANA WEST, the recipient of the 2022 Nancy Pearl Award for genre fiction, is committed to embracing diversity in her writing. That means she doesn't limit herself to a single genre. Instead, Eliana welcomes every story that comes her way with open arms. She aims to create characters that reflect the diversity of her community, with a range of social backgrounds, ethnicities, genders, and sexual orientations. Eliana loves to weave in historical elements whenever she can. She believes everyone deserves a happy ending.

From small towns to close-knit communities, Eliana West loves stories that bring people from different backgrounds together through the common language of unconditional love and acceptance. Eliana is a passionate advocate for diversity within the writing community. She is the founder of Writers for Diversity and teaches classes and workshops, encouraging writers to create diverse characters and worlds with an empathetic approach.

When Eliana isn't plotting her characters' happy endings, she can be found embarking on adventures with her husband, traversing winding country roads in their beloved vintage Volkswagen Westfalia, affectionately named Bianca. Whether it's traveling abroad or exploring locally, Eliana and her husband are always willing to get lost and see where the adventure takes them.

Eliana loves connecting with readers through her website: www.elianawest.com.

Follow me on BookBub

THE
WAY
Forward

MOCKINGBIRD BRIDGE

BOOK ONE

ELIANA WEST

Mockingbird Bridge Book One

The small town he couldn't wait to leave is calling him home....

Dax Ellis returns to Colton, Mississippi, a changed man. He traveled the world, earned a fortune, and made a lifetime of memories, but now he longs to put down roots. Time hasn't been kind to his hometown, and Dax wants to help—if only he can convince everyone he's not the same petulant boy he used to be. Especially the one woman who has every reason not to trust him.

Librarian Callie Colton cherished summers with her grandparents, in the town her ancestors helped build, in spite of the boy who called her names. Now that Colton is her home, life is quiet until Dax returns... and, along with him, threatening letters on her doorstep. He may still have the power to hurt her, but she's not the same scared little girl she used to be.

But as the danger escalates, Dax will have to face his past to find a way forward for the relationship they were cheated of once before.

Scan the QR code below to order

THE
WAY
Home

MOCKINGBIRD BRIDGE

BOOK TWO

ELIANA WEST

Mockingbird Bridge Book Two

A letter from the past will transform their future…

Taylor Colton always loved the crumbling plantation house passed down through his family for generations. Now he's bringing his popular renovation reality show to the small town of Colton, Mississippi, so he can bring the plantation house known as Halcyon back to life for the cameras.

After an ugly breakup, Josephine Martin needs a new start to heal her broken heart in peace. A hidden letter reveals a family secret that leads her to Colton to protect her family's history and honor a promise made before the Civil War… and to a house she didn't know was hers.

Suddenly, Josephine must decide if she's ready for the challenge of restoring a rundown mansion and its history, and Taylor's facing a challenge he can't charm away. Together, they must untangle a tragic history, a rocky relationship, and risk everything they love. Can they overcome the past to find their way home?

Scan the QR code below to order

Four
Holly
Dates

ELIANA WEST

An Emerald Hearts Novel

Four dates
A chance to reconnect
A different way to embrace the magic of the holiday season

Soccer star Nick Anderson is new to Seattle. He's thrilled to see the shy girl he remembered from high school when he visits the local Children's Hospital. Unfortunately, his excitement is one sided. With the help of her friends, he's got four chances to show Holly another way to celebrate the holiday season.

Holly Williams had worked hard to become a pediatric nurse at Seattle Children's Hospital. The only problem is she hasn't taken the time to enjoy it. Now the popular guy she secretly crushed on in high school is asking her out not just for one date but for four.

As Holly and Nick get to know each other again, they each learn what the holidays are really all about.

Scan the QR code below to order

Summer of Noelle

ELIANA WEST

An Emerald Hearts Novel

Star midfielder for the Seattle Emeralds, Hugh Donavan looks forward to his visits to Children's Hospital and spending time with the young patients. What he looks forward to the most is seeing one nurse who's captured his attention.

Noelle Williams is ready to open her heart again, but she isn't interested in dating a professional athlete after a disastrous marriage to one, no matter how kind and charming Hugh is.

With encouragement from friends and one special little patient to live her life to the fullest, Noelle agrees to one date with Hugh.

Will the magic of summer in Seattle lead to love?

Scan the QR code below to order

AN EMERALD HEARTS NOVEL

BE THE
Match

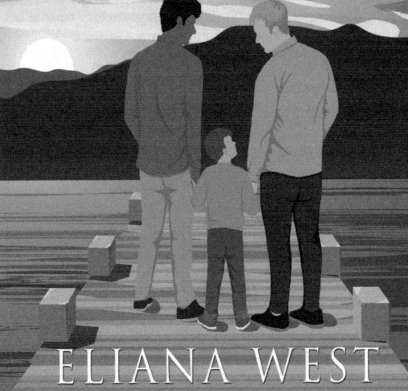

ELIANA WEST

An Emerald Hearts Novel

A senseless accident leaves Ryan Blackstone a single father. His son, Leo, survives, only for the hospital to discover he has leukemia. Ryan's only hope to save him is a bone marrow donor.

A donor registry reveals a perfect match for Leo but unearths an unsettling family secret: Ryan's wife's brother isn't dead. Then they meet, and Ryan realizes Dylan could save him as well.

Dylan McKenzie stopped thinking about his family's betrayal when they kicked him out twelve years ago. They would rather say he is dead than gay. So the news of his sister's death comes as a shock. Dylan is afraid being pulled back into the family will hurt him again, but meeting Ryan *and Leo upends his plan to keep his heart closed.*

Ryan almost lost everything. Now he must decide if he can gamble losing his family to have everything he's ever wanted. Together, he and Dylan could be the perfect match.

Scan the QR code below to order